CU01025194

PRAISE FOR LUCY CHRIS[

'Gripping and totally twisted—y(
engagements so you can stay home and finish it.'
Christian White, author of *Wild Place*

'A twisted tale of idealised love and sweet revenge as
victim becomes predator. Gemma/Kate is vulnerable,
fierce and unhinged as she sets about righting the
wro　　　 of her past. *Release* is an urgent, addictive and
provocative exploration of trauma, love and redemption.'
Lorraine Peck, winner of the 2021 Ned Kelly Award
for Best Debut Crime Fiction

'Dark, compelling and unsettling.'
Claire Kendal, author of *I Spy*

'Daring, edgy and electric.'
Samantha Harvey, author of *The Western Wind*

'Utterly compelling, clever, heart-stopping.
I can't stop thinking about it.'
Jo Nadin, author of *The Talk of Pram Town*

'Furiously passionate prose, clean as a bone.'
C. J. Skuse, author of the Sweetpea series

PRAISE FOR *STOLEN*

'Complicated and beautiful—this novel left me doubting
...y emotions and missing a place I'd never been.'
Maggie Stiefvater

'All the tension of lightning, all the terror of thunder.
A stunning, scary and beautiful book.'
John Marsden

Lucy Christopher is a British-Australian writer. Her first YA novel, *Stolen*, was a Michael L. Printz Honor Book, won a 2011 USBBY Outstanding International Book Award and received the UK's Branford Boase Award. Lucy has written several other novels for young people, was the director of the MA in Writing for Young People at Bath Spa University and is now a senior lecturer in Creative Writing at the University of Tasmania. *Release*, a companion to *Stolen*, is her first novel for adults. When not writing, Lucy spends her time daydreaming, walking dogs, and visiting family and friends spread across the world. She is passionate about the importance of wild environments.

lucychristopher.com

RELEASE
LUCY CHRISTOPHER

TEXT PUBLISHING MELBOURNE AUSTRALIA

The Text Publishing Company acknowledges the Traditional Owners of the country on which we work, the Wurundjeri people of the Kulin Nation, and pays respect to their Elders past and present.

textpublishing.com.au

The Text Publishing Company
Wurundjeri Country, Level 6, Royal Bank Chambers, 287 Collins Street, Melbourne Victoria 3000 Australia

The Text Publishing Company (UK) Ltd
130 Wood Street, London EC2V 6DL, United Kingdom

Published by The Text Publishing Company, 2022

Book design by Imogen Stubbs
Cover images by Roc Canals/Getty Images
Typeset by J&M Typesetting

Printed and bound by CPI Group (UK) Ltd, Croydon, CR0 4YY

ISBN: 9781911231387 (paperback)
ISBN: 9781922459473 (ebook)

A catalogue record for this book is available from the National Library of Australia.

The Forest Stewardship Council® (FSC®) is a global, not-for-profit organization dedicated to the promotion of responsible forest management worldwide. FSC defines standards based on agreed principles for responsible forest stewardship that are supported by environmental, social, and economic stakeholders.

For Rajiv, my heart

Supreme Court of Western Australia
PERTH

October 15th

I see you as I scan the courtroom. The familiar jolt hits deep in my stomach, and I twist in the hard chair to look properly.

Can it be you?

How?

You have a suit on. From behind, I see the white of a crisp shirt collar above a black jacket. A nice jacket, I can't help but notice, good quality, tailored. I always thought suits never suited you, but what else would you wear today? Ten years ago someone also found you a suit.

You're talking to a woman, bending to catch her words, your hair freeing itself from behind your ears. It's neatly trimmed and golden, rinsed with sunlight and shampoo, clean as morning. You've tried. Of course you have. Today is all about you. Today is what happens next.

Despite everything, I'm glad to see you. You shouldn't have come. You must know that your being here changes everything. The quake inside me enters my veins, bones, skin. You always were someone who brought change, like the rain. Tyler MacFarlane—the rainmaker, the firestarter, Loki in a rich man's suit.

I shut my eyes, clench my jaw, and try to contain this feeling. It's how I felt before, and I thought I'd gone beyond that. Perhaps you've come for me, like I came for you, for revenge or even forgiveness. Perhaps we're even.

I blink fast and return to this cavernous, wood-panelled room. My barrister, Jodie, is talking to me. She and I and my solicitor Mikael are standing behind a grainy table. Jodie is pointing at words on a blinding white page. Words about you. Words about me. These words are my story now; this is what the court wants to hear, or doesn't. When the jury decides, will they be with me, or with you?

Should we place a bet, Ty?

Me against You.

Jodie is frowning. She's asked me something, and I haven't been listening. She pushes the paper into my hands. So much black and white; you and I are so many words now. We are novels and films, stories in the minds of thousands.

'Have you read over this?' she says.

But I shouldn't have to practise or learn these words by heart. They should come from the core of me: my truth. What is that core of me now? Did I ever know?

'I've practised,' I say.

I dart around and look for you again, your shimmer of blond hair, your scar. But now, of course, you're nowhere. I've only imagined you.

My ghost man.

You are only inside me. Even after all these years, you are still here inside my head. Crazy? Maybe. You know, there are people who say I only exist because of you. Perhaps it is actually the other way around.

I shake my head to concentrate, study the dark brown wood beneath my fingers and press into it, lightheaded. I look up again when the jury files in. They settle and stare

4

like a bunch of wide-eyed owls. If I make a sudden movement, perhaps they will flap away.

I keep very still, and wait.

Were we always going to come back here, you and me?
Perhaps our story—my story—was never really over until
now.

Ten months earlier

LONDON

December 27th

A letter arrives through the slot with a snap.

I lift my head from the couch. Even from up the stairs, above the bakery, I always hear the mail come. I see the half-finished bottle of whisky on a cushion beside me, then look across to see that the cupboard—*your* cupboard—is still closed. If that doesn't deserve half a bottle of whisky, I don't know what does. Soon it will be a new year and I can't take you with me.

I say this every year.

And every year you come anyway.

If I could find the part of my brain where you hitchhike, maybe then the therapy would work. But, who knows, this year might be different. I check the time: half past nine, the post is early. My head is thumping as if there are a hundred hammers in there. In the cab on the way back from Mum's last night, I watched the Christmas lights go off one by one, as I tried not to be sick on the back seat. I have nothing else to do today but recover from a hangover. I'm not rostered on at the travel agency, even though I told them I could work over the Christmas sale period.

My phone beeps.

Nick. Of course.

You feel OK this morn? ;) x

Christ. What did I send him? I check through the messages from last night: several about wanting to see him. Then I went quiet. What I always do. Today I reply; it's the least he deserves.

Yeah, thanks. Went straight to bed. We should catch up soon.

Do I mean that?

I'm not sure.

I'm also not sure whether to put a kiss after my words. My fingers stay frozen. Was it you who took away my ability to decide on anything? God knows I've had a thousand sessions with Rhiannon, my therapist, but it never gets any better. Your fault. Whenever something goes wrong, it's easier to put your name on it. It's almost fun to blame you when the boiler breaks down, or the tube's delayed, or I get food poisoning...or drunk.

I shut my eyes and press send, without an x, and then feel sick about that too. I'm pushing him away, just like Mum says I do with everyone. True to form, I don't answer the messages from Anna and Neri, both asking about my plans for New Year's Eve.

I pad downstairs, feeling sorry for the postman who has to work the day after Boxing Day.

Another beep.

Catch up tomorrow? x

Nick's never dissuaded. I don't get that. I would be. I feel guilty, so I add:

Sure. Few drinks?

Still no kiss.

I bend down to the doormat and pick up a leaflet about a new dry-cleaning service on the high street, something from a political party, and then—

I'm not thinking anymore about Nick.

Under the leaflets, there is a letter. I stare at it as if it's alive and might bite. I'm suddenly anxious as hell, worse than I've been for months. This isn't a bill, or a late Christmas card. The envelope is too white, too official. And a part of me is not surprised to see it.

I'm surprised by that.

Get a hold of yourself. I say it out loud, pleased by the boldness in my voice. Then, I reach out and turn over the envelope.

The name above the address is my old name.

My dead name.

I carry the letter upstairs, between my fingertips, put it on the kitchen table and sit in a chair facing it. Perhaps someone else should do it—Mum, maybe. Someone else should know what's inside before I do. Once it's open, things will change; I'll have to decide how I feel, what I do…who I tell. There'll be other decisions, too: whether to see Rhiannon, or drink, or go to the cupboard. Decisions make me feel stressed. And when I feel stressed, I spiral. It's enough now that I'm not running screaming into the street. I can sit with this. I can breathe. A voice inside me says I should call Nick—that this is what he's for—but I can't. Then he might be the one who ends up running screaming into the street.

I stare at that name, so clear in black print, as if that old part of me is living here today, despite everything. I should have told the prison registrar about the name change, should have known this would happen, one day.

Eventually, I bring the letter to my lap. It isn't heavy, it doesn't tick. The postmark on the envelope is dated two weeks ago, but the post is always slow from Perth. There is a symbol

11

stamped in one corner; I could engrave it into my skin without looking—the crest for the Western Australian Department of Corrective Services, the department now considering your release.

I know what this letter will say. It's almost a relief.

Almost.

I'm shaking so hard I shut my eyes and grasp the arms of the chair. This could be a new kind of sentence. I rest the letter against the cyclamen on the table and try to breathe deeply; it's what Rhiannon would advise. Then I lurch from the table, stumble to the window, pull the curtains, open the latch. *Breathe.* The air is so cold it makes my teeth sting.

In.

Out.

In.

Out.

I clench my fingers into a fist and imagine pushing a knife. Your blood on my skin, sticky and hot.

You falling

down

before me.

I exhale and look out. The hazy glow of Christmas lights. Scrunched newspaper tumbling down slick pavements. A black cab turning its lights off as it speeds by below. For a moment, there's a sweet-soft numbness in the air, before the roar of the monster city comes back and I am hit by the stench of the drains. I make myself say it: *North East London. Barkingside.*

Nowhere to you.

One bed, a bathroom, a kitchen and a living room. Above the bakery. Why it's hot every morning.

It was only a few months ago when I filled in the victim submission form, when I answered those impossible questions about what impact an early release might have, the potential for contact, the conditions I wanted the board to consider. Surely it's too early for your parole? Maybe you've changed, and the letter will tell me about your good behaviour. Maybe you've changed more than I have.

I place my forehead against the window. A Christmas tree illuminates a front porch. Sal, my resident fox, slinks behind the bins, and the sickly sun begins to creep above the rooftops. I wipe my breath from the glass and watch Sal's fire-bright fur appear near the bus stop, her tail twitching in the nettles beside the alleyway. I see you when I move my gaze: you weave down the high street in a trench coat, your hair slicked back. I blink you away. But you slip inside a man dressed in overalls turning down Pinter Street. Then you're a guy leading a child towards McDonald's. You are the local chemist, unlocking your shop, sorting out my prescriptions for happy pills and painkillers.

You are everywhere. Still.

I bring my fingers to my neck and press until I cough, which makes me feel a little better, and now the glass is fogged up again, so I can't see you. I swallow and it hurts and it's satisfying. Not that I'd tell that to Rhiannon. When I shut the window and brush the crumbling paint on the sill, I feel the dry ridge of your scar against my skin. Even now, I can conjure you into my fingertips; you arrive like a trick.

I try to be logical and contain your presence with numbers. Nine years, nine months since I last saw you, handcuffed, your head down. And longer since my lips brushed yours and I tasted salt. Your sentence was twelve years. More than I thought you'd get at the time. Not enough now. But there's that thing called parole, good behaviour, and you always were a charmer.

I move away from the window. I need water, so do the ferns. I sprinkle the watering can over them on my way past and check the soil around the chilli plants. I whisper sweet nothings to the mint to help her grow. The holidays are always the worst, and coping strategies are so much harder. But I'd been doing well!

One glass of water, then another, then into the shower. I scrub hard. You're still inside me, like the grains of sand stuck in my boots—the boots in the cupboard in the living room. If I took them out, could I still smell the desert? I turn the hot tap on harder and blast you away. I gasp water and spit you out, down the drain. *Gone!* But if I shut my eyes, you could be right with me.

I don't look at the letter on the table.

I don't go to the cupboard.

I want to scream.

Instead, I put on the Christmas jumper Mum made me wear yesterday and the day before, and go into the kitchen, where I discover I've run out of milk and coffee. There is nothing apart from cat biscuits and the leftovers Mum packaged up for me. I tip some of both into a bowl for Sal.

Out the kitchen window, her glinting amber eyes stare back from under the bakery's old storage shed. She watches me as I step down the fire-escape stairs and crouch a couple of metres from her.

'No milk today,' I say.

Her nose wrinkles as she sniffs first, before sliding out, her body flat to the frozen ground. In summer, when she was little

14

more than a cub, she let me feed her from my hand. But now, as a winter adult, she is wary and withdrawn. I tell myself this is what happens with wild things, but the feeling of being abandoned by her still stings. Delicately, she takes a piece of turkey from the bowl with her neat, sharp teeth. She looks thinner today, though still beautiful: a flash of bright copper in this forgotten courtyard.

'There's a letter,' I tell her.

One of her ears twitches. Perhaps this is the day she'll reply to me. She'll tell me to treat you with the same disdain she'd treat a male fox, with angry calls and bites. She'll tell me to ignore you. I shift my weight from one ankle to the other as I consider her.

'It's not that simple,' I say.

She curls her lip, flinching from my words, then crunches the last cat biscuit and goes back under the shed. I long to touch her—to feel warmth and softness in this freezing air, to have flames at my fingertips—but I won't dare. Now she's all grown, I'm not sure she'll ever let me touch her again. I grab a discarded bit of roast potato and throw it in her direction, but she stays hidden. I pick up the bowl, go back inside and stand motionless in the kitchen for what feels like forever. Nick messages again and I ignore it.

Finally, I head to the mini mart. Milk, coffee, bread, tinned tuna, whisky, Hobnobs and cat biscuits: my standard haul for a few days. Eddie waves a hand above his wife's samosas, as he does every time, but I shake my head. They say people who eat less live longer. Do I want to live longer?

On a bench in East Park, shopping bag on my lap, I look for the park pack, inspecting the huge laurel hedge behind the swings where I know their den is. There are starlings and pigeons and even a small mouse, but no foxes. I leave cat biscuits anyway; it's too cold for hunting.

You're still creeping in, I feel you there, at the edges of me. It would be so easy to let you take over. I should have stayed at Mum's another day, should've met Nick or Anna in the city instead of coming home. I shut my eyes and concentrate on sirens a few streets away, on a man shouting down his mobile phone, on cars on the high street. You told me once how the land is waiting, underneath and around the city, always ready to return. I imagine the earth under the flashing lights and throbbing pavements. I remember. Even in Barkingside, even now.

I read Nick's last message.

We could have dinner tomorrow, not just a drink. My treat x

Why does he try so hard? I don't deserve him. Here is a nice boy doing all the nice things. I flick through more messages from Anna and Neri, and other half-forgotten friends from a lifetime ago, all wanting me to be *merry* and to have a *happy new year*. I still can't answer any of them. Today, I can't lie.

Back in the flat, I sit on the couch. No more text messages, no knocks on the door, nothing on TV but smiles and sparkle. I am a statue, still as desert rocks. I am all alone.

I look across at the letter.

Not yet.

I can't do it yet.

So I take the whisky bottle and make myself forget.

✧

16

In my dreams of your release, you're older, of course, and thinner, but there is still the same shine in your eyes, blue as the desert sky, the same shirt, and the scar.

Outside the grey, high wall, you go still, like one of my foxes. You stand smelling the air, watching the birds, checking that the world is as you left it. Your fingers twitch as if they want to hold something. Someone.

You are the same.

You are *exactly* the same.

I wind down my car window and hang my head out like a dog, panting and eager, but you don't see me. Not yet. There is a knife on my thigh, and the steel catches the light, makes me blink. I could blind you with it. Someone has given you shoes, new and gleaming; like you are now.

When you finally walk, you move fast. I shove the car door open, no time to close it behind me if I'm going to catch you. You don't look back, although you must hear the slap of my shoes on the tarmac. Maybe you want it, this release I'm about to give you. This pain.

But when I reach you, I stop. I don't stab. I drop the knife and I reach out to touch you. Finally.

And that's when you turn around.

December 28th

I wake, gasping. You are crushing the air from me. You are in the breath I breathe out. You arc in me, still. I cough, and pain flares in my throat.

Ty.

Your sweat in my sheets, your arms on my shoulders.

You and me.

Everything I can't have.

I reach out and find the bedside table. Here is the lamp, and the glass of water. I drink it down, replace the glass, then clench my fingers into a fist and imagine pushing a knife. I stumble from the bedroom and into the kitchen.

The letter is still on the table, propped against the cyclamen.

Soon I'll have to read it. Whatever happens, I need to do that first.

As I water the pot plant, I avoid looking at my name on the envelope. My anxiety is bad, as bad as before. I should tell Rhiannon. Or Mum. *Anyone*. I feel the familiar buzzing dread work up from my stomach as I remember my plans for tonight: seeing Nick. It's meant to be joyful, seeing someone new, someone handsome and funny, who actually seems to like me. Though he's not that new anymore. He's about to cross the threshold as the person I've been with for the longest time; he's about to break your record. Perhaps you're showing your anger by sending me a letter. Or perhaps the letter is to inform me that you've died. The dread turns to fluttering, a sharp-beaked bird trapped in my chest. If it's true, I will mourn, and I know it will feel wrong.

But it can't be true. You do not die. You cannot die.

Sal isn't here today, or doesn't come out when I go down to the courtyard. I leave food for her and go back inside. Now it's only a few minutes until nine, and I can't open the letter before work.

I turn on my laptop and check the briefings. The best sales are predictable—Caribbean, Tunisia, Turkey. But there, in the second tier of sales, Australia, too. It would be, wouldn't it?

There is a note in my inbox from Charli, the area manager, telling me what to push for and attaching the requisite stock answers that I will copy and paste when the questions come.

Is this fully refundable?
What sort of alcohol is included?
Can I pay in instalments?

It never matters if the questions come from the student site, the package holiday company or the bespoke adventures: everyone always asks the same things. Like Nick's messages, Charli's email finishes with a kiss. It looks so strange—a slip of her fingers no doubt. She wouldn't kiss me in real life, not even on the cheek. I remember Nick's lips. Gentle and soft. Christmas Eve. At the tube. He was hesitant, and I was surprised by the stab of emotion that came with it. Love? *No.* Now, I touch my lips and they are chapped and dry, winter all through them.

When I lick them, I taste yours. Your lips in the hospital when I said goodbye. Salty. Earthy. Dirty. I kissed you then, remember—my choice, not yours. And they told me it was all Stockholm syndrome. A 'psychological alliance'. A way to survive. Are you amused to know that I objected to that term then, just as I object to it now? Those words were just another way to make me a victim, another way of silencing me, moulding me into the shape of a good girl, the female they expected. To everyone else, we only had one story: you, the evil kidnapper, and me, the helpless victim. I was innocent and you the opposite. But it was always more complicated, wasn't it? Our story never fitted nicely into police terminology and courtroom procedure, and nobody ever listened hard enough to understand what any of it was really like. Besides, I wasn't helpless. It took me years to see it, but as Rhiannon always tells me, I was a girl who survived something traumatic, survived your coercive control. And I did it through love. Heroic, really.

I shut my eyes and have the moment: if I had stayed and if you hadn't released me, if things had been different...if you had only been good. But maybe you were. Is it possible the judge and the newspapers and my parents were wrong? Maybe you were the best thing that ever happened to me—how would I ever know?

Try to have a lovely festive season, hey?
Charli x

Try? Am I really so obvious?

I focus on answering the work chat-box questions, but every few moments I think I smell burning: the words inside

20

the envelope going up in smoke. I glance over at the table to check, but the letter remains unchanged.

I've been in this flat for almost the same amount of time that you've been inside. But what was my crime? That I let you get inside me, you and nobody else? Not even Charli knows who I really am. To everyone at Travel Solutions, I'm just a name at the end of an email chain or at the top of a chat window: *Kate Stone.*

Do you like my new name?

You won't find me here. You don't even know that *here* exists. I could hide here for the rest of my life, and you'd never realise. I shake my head, trying to shake you out. I'm stupid to think like this, to talk to you. I try not to, but there's something wrong with me, something missing. Or perhaps it's not actually something missing, it's something extra: an extra bit of brain that other people don't have. I've got you.

But you don't help me at all.

Another ping from a chat, the student site this time. I look back to the screen, take off my jumper. I'm hot and tingling all over; there are embers under my skin.

Kate@StudentTravelSolutions:	You are speaking to Kate, your travel expert. How can I help you today?
Hannah Davies:	I have a question about the sales.
Kate@StudentTravelSolutions:	Sure! Fire away, Hannah!

While *Hannah Davies is typing...*I check the sales myself. They're better than last year's. I almost laugh when I see the direct flight to Perth is on sale too: only a few hundred pounds and I could be outside your prison gates. It would be so easy. And so hard.

I glance at my phone: no messages. I pull a chunk from my fingernail. If Mum knew I'd just checked the flight prices to Perth, she'd be marching me round to Dad's flat for an intervention. And Dad would smile at me with his wide, blinking eyes, like he always does now, like he doesn't know me anymore, like he's some sort of mole. But then, maybe he never did know me. Maybe no one did. Mum and Dad would prefer the other thoughts I have about skinning you alive, or tying you to a tree, leaving you to roast, the way you left me.

I'd make you suffer. I've stood many times in the homewares section of John Lewis, looking at the chef's knives, wondering how firmly a person might need to press to kill. If Rhiannon knew this, she'd have me back on the hard meds.

Hannah Davies: I see there's a Red Fare that goes to Bangkok, Sydney, Auckland, LA. Tell me about that.

I copy and paste the standard response. Hannah pings back.

Hannah Davies: Sounds good. How long can we stay in each place? How long in Australia? I've got a cousin there.

For the briefest moment, red sand smudges everything, stains the keyboard, a snake slithers across the kitchen floor, and footprints from bare, hot feet colour the carpet.

I shake my head. If I believed in coincidence, Australia pinging up like this might have meant something. But I don't believe in coincidence, and I don't want to see you again. A life ruined once is enough. Anyone would agree.

Hannah Davies:	There're two of us. I'm travelling with my boyfriend, our first trip together. ☺

I recommend side trips to Darwin, and yes, even Perth. I'll get brownie points for upselling. As I wait for her response, I imagine what a first trip with a first boyfriend might be like— seeing Australia through untainted eyes. Could I ever have been a Hannah Davies, on a beach, drinking coffee without first checking if it had been drugged? My fingers hum against the keyboard.

Kate@StudentTravelSolutions:	Have you thought about a tour? You could see more of the country that way. Honestly, it's what I'd do if I could!

I'm such a liar. None of the tours we offer to the desert are any good, none of them go where we've been. I send her links, and sure enough Hannah Davies comes back straightaway:

Hannah Davies:	Wow, wicked!
Kate@StudentTravelSolutions:	I know, right?! If I could go to Australia for the first time again, I'd be all over this. Romantic too, with the stars out there. No light pollution! ☺

I'm good at making sales by being friendly with clients, and I'm always chattiest with the students. Sometimes it even feels like I'm their friend by the time they make their bookings. But this time there's a strange, persistent part of me that wants to tell Hannah Davies everything. All about the real desert. About me. About you. I want to write your name in the chat box and press send. But I don't. Hannah Davies won't want to know this story, or about my trip to Australia, or about me back then.

Hannah Davies: So, crazy thought—if we stop in Sydney, can we do an overland tour as well?

I imagine a stream of air travelling up my neck and into my brain: one of the techniques Rhiannon taught me. How does Hannah Davies get to do whatever she likes in a country she knows nothing about? Because I just told her to. I should send Hannah on a plane to join you. Then, when you get out, you can make her your plaything too: take her to the middle of nowhere and do whatever the hell else it was you wanted to do with me. *I've got the perfect tour guide*, I could say, *a real celebrity out there, he knows the place better than anyone.* My fingers twitch, but my history stays unwritten.

I send her the links she needs. I tell her the usual stuff about *finding yourself* and that *the big, wide world can offer more than a 9-5 job*—my proven lines for the student site. I push her towards a tour on the east coast, one that doesn't go far inland, not to the real desert. Hannah Davies won't see what you've shown me. I'm still protective about it, you know, the place you took me to. Is it still a secret, your *desert den*, that home you made for us? Or perhaps someone else lives there now, a shiny new kidnapper with his adorable kidnappee.

No.

It would be a snake pit now.

I've never found anything about it online, not in all these years. I've google-earthed thousands of kilometres of arid land across Western Australia: nothing. All I have is a hunch about how to find it again, the tiniest sliver of memory.

I ring Hannah Davies to verify her details. I never like the clearer picture I get when a voice replaces typing and makes a person different from how I imagined them. When she speaks, I almost don't hear her. All I hear is the rumble of your car over road corrugations, the jolting and swaying. It will be hot out there this time of year. Hot as hell. I switch back to Hannah Davies when I register her voice, so young. But I was young too. Younger than her.

You won't like it, I want to say. But I tell her to email me with any further questions, that I'm always here to help. And I am, I guess. Sometimes when I'm not even rostered on, I check work emails, do the chat box. It fills the hours, someone to talk to who is not you. That's how I rationalise it, anyway. Like I said, everything's always your fault.

I feel strange after Hannah hangs up; it's just as well no other serious enquiries come in. I imagine her and her boyfriend, her legs against the sand, her toes digging into it. I imagine her boyfriend fucking her under the stars, and how she'd smile. I think of her staring at the night sky and raising her middle finger at me.

When I hold the envelope, I want to cut it, burn it, swallow it whole. But I cradle it, imagining

> your death (accident in the exercise yard),
>
> another ten years (fight in the canteen),
>
> a diagnosis of cancer.

I get the whisky. When I finally poke my little finger into a corner of the envelope flap, the bottle is a fair bit emptier. I unfold the letter.

It's from the Victim Notification Register, part of the

Department of Corrective Services. The words are very formal, and you are referred to as Mr Tyler Andrew MacFarlane, and me as Miss Gemma Grace Toombs. There is no mention of you dying, or spending longer inside, or having a terminal illness. The letter states that you can't resume contact with me. Can't come within a hundred metres of me. Can't do anything to me at all. There are details of a Community Corrections Centre where you are required to report.

And then: 12 February. The date looks so formal on the page. I do the maths: six weeks, five days. So much earlier than I'd expected.

The news comes without fanfare, no reporters outside my door. After all this time: just a letter of notification about your probation, your release. I'm not ready.

I hold off for as long as I can, but eventually go to the cupboard. I pull out the plastic containers of clippings, turn my phone to silent, text Nick:

I can't do tonight. Feeling ill. Sorry.

No kiss.

I spread the articles around me until I'm an island and these papers are the sea. I bob on familiar words and images.

Gemma: found!

Gemma Toombs released from desert drifter!

Is this the face of a monster?

I trace the black-and-white line drawing of you in the courtroom, your hands clasped, your blue eyes black. You are beautiful and terrifying, and I can't look away. Something pulls behind my ribs, a *longing*. But for what?

Closure?

You?

For you to be out of my head?

But if you leave, what's left? You've been inside me longer than I've been without you. I read on through all the articles I know by heart.

Gemma Toombs, the 16-year-old abducted from Bangkok Airport, has been admitted to a remote West Australian hospital, apparently taken there by her captor. Her anxious parents flew from London to be by her side…

Tyler MacFarlane, a desert drifter with troubled past, watched Gemma for years before taking her. He said he was searching for the perfect life…

Tyler MacFarlane met Gemma Toombs in London when she was a child, then followed her years later on a flight she took with her parents. He kidnapped her and took her to his desert home in Australia where he constructed a fantasy…

The tightness in my chest is almost unbearable as I sift through the next articles about your trial. I look at one photograph of you leaving the courtroom, hands cuffed but eyes fierce and clear. Your hair had been cut by then, slicked back. You were wearing a shirt with a loose tie. You could have been an Australian poster boy, a surfer, a stalker.

I miss you.

I slap my face, and I like the sound it makes, the tingling it leaves. Sometimes I hate me more than you. I should be doing anything but this, I know, but I won't stop. Not until I've read everything, every single sentence. Not until this bottle is drained.

Here are the letters I wrote you: another failed closure exercise, suggested by another psychiatrist. Would things have been better if I'd sent them? Would you have replied?

I slap myself again.

Slap.

Slap.

Slap.

Until my eyes water and my cheeks are on fire.

In a gossip magazine, there's a photo of you as a golden, shaggy-haired child, standing beside a paddling pool in the sun. You can't have been more than six years old, one leg curled behind the other and mischief in your eyes, on your T-shirt a cartoon duck. The journalist talks about your loveless upbringing: how your mother left you and your sister when you were very young; how your father died from drink and left you too; how you spent time in a children's home and stopped speaking for months. The journalist says these are the reasons you looked for connection, why you thought you'd find love with me. She writes about your plans to find a soulmate, how you'd been searching the world over. In her article, you are the victim.

Slap.

Slap.

Six charges originally, though only five stuck: abduction, assault, false imprisonment, forgery, stalking. They never proved the last, and I never gave evidence for it: sexual assault.

Slap.

It feels like progress when I drag myself away and check your sites on my phone. Your sister hasn't posted on Twitter since last April; I wonder if she's given up. No matter how often I refresh the Australian news sites there's nothing, no words about your release.

I lie with my stinging cheek against the articles, against your faded face, against you. A sandstorm whirls inside me as I think about Hannah Davies, the *Flash Sale*. I could be waiting with the reporters. Or in your desert den. I could find it again, couldn't I? And you'd come back to it. Back to me.

Wouldn't you?

One move of my fingers and—click—no more drizzle or lying on newspaper beside the cupboard, and—click—it'd be you again, and—click—I'd be gone from here. Easy, really. I could kidnap myself.

December 29th

A momentary lapse, that's all it was, fuelled by too much booze. Quickly, I scoop up the papers, put everything back and close the cupboard door. If I don't act fast, I will only lose more hours, and I can't keep doing this. But when I turn my head and see the notification letter again, I vomit on the carpet.

At the kitchen sink, staring at my reflection in the window, I can make out newspaper print smudged into my pale skin, the space around my eyes puffy, and my new short hair sticking out sideways, too blonde, too quirky. The hairdresser thinks I'm funkier than I am. You wouldn't know me. My freckles have faded; no more rosy, baby cheeks; no more long dark hair. I am lean and muscular as a fox.

I will not let you be everything again. I repeat this to myself as I fill a soapy bowl and scan the courtyard. Sal is out there, chewing on bones. I want to sit with her and talk, but I turn from the window and scrub the sick from the carpet so hard my fingers sting. Half an hour later, I put the letter in my handbag and leave the flat.

The tube—so busy, as usual—clunks past where we used to live. Remember that big house? That leafy suburb? My school?

You should, you followed me there, too.

The pressure from backpacks and bodies builds steadily as more people get on, and I feel a familiar twist inside. A red-faced man is looking at me—just a perv, probably. I avoid his gaze and look up at the posters above the seats. My face was on posters like these once. Do they tell you things like this in prison? Do you know you made me famous too?

Missing. Gemma. The words accompanied by an out-of-date school photo in which I had green, clear eyes, and a hesitant smile.

The red-faced man is still staring. I want to be someone who shouts at men like him, but even though my heart is racing and my fists are clenching, I stay quiet. I shut my eyes and imagine somewhere else: hot sand, emptiness. My default land-scape. Why can't I imagine mountains, or babbling brooks, or rain in Wales? I text Mum.

I'll be another hour at least. Hope that's okay.

She replies instantly.

Of course, Sweet pea. I'm making your favourite! x

I squeeze out at Goldhawk Road and head for the faded glory of the West London Victorian Bathhouse. It's because of Mum that I started swimming. See, she's not all bad, despite what you thought of her. Back when she was fed up with my post-you moods, she took me to the local community pool near the flat we rented. That pool wasn't special like the Bathhouse, but there was something different about it. Transforming.

As it turns out, I'm good at swimming. If you hadn't come along, perhaps I could've gone professional, spent my days bliss-fully happy in water. Instead, I moved to Barkingside and got a job selling holidays.

'At least live with other people,' Mum said. 'Somewhere nearer the city, with other youngsters.'

She meant: somewhere with other young *normal* people, people who like to go out partying Friday nights, or who like theatre and restaurants and jazz.

'Too expensive,' I said. It wasn't a lie.

'At least live somewhere I can get to quickly. Not all the way out...*there.*'

She meant: live somewhere I can get to if you're going to top yourself, somewhere with a good hospital nearby.

I want to ask her why *she* can't live somewhere I can get to quickly, or why she can't live with other people. But perhaps it's a blessing anyway. This way, she finds it harder to invite me out for cocktails or shopping. And if I lived anywhere else, I wouldn't have Sal. I often wonder if Mum still thinks I'm going to top myself, even now.

In the Bathhouse I take off my layers of winter clothing and get into the swimming costume that's always in my handbag. My phone beeps before I have the locker closed. Nick again: I tell him I'm fine. How long will it take for him to realise there's something wrong with me? How long before he realises I'm not who he thinks I am?

Going for dinner at Mum's. I'll text you after, promise. x

I add the kiss this time, and he responds immediately with a kiss of his own. Guess it doesn't take much to fool someone. It even feels good. Could I spend a whole life with Nick like this? I shove the phone into my handbag, under the notification letter. You'll squash any more beeps, I'm sure. I walk fast to the pool. Swimmers part to let me through, as if they can see I'll die without this fix.

And then
the lowering in.
The release.
Oh!

No Nick. No you. No Flash Sale. No Mum. Just weight-lessness. Just water. My drug. I even take pleasure in the sting of the chlorine.

'I'm going to swim twenty laps every day,' Mum said after we returned from Australia.

She raced me on the first lap and won, of course. She always won competitions between us; she engineered it that way. And besides, back then I was like a drowning camel. But she stopped swimming soon after we started. Maybe she only ever wanted me to do it: something other than mope around that flat all day. But now I'd beat her. I'm stronger, paler and more stubborn.

On that first day of swimming, I clutched at the side of the pool, breathless, loving it. Thinking about…*nothing*. It felt like danger. I stayed on while Mum went to work, I did twenty laps, and kept swimming for over an hour afterwards. It was hard and my arms ached, but that cool, stinging water running over my face and into my ears blocked you out. The water made me forget, made me think only of my legs kicking, my arms circling. It was so different from everything that was you. Nothing mattered in that pool. With you, everything mattered.

Leaning over Mum's kitchen bench, I watch her assemble a lasagne. I've already been to her bathroom cabinet and stolen as many sleeping pills as I think I can get away with. My handbag feels as if it's glowing with all the things I've hidden there. I should've told Mum about the letter as soon as I got in the door.

33

But when I looked at the post on her hall table and saw nothing from Corrective Services, my first reaction was relief.

I jump as Mum uncorks a bottle.

'All okay, darling?' she asks, pouring me a glass.

I nod, reading the label. French red, never Australian. 'All fine.'

We tiptoe around each other now. It was easier when we met at Rosario's on the corner. At least there I could pretend we were work colleagues, or distant cousins catching up—I'd make up a different scenario each time.

'The company's got a lot of sales right now,' I say, if only to break the silence. Then I add, without really thinking about it, 'Maybe I should take one.'

Her mouth is on the wooden spoon, tasting the meat sauce, as she spins around to look at me. I haven't left the country since you. I tell Mum it's because I'm scared of planes, which is sort of true now, but it's more than that. What if it happens again? What if it happens again, but without you?

'Anywhere nice?' She is trying to keep her voice neutral, light. As if this is a normal mother–daughter conversation.

I study the cheese grater, thinking about that student, Hannah Davies, kissing her boyfriend under the stars. The click of the mouse, the ease of it. Why haven't I told Mum about the letter? There *is* something wrong with me. This feeling I have… this *longing*…I don't want anyone else to know, even her. Especially her. Even now, I want you all to myself.

'You could take this Nick, wherever you go?' Mum smiles, almost smugly. 'When am I going to meet him, anyway?'

I shrug, I have no intention of letting that happen any time soon. Maybe I want him all to myself too.

34

'Soon,' I say, attempting a smile of my own to placate her.

Mum would like Nick; she'd think he was sensible. She'd appreciate his shiny leather shoes and salmon-pink shirts and wide, confident smile. She'd like his beautiful, straight teeth. Would she like his blond hair and blue eyes, though, the resemblance?

'I think I want to go somewhere alone,' I say. I'm trying this out, exploring the hesitant desire I have inside me.

Mum tilts her head as she watches me. Is it possible that she received her own notification letter, which she's since hidden? Maybe this dinner is to talk about the next step, or to commiserate.

'Like a gap-year thing?'

'No,' I say.

She can't have a letter. I changed the details on file years ago, stipulating that I would be the only one notified about developments in your sentence. But why didn't I change my name too while I was at it? Why keep my dead name just for them?

'Bit old for a gap year, aren't I?' I say.

'You're only twenty-seven, sweetheart, still time.'

'Mum, I'm on the minimum wage.'

She flinches. 'Not quite minimum, you told me—'

'Close enough.'

She frowns as she puts grated cheese on top of her creation—first cheddar, then mozzarella, then parmesan—and shakes the dish once, twice, as if to shake some sense into it. She must be off her diet.

'If you go away, you might feel like a change when you return. University?'

'You never know.'

She licks the wooden spoon again and studies me. 'So, where do you want to go?'

There it is: the million-dollar question. Unless she is doing a really good job of disguising it, Mum doesn't know anything about your early parole. She'd be acting very differently if she did—freaking out, making me stay in her spare room, not letting me out of her sight. She'd be on the phone to Dad, saying we all need a family meeting. She'd be contacting her anxiety coach. I can't do that to her again. Not to any of us.

I should tell her.

I should.

I reach into the fruit bowl for a grape, roll it around my mouth. You once called me your little rebel, said I'd never be like them, not like any of the cardboard cut-outs who live in cities. But you manipulated me—that's what they all said. What would you think of me now? Not much of a rebel, not enough for you.

Mum walks around the bench towards me, still carrying the wooden spoon, unaware it's dripping sauce on her expensive slate floor. She's smiling. She remains Ms Positive Thinking, even as your release date is burning holes in my handbag.

'You know, I've actually been thinking lately that it's time we went somewhere together,' she says. 'Maybe a nice beach holiday? You know, cocktails and girly chats, and…'

Shoes? I feel like adding. *Fake smiles?*

But I nod and listen like a good daughter. There's power in this, knowing something that she doesn't. I kind of like it.

'We can even bring Dad along?' she adds. 'Of course, he'd stay in another room, another hotel even—'

'Australia?' I say, interrupting, and surprising myself.

I regret the word as soon as it's out. Her mouth opens, then she goes as still as the lasagne dish. I want to wrap my fingers around the release date numbers in your letter, hold them tight in my palm, keep them only for me. If she sees them, I'll lose this tiny shred of power. She'll see inside my head and find you there. She'll own you, too.

She holds my gaze.

'No,' she says quietly. 'Not there.'

I reach for a dish cloth and wipe the sauce drops off the floor, avoiding eye contact. 'It might be good for me to go back. A kind of purging. Cleaning out the system.'

I shrug. Why don't I just take the letter from the handbag, show her and tell her I don't know how I feel about it? Tell her I need help.

Because I'm a coward.

Because I hate her hold on me.

Because you're the secret she doesn't have. You're my power.

'No,' she says again. When she drops the spoon, it bounces on the tiles and sprays globs of sauce onto the cupboard doors. 'You're going back to the psychiatrist.'

I glance at my handbag. It wouldn't take much: just dip my hand in, take the letter out, unfold it and lay it on the bench. She would do the rest, take over and sort everything, like she always does. I stare out the window so I don't look at her. I can't.

It's dark as midnight outside, though it's not late. Perhaps there's another stalker staring in at us as I stare out. Perhaps the letter is wrong and you're already here, waiting for me to leave Mum's, ready to follow.

Would you?

You said once that you could never let me go, that you'd find me anywhere.

Mum is frowning, chewing her lip, the way she looks at art she's considering for her gallery, the expression she uses when she's trying to work out if it's a fake.

'Dad said Sydney was nice.'

I hear the question mark in my voice. Even now, asking for approval. And why Sydney? I've never wanted to go there. Sydney is just another big city; the only difference is it's closer to you. Sydney is where my parents went for a weekend when I was recovering in hospital in Perth.

'It won't help,' she says. 'Going back there.'

Maybe she thinks I'm regressing, choosing you over her again. You over the world. I guess that was always her biggest fear: that your hold on me would trump everything.

'I thought you'd stopped thinking about all that,' she adds. 'What's happened?'

'Nothing.'

My heart's beating so fast I think it's going to explode. I can't do this. I don't want her to know. Not your release date, not anything we share.

'You can't go back,' she says finally, firmly.

And she's right, of course she is. I know it with the certainty that snow melts, spring comes. But she's also wrong. And I want to shout at her until she knows it too. I want her to feel what it's like in my head: wanting something awful and wrong and not knowing what to do about it. I want her to know what it's like to be me.

But I'm not strong enough. I need Mum to shake sense

38

into me, like she did to the lasagne. I'm only strong enough to work for Travel Solutions, to swim in the evenings and to have dinner with Mum afterwards. I'm certainly not strong enough to see you again.

The fury comes fast, like hot coals in my throat. I need to get away. Away from this flat, from Mum and all that she's done for me. I lunge for the door, fumbling with the keys she always leaves in the lock.

'Why does anyone lock a third-floor flat? You're paranoid!' I shout. 'WHO WANTS TO COME IN HERE ANYWAY?'

She grabs my arms and shakes me. Now I'm split in two. I know this feeling: it's when I'm not here, not there, not with her, not with you. Not anywhere. Not anyone.

'Kate!' Mum yells. And then, 'Gemma!'

She never uses my dead name.

'It's okay, calm down. You're here, in my flat.'

'No,' I say. 'NO!'

Because you are here now too. So close I can't see anything else, your hands over my eyes, down my throat, scooping me out.

'You have to stop, Gemma!'

Her face is right in front of me, and I see the lines of make-up around her eyes. The green eyes you liked so much in me. She holds my wrist with one hand, tries to wrestle the key from me with the other, but I grip hard and turn it in the lock. Panic constricts my throat as I tumble out into the hallway.

Mum grabs at me as I hurtle down the stairs. The concierge at the front desk sits up in his chair, staring as I skid past. I want to smack his face until he lowers his eyes.

'Kate!' Mum yells. 'Gemma!'

I can't respond to either of my names. I hurl myself out of the heavy wooden doors and onto the quiet street, where I can breathe and there's only the dark presence of the park opposite. I make myself listen for foxes, vixen calls, night-time birds.

'I'm sorry, I was stupid,' I say, trying to be calm. 'I don't want to go back. You're right.'

Mum looks around—likely checking for prying passers-by—then touches me lightly on the shoulder. I've returned to being breakable.

'I can bring Nick round for dinner,' I continue. 'Next week, soon…' I stumble for what she wants.

She's smiling now. I'm fooling her again, fooling myself.

There were rules in the Victim Impact Box, I remember:

Don't resume contact.

Never react to communications.

Inform those close to you of any new developments.

I should tell her. I look at cracks in the pavement. Mum reaches her hand out again, but I stumble away, steady myself on the window of her local florist. I press against the cold, slick glass, and stare at the flowers.

'You'll be okay,' Mum whispers. 'Time helps, remember? Breathe.'

But time hasn't done shit. You took me for only a few months, and it's been ten years since then. Time is making things worse. Time has made a deeper chasm, one I'm still stuck inside. And there are no handholds here. There's only a freezing high street in West London between Christmas and the new year, and a florist's expensive window display, and no fox calls from the park. Roses. Carnations. Lilies. There is nothing here that would grow near you. Only weeds grow there.

Mum rubs my back like I'm a child. '*Shh*, it's okay. Soon you'll settle down and find something real, and it'll feel just right, you'll see.'

But you were the only real thing.

'No,' I say. 'I can't…!'

I make a strange, strangled noise when my words run out, not quite a scream. Mum's eyes widen. Her hand comes towards me, as if she wants to muffle me, like you did once, but she drops it almost immediately. I want to run, like I wanted to run from you.

Why can't I tell her?

Why won't she let me?

Why won't you?

In the end, we settle for Rosario's. Mum orders lasagne, and I order a salad and try to chew slowly, focusing on simple thoughts. A simple life is what everyone says I should hope for now, but simple is the only thing more impossible than having you.

'Are you still seeing Rhiannon?' Mum leans in closer, after checking the whereabouts of the waiter.

Rhiannon's specialty is trauma. Mum can't afford her, but puts a monthly 'allowance' into my account so I can pay.

'When I can,' I lie.

I'm retreating, I feel it. It's how these visits usually go, at some point. I often wonder why she only ever focuses on you and me as the great relationship tragedy of my existence when there's another right here at this table. I dig my fork into an oiled-up tomato, and it shoots across the table. Mum glances at the waiter again.

You were the one who took her from me. Took Dad, too. And my friends. You took all of them, although you'd argue the opposite, I'm sure. And you know the cruellest thing? After you'd made me love you more than any of them, you went away anyway. Or they took you away. But you know, Ty, on that final day, I was coming around to what you wanted. I might've even stayed with you forever, like you asked for. Does it kill you to know that? That on the day you finally took me to a town and left me at those hospital doors, I felt like an orphan for adoption. A nobody. You were covered in sand and smiling, and I left you to be arrested. Now I don't have you, or anyone. Only Sal, my parents, my plants, and Nick, sometimes. I don't know if that's enough. Mum would throw her lasagne at me if she knew what I was thinking, but she needn't worry. I'm meek again, handcuffed to her Ted Baker tailcoats, fork diligently going back for more salad. A good girl. I'm so expert at playing this part.

We order more wine, talk about Mum's latest gallery acquisitions. I hear my phone beeping in my bag and know it must be Nick. All of a sudden I do want to see him; I could forget all this with Nick, perhaps erase your release date numbers completely.

'Next week then?' Mum says afterwards, as if nothing unusual happened tonight and I didn't make a gaping hole of everything again. She's already reaching for her diary. 'There's New Year's Eve, of course. Are you busy?'

I nod. 'Anna invited me out. I'll be with her.' My lie feels as oily as the tomatoes.

'Oh, that's good, darling, great! Then let's go with Jan the sixth. It was nice here too, wasn't it? So, here again? You free?'

42

There is nothing in my diary, apart from my shifts, for as far into the future as I can imagine. I don't even own a diary.

'Sure,' I say.

As I walk away from the restaurant, I remember how people wanted to fuck me, in pubs, and parks, and in supermarket aisles, back when they recognised me, when they realised I was *that girl*. Proper *It Girl* me. A celebrity, but dirtier. Sand under my nails. It didn't matter that I was a teenager, barely legal.

You're the one from TV.

The one with him.

As if I was hewn from you. As if they only saw me *because*.

They asked if I was damaged. They asked what you'd been like, as if I was a sexpert at seventeen. I didn't tell them I was a virgin. They wouldn't believe it. Besides, I didn't know. Women tried too. Someone called Mary said she wanted to *right me* from you, fix me from my misguided desires, whatever that meant. Others wanted details, always more details. We were a story that sold, and they all wanted more of it.

Then there were the ones who didn't believe. They said I wanted to be taken, that I was gagging for it. They said I wanted attention and had created the whole thing. They said I was fair game, that they could ask me anything.

They did.

Finally, there were the real perverts, men more than twice my age who bought me drinks. I took them because I'd lost most of my friends by then anyway, and they seemed concerned about me, as they slipped arms around my shoulders instead of drugs into my wine. Perhaps they wanted to *right me*, too, perhaps they wanted to be you.

It started then, the mindlessness. I can't remember who I first fucked in the end, but I do know I was getting away, finding a different part of me, finding someone new from you.

Maybe if we'd done it beneath the stars like they all thought, then that question inside me might've had an answer. Or maybe I'd be worse. How would I know?

I found Nick on some dating app. I swiped and swiped until I found you. Only he isn't you, is he? He's a banker who has kept a job down for years, someone with a normal upbringing, who isn't obsessed with living in a desert. Nick hasn't stalked me or kidnapped me either. Not yet. But, like you, he does have dirty-blond hair and bright blue eyes. And he seems to like me. Really, he does. Tonight, maybe this could be enough. Nick knows nothing about my life before. I like it that way. A person can know too much about another before they get together, don't you think?

I check my phone as I'm walking. Sure enough, it was Nick pinging.

So tonight? x

The first time we hooked up was after a couple of bottles of wine in the scabby pub near my place. We fucked in the alley behind the pub because I didn't want to bring him back to my flat. I remembered the slightly hurt look in his eyes when I said goodnight, but not much else.

I can't remember the first time you and I were together either, after you drugged me at the airport. You said it was just a kiss. It's what you told the court months later, too. You swore you hadn't touched me without me being aware of it, not that night or any night. But, thinking now about that first night, those first nights, when you'd drugged me to amnesia, how could anyone prove anything different? The medical examinations I had in Perth were months after you took me. The only person who knows what happened is you.

And how do you remember things now? Do the memories get messed up? Have I twisted in your mind? Has a psychiatrist asked you to draw me, the way Rhiannon asks me to draw you? And do I look like a dark, jagged shadow, like you look in my pictures?

Another ping.

I could meet you in the city this time? I'm at drinks. Come! x

So, Nick is drunk. He wants a booty call. He doesn't want a quiet drink to talk about my past or who I really am. Maybe that's just as well. You wouldn't get drunk before you saw me, and you would love a quiet corner to discuss my past as a victim. That was your favourite topic, after all—me as a victim of my parents' capitalist, shallow lives. You never thought I was your victim.

I shouldn't see Nick now, not after these last few days, and not with that letter in my handbag. But I also have a fantasy that always makes me feel better, and I've never properly enacted it. Nick looks like you, as close as I could find across several dating apps. Maybe there's another way to exorcise you without having to see you again. What is it that Rhiannon always says? *If you can't get rid of him, how does it feel to bring him close instead?*

It might feel good.

On the way to the tube, I buy a half-bottle of vodka from the off-licence and swig until I start to feel pleasantly numb, a little like how it used to be, back in the old days of the bars and the men. I keep Nick's message open as I walk, then reply.

What are you wearing? Don't suppose it's a dirty old shirt and boots?

45

I laugh at what comes back.

Role play? I can do that.

Plenty of women have fantasies of being tied up, dominated. What I want isn't so new. Besides, if I use my imagination, it could be you texting back to me, couldn't it?

Kidnap me. Do it like you mean it.

I don't feel weak, the way I do when I talk with Mum, or Dad, or even Rhiannon. Perhaps it's the wine and the vodka, or the breakdown with Mum, or perhaps it's just a new kind of desperation that comes from knowing your parole date. Whatever it is, I get a thrill when I read Nick's next words.

Where are you?

I'm buzzing all over, bees under my skin. I haven't felt like this for years.

It won't take me long to get ready.

My chest tightens. I still don't know Nick that well. But if this goes wrong, I could ignore him, I could block him entirely.

Hammersmith and City. Just on.

I share my phone location. I'm still a needle in a haystack, a gem in a stone. But you could find me in this city. It wouldn't take you long to work out my routine, to know to watch me at Mum's from the park across the street, to follow me on this line. People pile into the train—too many people, too little space. But you kidnapped me in a busier place than this and got away with it. And if you did it again? If I saw you here? You'd look older, and rougher. I hear prison isn't kind to kidnappers of teenage girls. But you would have tried to keep to yourself, stay out of fights, keep fit. The thudding inside me builds, and now it feels like I am glowing, like you really are here.

I jump when my phone pings again.

I'm coming.

Then again.

I'm close.

I share my new location.

Everything is pinging and buzzing, and maybe this is enough: you being here like this.

I look up at each new station. Only a few more and I'll be off at Liverpool Street and changing to the Central Line. Could you find me before I get to my flat? My head spins as I imagine how many trains there are on this line right now, how many carriages, how many thousands of chances there are of you not finding me at all. It's impossible. It can't happen, I know.

But you are there when I get off. Right there on the platform where the door of my carriage opens. You are nervous, I can tell. My breaths catches as I wait one second before you meet my eyes, two, as the doors open. I gasp as I step out. You look different, of course. Cleaner. No older. But you have come for me. Found me again.

Invite him into your life—Rhiannon in my head with her psychiatrist permission—*see what it might be like.*

'Ready?'

I give a slight nod. This isn't quite how it's meant to be; I should be struggling, and you chasing.

You start talking about how you had to buy a checked shirt from some late-night shop in Soho, asking how I like it, but I ignore that, turning away.

I run.

When I glance back, you're staring after me with your mouth in a perfect O (not your most attractive look). But what did you expect? Did you think I'd give it all to you so easily, so soon? I tilt my head towards the stairs, give a little smile. And that's all it takes. You are running now, too. We slide through the bowels of the underground, dodging revellers and tourists. I hear your laugh behind me as I speed up, though it's different from the laugh I remember. It's freer now, lighter. Perhaps prison hasn't been so bad, after all.

I just make the change. You don't. I see you staring after me again as the Central Line train to Woodford pulls away. I keep your gaze, daring you to think you've lost. But you will be after me, I know. You will be on the tube just behind and coming for me. I'm smiling so hard I have to bury my face in my gloves. I'm marvelling: me, smiling so wide when I didn't think I could anymore. Maybe this—you like this—is an answer.

In the time it takes to get to Barkingside, I drink more of the vodka and the doubts swagger in. Perhaps I should see Rhiannon sooner rather than later, like Mum said. Maybe I am drunker than I think. Maybe what I'm doing right now is the first sign of being crazy.

I turn right when I come out of the tube station and buy another half-bottle at the mini mart for later. Mum slipped twenty pounds into my pocket as I left: what else am I going to spend it on? *Do what I want and you get this,* that money said. *Be a good girl.*

No sign of you. But of course, there isn't. It's a dream, all this. A dangerous fantasy.

I take the short cut, through the alley between the park and the supermarket. It feels different tonight, darker and quieter than usual, much colder too. I'm shivering. But I can smell fox scent, fresh and strong, and that calms me. I check around an abandoned shopping trolley for any of the local homeless people, who all know me. I'll give up my vodka if they're here, and maybe the rest of the twenty. When I first saw you, when I was a child, you were homeless too, living in the rhododendrons in Prince's Park near my house. You came looking for your mum, all the way from Australia, isn't that what you told me? She sent you a letter, said you should live with her. And you came. Only you could never find her, and by the time you heard she had died, you had no money left. Did anyone ever stop to give you vodka and coins then? Did anyone apart from me even notice you? Would it have been any different if someone else had?

I watch the trees, winter-spindly and creaking, but no one stares back. I take a swig and almost cough at the liquor's sudden heat against my cold lips. I keep walking.

'You shouldn't be out here alone.'

I jump, skitter off the path, then look behind.

You?

You.

You've followed me, after all.

In the streetlight, I see the shirt is a little bright, a little too cowboy, but you are almost perfect.

'I said, you shouldn't be out here alone. It's dark, and late.'

Your voice is not quite deep enough.

You come towards me. Something isn't quite right about your half-smile, but…almost. I step backwards all the same. You could still hurt me. Maybe I was stupid to think this version of you would work. But then I smell the aftershave on your neck. You've made an effort. For me. I let you come up close. I can hit you over the head with the bottle if I need to, spit fire in your eyes. I'm always ready. Many of the men I was

49

with early on required push-back, too.

You frown. You think you're doing it wrong.

'Grab me,' I growl.

I have to say it again, more forcefully, before you take my right arm behind my back and lean your body over mine. I hear your breath in my ear, feel its heat on my neck.

'Come on,' I say.

Still, you don't do anything.

'Take me home,' I insist. 'Now.'

I twist out from your grip, and you let me. You let me!

'Come on!' I shout, shoving you. 'You know where I live. Take me!'

Your eyes are wide, but after a moment you pin my arms and push me off the path, so hard I stumble against one of the spindly trees. I reach out and catch a branch, catch my breath.

When you frown again, I pull you to me and kiss you hard, angry and desperate. And you kiss back roughly, too. And then you are pushing me down the path, towards my flat, towards my life as it is now and everything I want you to see. This is good. This is…

'Wait.'

I grab the hair at the base of your skull and push you away from me, gripping your neck and peering into your eyes. Staring back in the weak light, these eyes are paler than I remember. There is no scar on this cheek. It must have faded over the ten years. I blink. It isn't you. I know it. I don't want to know it.

'Is this…?' you start to say. 'Is this what you—?'

'Just do it! Try.'

I'm surprised at how firm I am, at this power I have. The release date in my handbag doesn't matter now, my anxiety has vanished. This is all there is. It has to be.

'Take me back,' I say, smiling. 'Do it!'

And you do. You push and I pull, and it feels good. Bright somehow. As if you are shining beneath the streetlight, making the alley glow. As if we are both golden. Because this time, you saw me waiting: you found me. And I saw you, too.

December 30th

I don't have a hangover, not a terrible one anyway. It's the first thing I notice when I wake. That, and the calm. I've slept *well*. My second thought is that there is someone in my bed. I sit up quickly, pulling the covers around me. This doesn't happen. No one ever stays over.

'Nick?' I say.

'You remembered.' He bows his head, sits up and smiles slowly. His eyes—grey-blue, not vivid enough—are laughing at me. 'But what were you calling me last night? Another name, your ex?'

I'm naked, and I'm cold. I have nothing at all to say to him. There is also a strange light in the room, as if it is already mid-morning. Have I slept in?

'You stayed,' I say, like an idiot.

'I did.'

He doesn't ask if that's okay.

'Shouldn't you be at...? Shouldn't you?' I can't remember where Nick works. In this strange daylight, he doesn't look like you, not *enough* like you.

He laughs. 'Look out the window, Kate.'

Everything is white, more like the moon than Barkingside.

We're in a clean, blank page. Or endless bedsheets. I can't see a single person. No cars, no foxes, no birds. You aren't anywhere, and it is all so quiet. A new world.

I scrunch my face as I remember: last night, what I did... with Nick.

Not you. Never you.

I shake my head to drive away the images.

'Snow day,' Nick says. '*Bed* day.' He reaches over and wraps his arms gently around my waist, which is almost nice, the feeling of his skin against mine. 'Is this the day we finally spend some time with each other?'

My body goes tense, and even though I breathe deeply, I can't relax like I did last night. This soft, quiet morning unsettles me, it's different. Can I reciprocate, wrap my arms around Nick? I touch his wrist, trace his veins with my fingertips. I'd forgotten about the tattoos on his arms—a woman with thick, wavy hair and big lips, which looks comically old-fashioned but is probably ironically cool. You have no tattoos; you believe in different kinds of images. You always said that the only art worth anything was made directly from the land, about the land—*was* the land. You'd never paint a woman who wasn't me onto your skin.

'I need to go to work,' I whisper.

'You can't. Didn't you see outside?'

I stare at him: so, I haven't told him I work from home. I find my coat on the floor, wrap it around me and walk to the bathroom. I don't feel as sick as I usually do after one of these nights. At the toilet, I don't throw up. But I feel tender. What had I asked him to do to me last night? Who had I been? I press my forehead against the toilet roll and remember.

Tie me up, I said. Take off my tights, knot them round the bed posts.

He was hesitant, but I insisted.

He did it for me.

I angle my mouth and bite the paper, use it to stop my scream. But no scream comes. I feel calm again. *Weird.* I haven't felt this calm for years. Not drunk. Not exactly numb. And I can remember what happened, most of it. Nick kissed me in the alley, then took me back here to fuck, but it was you doing it too. You were rough, but I asked you to be. I straddled you and rode you as furiously as if I were erasing a stain. And it felt good.

But it wasn't you.

I spit the toilet roll out.

Mum's right: I should see Rhiannon. Finding you in a crowd is one thing, imagining a whole night with you, believing it...

And now Nick is in my bed, propped against the pillows as if he is waiting for breakfast. Does this mean he thinks he's my boyfriend now? Is he?

He's still grinning at me when I come back, practically bouncing like Tigger. 'So, what shall we do today?'

You would never bounce. You'd be more like Eeyore.

'I told you, I have to work.'

If it's possible, he might grin harder. 'Ah, c'mon, Kate, no one will be at work. We haven't had snow like this for years, not in London. We could...build a snowman? Snowball fight?' He looks at me from beneath his blond hair that falls over his eyes like yours used to, maybe a little more artfully. He's my age. You would be older now; you would have wrinkles. You

54

wouldn't be this pretty; your teeth wouldn't be so white.

'Amazing, isn't it?' he says. 'The snow wasn't forecast to be as heavy here.'

'This was expected?'

His smile is cute if I let it be. His smile tells me to come back to bed, this time for something gentler. I consider it. Could this be my life now? Roleplaying you back, fucking your shadow, and then, over time, morphing you into somebody real, letting you change? Could this new world start now?

He throws a pillow at me. 'Don't you watch the news, Kate? It's been saying snow for days.'

'I watch the news,' I say. The Australian news. The internet news. I watch for news of you.

My eyes flick from his face back to the tattoo. Could I ignore it?

'Remind me what you do?' he says. 'What's so important that requires you to work on a day like this?' He reaches for me again, runs his fingers up my arm until he's clasping my shoulders. 'I know, you're a spy? That would explain everything, why you disappear at a moment's notice, your mysterious exterior...'

'I work from home,' I say, still contemplating the ink on his skin.

'Aha! Spy, website-maker, writer maybe. I know, raunchy blogger!'

I laugh, can't help myself. 'I work for a travel agency.'

Panic grips immediately: he knows too much; he's getting too close. I turn away from him and pull on a T-shirt.

'I don't have any milk,' I say. 'Or bread.'

His smile drops as if I've slapped him. But rather than leaving, he pats the space on the bed beside him.

'C'mon, Kate, I don't want your milk. It's you I want.'

I flinch and he sees.

'Sorry,' he says. 'That was corny, wasn't it?'

I raise my eyebrows. 'A little.'

I see the blush in his ears. Perhaps this is the kind of cheesy conversation that happy couples look back on for years, the kind of thing to put on anniversary cards.

'It's okay,' I say. 'But I do have to work.'

He gets up, throwing off the blankets. 'So, I can get the milk, then make you tea as you work. Simple!'

When he reaches for his jeans beside the bed, I see his arse: bigger than yours, though not unattractive (you always did have a scrawny one). I could get used to an arse like that. I could even get used to a boy like Nick, in time. He sees me staring at him, and I hate myself again.

'Full of secrets,' he says as he passes me, reaching out to touch the tip of my nose. 'I want them.'

And I want to tell them to him, but I know that if I do, he'll be gone. And you'll be gone too. That scares me more than anything.

'It's only just past eight,' Nick says. 'Plenty of time. Have a shower, Kate. Let me make breakfast. I know you have bread; I saw it when we came in last night.'

'How?' I frown.

'I wasn't as drunk as you.' He winks. 'It's fine, seriously. You're fine. Just breakfast, then I'll go. Promise.' He sighs dramatically. 'I'll brave the blizzard by myself, make a snowman alone.'

I almost nod, but somehow manage to keep his gaze. I think I want him to stay. What's happened to the woman I was

56

last night? Does he not hate that I'm now so different? I think I hate it. He grabs the towel on the back of the chair, passes it to me.

'Why are you being so nice?' I say.

Is he being nicer than you?

'I guess I hope someone would repay the favour for me when I'm hungover,' Nick says.

'Right.' I hope he doesn't think that someone is me, and I also hope he does. I don't know anymore.

'Anyone ever tell you you're cute when you're puzzled?'

'Hmm.' I turn for the bathroom. 'Just a cup of tea. There's milk in the fridge.'

He grins. 'Knew it.'

I almost smile.

As the water slides down my body, I think
    of him
    not you,
    taking over my flat and cooking
    (not lizard but toast),
    and of him in my bed, only taking up a little room
    (hardly touching, really).
    His shirt is wrinkled now, his hair is dirtier than blond,
    his smile wide and entirely his.
    Maybe, I think.
    Maybe.

When I come out of the shower, there's no sign of Nick. No boiling kettle, no click of the toaster. It's as silent as outside. But he's still here, I know it—I feel it. Anxiety swirls inside me.

57

What's he doing? Throwing on a dressing gown, I pad to the kitchen, where I find him stooping over the table, his back to me.

'Couldn't you find the teabags?' I say.

He jumps up, his shirt hanging open as he turns to me.

'I…ah…uh…'

I almost laugh at how flustered he is, then I see what is in his hand. The letter. Your release date. I stop still. He's been looking in my handbag.

'What are you doing with that?'

He comes towards me, his arms outstretched, as if he's apologising, but he doesn't say sorry, only gives an embarrassed laugh. 'What is it?'

I shake my head. 'Nothing.'

'Who's Tyler Andrew MacFarlane? Who's Gemma Grace Toombs?'

Fuck. Fuck. FUCK.

'You didn't even boil the kettle,' I say, sharper than I mean to.

'I was about to.' He doesn't move. He keeps his hands up, placating, the letter just out of my reach. 'I was looking for the door key in your bag. I wanted to go out and get us croissants.'

'You were snooping.'

His eyes widen, as if I've slapped him. He looks like a little boy.

'I'm sorry, but I saw the logo on the envelope and the strange name, and I…'

I push him, slamming him into the table. But I'm not being sexy this time and Nick knows it too.

'Shut up,' I say. 'You shouldn't snoop!'

Has he read all of it? Does he know who you are, your release date?

'Whoa,' he says, watching me warily. 'I didn't read much, cool yourself. But hey, if there's something you want to tell me...'

I shake my head. He can't know anything about me, and nothing about you. I slam him into the table again. 'You need to leave!'

'Jeez, don't go scary on me!'

His hands are up again, still holding the letter. He's ruining everything. Thank God I never introduced him to Mum, never brought him any closer. I've backed him into the kitchen now, but that's not the right direction: he has to go down the stairs behind me. My heart's beating too fast, panic shooting up my veins.

'Please, just leave. I mean it.'

He frowns and stands to his full height. 'I don't get you,' he says, his tone of voice now serious. 'One minute you're all over me and the next...'

'Leave.'

'What're you hiding?'

'Nothing!'

He still has it. He won't let it go. He's crushing the envelope.

'Give it back!'

I make a dive for the letter again.

'What is wrong with you?' he says, pulling his arm away as I try to grab at it.

The envelope tears.

I snatch a knife from the bench, by chance one of my sharpest. I hold it up in front of him, pleased by the sudden shock on his face.

'What the hell?'

Now he's listening.

Instantly, he drops the letter. With my left hand, I push the letter away from him. With my right, I grip the knife harder, moving it towards his cheek.

'Don't snoop in my stuff, ever!'

His mouth turns down, his expression nasty. It's what all the men do, eventually, when they realise I'm not who they expected, not who they want.

'What's going on, Kate?' His hard, angry eyes swivel to see the knife. 'You're some kind of crazy now?'

I stare at him. Can he see Gemma behind Kate? Can he see me like you did?

'I don't get you,' he says again. 'Do you even like me?'

When he turns back to me, there's a pleading look in his eyes, which catches me for a second. I start to lower the knife, start to apologise, but can't do more than mumble a beginning. I stare at his shirt, at his pale skin. His snow skin. English skin.

'You know you never even said thank you,' he hisses. 'For what I did last night.'

My fingers fasten around the knife again. 'You should be the one thanking me.'

And he should be, for allowing him to be anything like you.

The glint of the blade is back near his skin. Could it feel like it does in my dreams, when I push the knife into you, the warm, sticky heat over my hands? Could I have the release? The knife is quivering in my fingers. I'm scared now.

He keeps eye contact. 'I should report you.'

Quickly, he reaches for the knife, but I push my shoulder

into him, shoving him away. Then he snatches for my wrist and squeezes, as if he owns me. I won't let him. I hold the knife back to his face. And I cut him. Just a scratch, on his cheek. Just enough to draw blood. Enough to make him leave. And, yes, he steps away from me. He touches his cheek. When he pulls his fingers away, I see the blood on them. I did that. Perhaps I'll leave a scar. There's a voice inside me that says, *You'll look better with that.* Then I start shaking.

He looks scared as he takes another step away. I lower the knife; I'm scared of me too. He stumbles backwards, out of the kitchen. I go after him, still with the knife, still wanting him to leave, and yet…He staggers down the stairs.

'You're seriously nuts, Kate!' he shouts, glaring up at me.

And you know what I do? I laugh. Because I must be nuts, to be doing this, to do what I did last night. At least he's now seeing me as I really am. But I'm shaking all over, and I can't trust myself with this knife. With him.

I stare down at his wide, confused eyes and I want to cry, want to say sorry. I want him to understand. But it's too late. Nick has blood on his cheek; he's probably thinking that he is fleeing for his life.

Is he?

Why did I have to go and ruin it all? If he'd left before it got awkward, if he hadn't found your letter…

I skid down the stairs after him, but he's already out the door, slamming it shut behind him. I lean against it, try to listen for his footsteps outside, but the snow has muffled all sound.

What just happened?

What the hell just happened to me?

I think I've turned into you. Someone who should be locked up.

I stick your letter back together, smooth it, fold it and prop it back up against the cyclamen. Now that it's in one piece again, neat and safe, I feel calmer.

When I go down to the courtyard to feed Sal, she stares back at me with unblinking amber eyes, those tiny fires inside her. She's questioning me, accusing me.

You've got unfinished business. You should sort it.

'And what makes you so perfect?' I ask. 'Where do you go when I don't see you for days?'

She has secrets too. She's a hypocrite, that fox.

When she returns under the shed, I wish I could crawl in with her. But I wait with my breath hanging in the freezing air, watching more snow fall.

Would Nick go to the police?

Does some part of me want him to?

December 31st

> Stop ignoring me.
>
> You need help, Kate.
>
> Tell me why you did that.

Delete. Delete. Delete.

I can't call. Can't speak to anyone. When Anna messages about a New Year's Eve party tomorrow, I say I've already got plans with Mum. When Neri messages, I say I'm seeing Anna.

January 1st

No police turn up. Only more snow. Record-breaking, they're saying, London's Big Freeze. New Year celebrations all called off. But it's summer with you, *Perth Today* reports a heatwave. Climate crisis everywhere.

Even Sal has disappeared. I leave food out for her anyway, and I check the park. There is evidence of the other fox pack, so I wait on the cold, damp bench, and stare at the muted colours of the undergrowth. The small greyish fox I like to call Moonlight is digging in an old bin bag beside a drain. But no Sal. Before I leave, a charm of red-faced goldfinches arrives swiftly in the bare-branched oaks, squeaking like hospital trollies. Then night comes quickly and with more snow.

January 3rd

There is a knock on the door in the middle of the night. Only one. I wait, but whoever it is doesn't knock again.

And Nick persists:

What the hell, Kate? I don't understand you or what's going on.

You knifed me!

I can't answer.

January 4th

Back at work, I decide to focus, concentrate on what I'm selling. It helps to think about other people, not about me, not about Nick. Not even about you.

But who am I kidding?

January 5th

Kate! Stop being so fucking stubborn and just answer!

Delete.

Who even are you?

Delete.

Why're you such a crazy bitch?

I delete my profile on the dating app. He was a mistake anyway, not really like you at all. I don't know what I'll tell Mum. *I knifed him.*

I stand on the doorstep and watch kids throwing snowballs in the middle of the high street, adults holding mugs of tea, talking in groups. Eddie's mini mart is open, brightly lit against the grey day. I wonder what his wife has cooked this time, but I don't go over. No one looks across at me, not even when I roll my own snowball and throw it to land near the kids.

January 6th

Five weeks.

Rather than heading out in the cold to meet Mum, I call her. 'Too much snow to come,' I say.

Sal still hasn't returned. As I wait for her in the courtyard, I watch hundreds of starlings flying in a tight, dark cloud.

The city has shut down.

January 7th

Today, finally, sunlight leaches through bony branches, and through me. I text Anna, then Neri, to see if either of them wants to go for a drink, but they're both already booked up, burnt by all my no-shows no doubt, and who can blame them. I walk to the park and catch a glimpse of Sal in the far corner. I call to her, but she keeps her distance. I wonder if she knows what I did to Nick, if she's scared of me too. No goldfinches or starlings. No birds at all. No living creature wants to come near.

January 9th

The snow has thawed enough for me to travel to the Victorian Bathhouse. Once there, the water releases me; I dive deep and forget.

Afterwards, I visit Mum and pinch more pills from the bathroom. Does she ever think she's going mad, taking more than she should? I'm sure she'd be too scared to tell her GP about her forgetfulness; she never wants anyone to think she's slipping.

We don't talk about you, or Nick. She doesn't even ask. I smile and tell her about the sales to Greece.

January 10th

You're a child, Kate.

You don't get to have everything your own way.

I delete all his messages, delete him. Perhaps it's just as well to whittle things down, become lean, like a fox in winter.

There's another knock on my door at night. I don't bother to check. I tell myself it's just the pub kicking out, just drunk kids. I put the deadlock on.

January 12th

One month.

I sit up in bed and stare at moonlight on snow. I tell myself I am watching for Sal, but really, I am frozen. Anxiety is all through me, eroding me. If I erase you from my life, what's left inside? What parts of me remain that are mine alone?

January 13th

The work emails and chat boxes are about the winter sun in Ibiza, or the recent case of food poisoning in a resort in Tenerife. It's all pretty standard, until this one:

> Hi Kate,
>
> I hope you can help.
>
> I've recently had some bad medical news, and I'm thinking about going on a special trip before my treatment starts properly. Could you talk me through some ideas? I see you're listed as an online Travel Adviser for Australasia. I've always wanted to go down under. I want to see something beautiful—something to reset me. I would value personal recommendations. I love wilderness, tranquillity and travelling solo.
>
> What would you advise?
>
> Rose

My fingers hover. I could forward this enquiry to Charli or another of my colleagues, but already I'm starting to imagine Rose: my age, actually maybe a little older, never married, but never had any real life of her own either, and now with a surprise cancer verdict, or something else horrible. She'd have a red headscarf on, a cup of coffee in her hand. She'd have cats, I think, two; she'd like a dog, but they're not allowed in her tiny London apartment.

I often imagine lives for the people I sell holidays to, whole complicated backstories and family sagas, and today it's easy to let my mind run away. I conjure up the parents who gave Rose such a lovely name and imagine how gently and thoughtfully they brought her up; all organic food and regular trips to the woods to play. I think I would've preferred a name like Rose. Something gorgeous that grows. Something thorny. I go back to the email. If I was really sick and could visit only one final place, I know where it'd be.

Maybe I don't need you to take me there.

January 14th

It's almost impossible to get to Rhiannon in this new world of white. I take the tube as far as I can, then walk the final stretch. Lampposts emerge from the snow, fallen leaves peer from under dirty white covers. Barely any sound but the crunch of my boots.

A maintenance dose, Rhiannon calls it. Enough to keep me steady but not fix anything new, an appointment every month or so. Soon it'll be coming up to my ten-year anniversary with Rhiannon. Is that the kind of thing a client celebrates with her therapist?

I stretch my gloved hand into the space beside me and thread my fingers through the air. You would like this weather, forcing the big city to a standstill. Snow in London is like rain in the desert; they both make everything stop. You'd say this was nature triumphing once again. I imagine you here, drawing pictures with the tips of your boots, making arcs and loops in the whiteness. You'd colour the patterns with winter berries, holly leaves and ivy stolen from parks.

As I walk, I think how small London is compared to the land you took me to. If a scale map of London were placed inside a scale map of your desert, and my regular routes traced across yours, how little my life would seem, must always have seemed.

68

My phone pings.

> More snow coming! This really is the most beautiful country—we are so lucky! Xxx

But I don't see a country. I see white smothered buildings, and a veiled message in my mother's words—England is better than Australia, why would I ever want to go back there?

On the next corner is a man begging for change. He is you, of course. But when I get close, I see he is old; too old to be you, and too old to be on the streets in the snow. I give him the few coins I have. He shivers on the wet pavement as he holds the money in his bare, blueish palms.

'My gloves?' I say, pulling them off and placing them in his lap.

'Bless you, lady.'

I imagine taking him home, bathing him and keeping him warm. I could cut his hair and dress him in new, dry clothes: a shirt and boots. Perhaps I could call him Ty. And then he could report me to the police too.

I am crazy, like Nick said.

Longing for warmth, I pull my coat around me as snow slips down the back of the collar. We're not as lucky as Mum says. Perth has 3,212 hours of sunshine each year; London has only 1,481. How many hours of Perth sunshine have you seen where you are?

Rhiannon asks about my dreams, and then, as usual, if I would like to bring you into the room.

'You could draw him, or talk about him?'

I don't tell her that I see you everywhere now; that it is getting worse; that on this journey to her, you were the bus-driver, the

69

pot-washer I saw through a window, a dog-walker, the homeless man. I don't tell her you were Nick. I don't talk about Nick at all. I don't say I've been stockpiling Mum's pills, either. I should say all of it—it's what Mum pays for. I used to say those things.

'Well, if you can't bring Ty in, what about expelling him completely?' she suggests. 'This in-between space doesn't seem comfortable for you.'

'I should expel him,' I say.

She waits and watches, endlessly patient. 'And how might you do that?'

With a knife.

With a car swerving across the street.

With a blow to the head.

Outside her window are the dark tips of bare trees, snowflakes drifting down; whiteness smothering, quietening everything. I'm not strong enough for this. It's been useless coming today. I'm useless. I clench my fists inside my coat sleeves. I want to be Rose, the dying woman who emailed me, planning a final trip to somewhere beautiful and far away. Then nobody could tell me I was wrong for wanting to go to Australia, not if it was my dying wish.

On my way back, I look for the homeless man, but he's moved on. Sipping the coffee I'd bought for him, I hover at the spot where he'd been. The words from Rhiannon's session are like an axe in my head: *expel him.* As if it were as simple as letting out breath.

I take a detour. It's not far from Rhiannon's office to Prince's Park, where you used to live; sometimes I think it might be the reason I picked Rhiannon as a therapist in the first place. Today, in the snow, your park looks like a picture. I sit on the bench near your rhododendrons, where you once made your bed. Although cut back for winter, they still have green leaves. In the early years, after I returned from you, I sat here a lot. Sometimes people took photos of me, or left trinkets for you in your rhododendrons. Sometimes I hid and watched.

I shut my eyes and dig my nails hard into my hands, suddenly furious at myself. Will I spend my whole life trying to let go of you? Will there never be a time that's free from you? I bend down and gather sticks, leaves and berries, shaping them into a wreath in the snow, imagining it glowing with candles. I write your name in the centre.

Ty.

A berry for a full stop, red as blood.

Even when it starts snowing again, your name remains. I dig my nails harder into my palms as I realise what I've done. A shrine, a fucking shrine! So much for expelling you. I stand up, scattering the berries with my boots, trampling the leaves into the snow. You do not deserve a shine. I kick until the snow turns dirty, the cuffs of my jeans sodden, and my fingers numb.

January 15th

Dear Rose,

I'm sorry to hear of your recent medical news. I would be happy to chat about a trip to help you at this difficult time. You mention you like wilderness and beauty and travelling solo: I can understand, I'm much the same.

There are many magnificent places I can suggest; places you should be able to get to without too much strain on your health. The isolation and beauty of the Western Australian deserts are like nothing else on earth, such vivid colours, and endless horizons…

I pause.

Why the hell did I just write that?

I press delete and tell her about the Great Barrier Reef.

January 16th

Dear Kate,

Thank you for your suggestions. I like the idea of the Barrier Reef, but it seems a bit well-trodden. Or should that be well-swum? I want something truly unique for my last solo trip. What would you recommend that you don't recommend for just anyone? What would you pick? Inspire me!

I wait at my laptop.

Not quite four weeks. It will be hot when they let you out. Late summer, the hottest time of all. My mouse hovers over Rose's email and then I type fast:

Have you thought about the outback? The vast Australian deserts?

Maybe Rose could go instead of me—find you, your den, and relive what I can't. But how would she get there? There are no commercial tours to where you took me. From Perth there are only 'desert tours' that go sandboarding or to visit rocks near the coast called the Pinnacles. The sand on these trips is golden, not red; no bloodied smudges on the soles of feet. The roads on these trips are tarmacked, not dirt.

Maybe I could start the first tour to our desert—to your den—and Rose could be my first client. Surely there's a market for sick tours like that. My ridiculous fantasy becomes another excuse for getting back onto Google Earth. Soon I'm zooming in, satellite mode, to where you took me—where I think it is, anyway—where it's blank, unmapped. There are more roads leading out to more mine sites now, but it's too blurry to locate any smaller buildings, one of which could be your den. But I'm close, I know; each time I zoom in I get a better scent.

January 17th

Pleased with the sales I've made this month, Travel Solutions gives me a New Year bonus. I stare for a long time at a new set of numbers: enough money for a flight. Dad could water my plants. I could bring Mum's pills. This time, I could do things my way.

January 18th

I peer under the old bakery shed for Sal, but she's disappeared again. The cat biscuits I left last time are gone, but it might be some other cheeky beggar taking them. A rat, probably.

At the laurel hedge in the park, I discover scuff marks and fur in the slushy mud, but still no Sal. At dusk, I wait. With my binoculars, I can see all the way to the overgrown vegetation by the stream. And there, in the last glimmers of daylight, I see her. She's not alone. Tight to her fur is a much bigger, broader-skulled fox, not her usual mate. I almost smile for Sal: an alpha male! She's done well.

'He'll get you in trouble,' I whisper. 'Be careful.'

Her ears twitch at the sound of my voice, but she doesn't turn. She might come back to the shed to have her cubs in spring, but I know she doesn't need me now. As I move away, tears cling to my cheeks like ice.

January 19th

Three and a half weeks.

I take some of the plants from my flat, the hardiest ones, find a spot near the shelter of the laurel hedge and dig them in, my best compost on top. I hope Sal smells me here, lingering in her world, and leaves her scent against mine.

You told me that plants sometimes lie dormant for years, waiting patiently for as long as it takes to grow. As I dig the roots in deep, I too feel like a seed underground, waiting for light, for rain. I sit back on my heels, surveying my work as the snow melts. There is the smallest shred of hope inside me.

January 20th

I often sell a particular small Greek island to students, a paradise where they can help orphaned turtles, those forgotten in the older turtles' rush back to the sea to catch the currents. The students walk along the sand and pick up the stragglers, place them in buckets, which they then empty into the water. The hatchlings swim to find their parents again.

But Kefonias is hard to get to: first the flight to Athens, then the bus to the port, then a ferry to a first island, followed by a connection on a smaller boat. Finally, a taxi or a long walk to the volunteer centre. It's more difficult to get there than to you. Internet and reception are not always reliable, I warn the students. *Perfect,* they say: their mums can't visit.

I have always been a sucker for creatures left behind, orphans and strays, and Mum knows it. I need space: I'll tell her I need hot, white sunshine and time alone.

January 22nd

Three weeks.

Mum is waiting in Rosario's. I kiss her, both cheeks, and order us both a prosecco without asking her first. She raises her eyebrows and smiles but doesn't say anything. Perhaps this is the kind of daughter she has always wanted, someone bold with their alcohol choices, bold with everything.

'I've got an idea of something to do,' I announce as soon as I sit down.

I need to find that spark of fire inside me and fan it while it's alight.

'Sounds good, darling.' She smiles encouragingly. 'What is it?'

For a moment, I have an inkling of what my relationship with Mum could have been if you hadn't happened, if I'd grown up as planned: Mum supporting me out into the world, me accepting her encouragement. I'd be like one of the hatchlings on the beach, following her mother's path. We would swim together.

'I'm going to buy a fare in the Flash Sale,' I announce. 'From the student site. They still have them.'

She stiffens, puts down her glass of prosecco. 'Oh, yes?'

'It's fine! Let me tell you about it.'

It helps that I've already planned the trip so many times with clients; I recite my script like one of my sales pitches. I tell her about the turtle orphanage and the volunteer centre; that there'll be other people my own age around me the whole time; that I'll be like a gap-year student, finding herself, getting back on track. I can play this part.

'I've been thinking about what you said a few weeks ago,' I

continue. 'About trying something new.'

She doesn't move, but if her ears could twitch, she'd look like a fox. And here I was thinking it was just you and me who were like foxes.

'And your job? They're okay with it?'

Of course she would ask about that first. I clench my jaw, angry that she's not simply happy for me, before I remember that it's a lie I'm wanting her to be happy about.

'It's fine,' I say. 'They're encouraging it, in fact. *Research*. I'll be able to sell these trips better if I know them. Anyway, I can still do some work from out there.'

When I tilt my phone and show her my return student ticket to Athens, she gets excited, just like I knew she would, clasping her hands together and almost taking out the waiter arriving with the breadsticks.

'Perhaps I can visit you?'

I tense. Even my time alone is still, it seems, about her, *includes* her. Like you, she can never let me go. When I tell her about the bus and ferry and the smaller boat too, she frowns.

'You can only get there by boat?' she asks.

'It *is* an island.'

She doesn't need to know about the other ticket. She doesn't need to know I haven't told the company anything. Mum watches me across the breadsticks.

'And you feel okay about it?' she says. 'Going away by yourself?'

That's a harder question. I snap the end off a breadstick as I consider my response.

'I need time and space, something new. You said it yourself. I'm sick of being stuck. I need to move forward.'

Mum smiles. It's exactly what she's wanted me to say for a long time. Then the questions start.

Shall I fly with you to Athens?
Are you sure you'll be okay on the plane?
Isn't there someone you can go with?
Tell me about women travelling alone in Greece.

And I can, because I've done it so many times with so many anxious students, and sometimes their parents. Finally, all those years at the job have paid off.

'It'll be okay,' I say. 'If I don't do it, I'll never know if I can. I'll think of it as a challenge.'

Mum gets up, comes round to my side of the table and hugs me like she means it, like she's proud of me. Suddenly, I have no breath at all.

'I'm happy for you, darling,' she says, 'For sorting yourself out, for deciding what you need and going to get it, for growing up.'

And I'm a hatchling on the beach, running for the sea. But I'm also waiting to be picked off by gulls.

January 23rd

Dear Rose,

You asked what special place I'd chose for my own trip? Well, there is somewhere: a place I daydream about. A desert in Australia. Most people think of it as immense and desolate, inhabited by deadly snakes, and it is vast, sure, but it is also vulnerable, with one of the world's most fragile ecosystems. It is spectacularly impressive, but you have to work for the privilege of witnessing its beauty. This desert is not easily packaged for a trip.

What am I doing?

I sit back and stare at the screen. Why would Rose want to know my thoughts about our desert? If I'm going to tell her about the outback, I should tell her about the luxury train journey on the Ghan from Darwin to Adelaide, about Uluru and Kings Canyon. But nobody else is asking me what I think about anything that matters, and I have so much to spill. The cursor blinks. Why do I really want to tell all this to Rose?

While I hover in front of the screen, bushfires rage across the land towards you. Perhaps, before I get there, they could burn you alive, your prison an oven.

January 31st

Around ten p.m., Nick turns up at my door. I see him in the peephole. I've had a few whiskies, so I don't even think before I open the door, leaving it on the latch. I stand there, waiting for him to smile at me, forgive me.

He's drunk too—I see that right away. But he's clean-shaven and wearing a fitted blazer, brown winklepickers and white ankle socks. Work drinks again? My cut on his cheek has hardly left a mark. I peer closer: just a tiny bit of scab on his cheekbone.

'Kate,' he says. 'Hi.'

Businesslike.

'Hey, Nick.'

A part of me wants to pick the scab, tease that wound open. Another part of me wants it to heal and disappear, and for us to go back to what we were. I want him to smile like he used to and say that he wants me. But you see, Ty, it seems you've ruined this too. Maybe it never was just him and me in this, no matter how hard I tried.

Did I try?

He's not like you tonight. Too clean. Too monied. Mum would like the look of him now, a neat city boy. Mum would also like Nick and me on a Greek island together saving turtles—I really could turn into the perfect daughter. Clumsily, I start to apologise, but then I notice his cold eyes staring back, his unsmiling mouth. I'm naive, stupid. He doesn't care about me anymore. And that's how it should be after what I did. I swallow my garbled apology.

'Why'd you come back?' I say instead.

He flinches, as if I've hit him, and once again I want to say *sorry* and *please come inside*, but the words stay stubborn in my throat. I'm scared of him, but not in the way I was scared of you. This fear is different: this fear is about me, too. As he sways, still staring, I see dark circles under his eyes, a pimple on his chin, a faint shaving rash on his neck, and some part of me wants to look after him, to protect him—from me.

'Sometimes I hate you, Kate,' he says quietly. 'You know that? I've hated you these past weeks.'

I shrug. I know. I've hated me too.

'I don't understand you,' he adds, 'who you are, why you threw me out, why you…'

He gestures to his cheek, and I look away. He's slurring like an amateur. I want to sit on my couch with him, with whisky, and make him slur more; I want to do more than that. But I'm not ready to play the vixen tonight. And besides, I did that to his cheek. And besides, he knows about you.

'Maybe you shouldn't try to understand,' I say, more firmly than I mean. 'Maybe you should get away from me.'

His eyes widen, and he leans forward into the space between us. I could lean forward and kiss him, or he could kiss me. Neither of us does.

'Tell me then,' he says, 'tell me what I don't know about you.'

80

'You're drunk,' I say.

'You're always drunk.'

'You'll forget this in the morning.'

'I won't, that's the problem. I don't forget you.'

Does he want to save me, tip me back from the edge? Or is it simply that, if he can't understand me, he can't control me? What is it with men always needing control?

'Have you been to the police?'

He leans back, off balance. 'Haven't decided yet. I have the evidence.' Again, he thrusts a finger at his cheek. 'Are you going to tell me why you did it? Maybe I won't go then.'

Blackmail? Or does he want something much simpler?

I put my hand back on the door handle, ready to shut it again.

'Nick, I can't be a girlfriend,' I say. 'No *us*. I'm not...ready.'

His face hardens. 'I wasn't asking you.'

He jams the tip of his shoe between the door and the frame, leering at me. He wants something else. Something I can't give. Answers. I'm trembling. I want to slam the door against him, break his bones. I could do it.

'Don't come any closer,' I whisper.

'Or what?' He thrusts his face forward, all alcohol fumes. 'What're you hiding from? Why're you hiding from me?'

I get it: I'm the itch he can't scratch. The answers he doesn't have. He's not in control of me, and he hates it. Now I see who he is—with his perfect suit and expensive shoes and ordinary banker's world—and I don't fit him at all.

'I can't be with you,' I say. And then, before I try to close the door, 'Thank you for not saying anything.'

'I haven't decided yet.'

The door thumps against his shoe. He won't let me close it, won't let me return to the safety of my flat. He's right in my face, with his sweet-sour breath, his swaying, his bulk.

'There's something wrong with you, Kate,' he hisses. 'Do you know that?'

I shuffle backwards. Of course there's something wrong with me.

'Just go,' I say.

'I'm giving you a chance. To get help. Not everyone would offer that.'

'I don't need your help.'

I shove the door. But again it hits his foot. Why can't he just let go?

'Why do you always have to be so nasty to me?' he says. 'I know you can be nice; you were before I saw the letter. What happened?'

Is that kindness in his face, or pity? I shake my head at the memory of *that night,* roleplaying you back, him fucking me from behind. When I wanted him to go harder, he pushed deeper, got rougher: he liked it when I wasn't nice then.

'You've been pretending with me.'

I shake my head. 'No.'

It doesn't feel like I'm completely here: I'm floating, looking down at him and me. I step back, blinking to make things clearer.

He knows.

When I don't continue, he throws his hands up. 'There's something missing inside you,' he says. 'And you know what I think? You can't love. You can't do it. You've lost what it takes. There's something wrong with you.'

He taps his temples in time with his slow words, like he means I'm crazy.

I blink at him. 'I don't love you, if that's what you mean.'

'Nice,' he says, his mouth twisting. 'I was just trying to help you, Kate. Nobody else seems to be doing that.'

'I don't need it.' I keep pushing the door against his foot until, finally, he steps backwards, his hands up in a placating gesture. 'Piss off, Nick!'

His expression turns hard immediately.

'You're a bitch,' he says. 'You're so fucking weird.'

He stumbles away from me, still cursing. Breathing fast, I shut the door and feel my way down the wall to the carpet, my feet slipping on the shiny surfaces of the pile of junk mail. Tears are already on my cheeks. But why do I care about him? He doesn't see me like you did; he doesn't care about me. But he is right about one thing: there is something missing.

You took it.

I want it back.

February 5th

One week.

Mum and Dad drive me to the airport, Dad talking non-stop about the deal he got on his new black Audi. Mum and I tune out, like how we used to before it all went wrong, before you, back when we were just an ordinary family. But I feel different today, as if I now have spine where before I was just skin. I'm leaving the old me behind.

Dad finally stops talking and Mum reads us the weather forecast for Athens from her phone. I stare at the wet roads.

'I'll go in alone,' I say. 'Check in by myself. That's okay

with you both, yeah?'

I've agreed this with them already, but I need to confirm it. Mum smiles at me warily, but Dad nods solemnly as he glances at me in the rear-view mirror.

'You won't forget to water my plants?'

Another solemn nod. The plants are in the back seat with me, ready to go to his flat. I brush my fingers against their leaves and wonder if it's possible to miss plants more than people; a very *you* thought. Then Mum starts up again with questions about the turtles and volunteers and the safety of the accommodation.

They still don't know about your release date. It seems unreal that the prison kept me, and me only, on file for notifications. It's like a sign.

I don't let Mum and Dad come beyond the drop-off zone.

'I'll be fine,' I say, as we get out of the car. 'I need to do this.'

'Let her be, Kristen,' Dad says, and for once Mum listens.

Dad passes me my bag, his hands shaking. His watery eyes and his soft, hesitant voice almost make me stop in my tracks. He's changed too these past years. I don't know why everyone is so focused on me as the only one needing help; we've all been chipped away by you. You've got into us all, made us all less than we were.

'Be safe…ah…Kate,' he says. He always stumbles on my name now. He pats me on the head like I'm a toddler. 'We're proud of you.' When I hug him, I hear him murmur, 'Love you, girl.'

Those words are new from him, and my mouth jams before I can say them back. Almost immediately, he steps away awkwardly. My throat is so tight that I can only nod when

84

Mum tells me, again and again, to be safe. When Dad places the biggest wad of cash I've ever seen into my hand, I hug him again. What has happened to me that I can leave them like this? Does it mean you've won? I feel as if I'm being torn apart as I step away from them, but I can't turn around. If I do, I might run back into Mum's arms and play the little girl. I must do this. It will be better in the long run, for all of us.

I think of Nick's hard expression as he stood jammed in my doorway.

You can't love.

There's something missing.

I think of Rose and how brave she is to plan her last trip to somewhere she's never been. I need to be like her now.

Before I step through the sliding doors to the ticket desks, I look back one last time. Mum is crying but trying to hide it. She even wraps her arm around Dad's waist as she smiles at me. It reminds me of the last time we were all at an airport together. After you. After the court case ended and we were coming home. There were so many reporters; we were famous. I remember Mum pushing the cameras away as we headed through the crowds.

Now, as I wave goodbye, she buries her head into Dad's shoulder, the way she used to. I wonder whether her confidence and positivity with me is just an act, whether she plays a part like I do. At least in this final image I have of them, they're together. My leaving could be a good thing for them, too—the gift I give after taking so much.

When I get to Departures, I lean up against a pillar near the toilets, listening to kids screaming, a machine whirring and whirring, endless announcements. I've turned to water again—I'm made of rivers breaking their banks. I have no spine left. I can't do this. But what else is there? Even if I turned left and took that flight to Athens, I'm not booked in at the turtle orphanage. So I turn right towards the Qantas desks.

'To Perth,' I say.

To you.

I will remember it all, this time. No one is holding me steady as I wait to board the plane, pretending I'm only drunk. I don't throw up in the toilet. No one is leading me through the transit lounge showing a fake passport.

Last time, flight attendants gave us champagne. Do you remember that? I don't, and it would've been my first taste. I only know about it from the court transcripts—*celebrating*, you'd said, *newly engaged*. Sixteen and drugged to the eyeballs, and not even a question? How did the staff not know? How did you get that kind of luck?

I keep my nerve as I board the plane, reminding myself that I have to do it, that Mum and Dad will understand. Anyone would. Although *The Daily Mail* would have a field day if they saw me here. I can imagine the headlines:

Stockholm syndrome or masochist?

Back for more.

Victim still controlled!

Or would they write about me burning for revenge, returning for payback?

Now it's her turn.

I booked a window seat so I can watch the land as we descend into Perth. I remember the views from the air on that final flight: swirls of brown and orange, the dried-out creek

86

beds curling like snakes, so like the Indigenous art you told me about and I've researched since. But memory swirls in patterns too, and perhaps I never saw all that when I left. Perth is on the coast; surely it's the sea I should be remembering, not desert.

Perhaps my memory of your arid home—of you, even—is also like a painting: a constructed landscape, a vision, but not the real thing. *My* vision. Which means that what everyone else assumes about you and your desert is also a construction, their vision. I guess there is no such thing as a true vision; everything is always just a *scape*.

The older man beside me turns to talk as we take off. 'Going anywhere nice, love?'

'Work trip.'

'To Australia?' He raises his eyebrows, clearly impressed, then starts on about his daughter who's married an *Aussie bloke* who is building a house, *only right on the bloody beach*. I smile politely. 'You been before?' he says.

'When I was sixteen.' Instantly, I hate myself. Why am I telling him? I should be minimising my trace.

He laughs. 'You still look about sixteen.' I think he's expecting me to take this as a compliment, but I don't acknowledge it. 'Bet it's changed a bit,' he adds eventually.

'Some things might have.' I turn on the screen in front of me and stare at it until he gets the hint.

You're close now, days away. I feel you in my blood, making my pulse race. Now I can't imagine a version of my life in which I don't make this trip: I'd only ever find a way to return. And why shouldn't I let you in properly after all this time?

Supreme Court of Western Australia
PERTH

October 15th

There are so many people in this courtroom, so many different voices. But not yours. There are men here who are tall, tanned, who have the requisite blond hair. But I know I've been wrong: it's not you here today to see me. It's just the memory of you, clinging, lingering. If you were here, there'd be more fuss, media; everyone would notice. But still I can't shake it, this sensation at the back of my neck. Someone is watching. Something is different from what I expected.

Jodie touches my right wrist. 'You need to listen to what's being said,' she reminds me.

As if I could forget. As if there is anywhere else I could be right now.

She gives a little sigh. I know she's worried I'm not taking it all in. *But I'm an old hand at this,* I want to tell her. *I've been here before. Chill, Jodie.* But I nod, my lips pressed tight. She is right. Things are different this time, and I'd do well to remember it.

When the judge calls my name, I hold onto the edge of the table in front of me, aware of the many eyes at my back, as the court clerk reads the charges. The first two are the same as yours were—ironic, really—but the last one is much, much worse.

'Not guilty,' I say, to everything.

The feeling of you being in this room with me is growing stronger. Is it guilt? Longing? A little of both?

The judge is addressing the jury now, outlining the order of the trial ahead. But I know what will happen next. After the opening speeches, the prosecution team will present their case and witnesses, and then it'll be our turn. All the truth and lies of us will fill the spaces in this room. Finally, when Jodie calls me as a defence witness, I will place my hand on the Bible, and I'll say my last words: my testimony. Then, the decision, agreed upon by twelve random people who think they might know something about us, but don't and never will

My skin is hot and clammy, even though the day is cool, unusually so for Perth in October. The forecast said rain and a strong breeze, more like English weather. When I look around, I see winter coats, scarves. Everything is upside down. I feel Jodie's eyes on me. Why is she so worried anyway? Will the result of this case affect her career, change her life like it will for me?

Mr Lowe, the barrister for the prosecution team, stands, and the room quietens. The prickle at the back of my neck is still there. I start scanning again. And suddenly I think I understand: it wasn't you I saw, it was Nick.

Eight months earlier
PERTH

February 6th

Six days.

Once I'm through customs, I stand for a long time on the pavement outside Perth airport. The early-morning air is hot and sweet, and I squint against the sun. I'm waiting for the anxiety to start in my stomach and move like wildfire through my whole body but, apart from a strange fluttering in my throat and chest, it's not as bad as I expected. I keep breathing deeply anyway, then turn my eyelids to the sunshine. I'm finally warm. This feels okay, *good*. I sit on a bench and tuck my smile into my shoulder. After all this time, I've done something by myself, not Mum's decision, or Rhiannon's, not even yours. Nobody knows where I am. Perhaps there's more to me than anyone has ever assumed, even me.

I'm back.

The four-wheel drive hire car I choose is top of the range, better than I need, but I have Dad's money now, so why not? I drive out of the airport onto the highway, heading straight for the prison, drawn like a moth to light. It's crazy, but it also feels right. Is that how you felt when you took me, knowing it was crazy, but realising you had no other choice? An inevitability.

I haven't driven a four-wheel drive since the time I tried to escape in yours, and that didn't go too well, but I like being up high and how the car hogs the streets. Here, I can drive through the middle of the city centre; there is hardly any traffic. I can't imagine doing that in London. They call Perth a big country town, as many people in the whole city as in a few London boroughs. I don't feel as if I'm really here: someone else is driving this car, not me. I'm in Athens, transferring to an island ferry, hanging off the side of a boat, watching for dolphins. I wind down the window to the sound of the lorikeets, loud and rude, so different from the polite English birds. The heat on my arm against the window frame feels good; the pores in my skin are opening up. I want everything this heat can give me.

I've googled where you live many times, but there's not a lot to go on. The prison website contains only a few images of buildings along with a short accompanying text. Apparently, you have a nailed-down bed, a small desk, a chair and a toilet. I drive into the sunlight, my fingers on the steering wheel tapping along to songs on the radio that I haven't heard for years.

The first thing that surprises me is how soon I arrive: less than half an hour from the airport to the prison turnoff. The whole trip from my place to yours, door-to-door, takes only about a day. Easy. The second thing I notice is the long, tree-lined driveway up to the prison buildings. It's as if I am driving into a nature reserve, not a secure unit. I take it slowly, looking for wildlife, wattlebirds, mynahs, Australian magpies. Seeing them is like greeting old friends. There are no foxes, but I know that in Perth, like the rest of the country, foxes are imported vermin; this state has the biggest fence in the world to keep them out. If my Sal were here, she'd likely be poisoned. Gums rush past on either side of my car: ghost gums, she-oaks, untucked paperbarks spilling their pages. You would like them. Did you notice all this when they drove you inside all those years ago? Can you hear the magpies and mynahs from where you are?

My shoulders stiffen as I get closer to the buildings. What if I'm not allowed to drive here, or someone recognises me? After all, I don't have an appointment, no plan. But it's so easy. Soon, I'm at the entrance to the prison, which appears at the end of the driveway like a stately home.

It shouldn't be this easy.

I take a deep breath, and the tang from the eucalypts stays in my throat.

Along the high grey walls are watchtowers with windows, barbed wire and rotating cameras. There are palm trees too, tall and beautiful, and more gum trees, tuarts perhaps, with swirling pale bark. They look like old gentleman, bending together in the afternoon breeze to discuss the day. Their leafy crowns stretch over the prison wall. I imagine you on the other side of this concrete divide, looking up at the same trees, listening to the same birds.

We are so close now.

We breathe the same air.

According to the website, visiting hours are already over for the day, but I pull into the car park anyway. Today I just need to be nearby. Waiting. In front of me are two low buildings, between them a square of vivid green grass leading to a large door. I watch a woman around my age walk through the car park, pass right next to my car, and go straight in. Nobody stops her. Beneath the prison walls are beds of native plants, banksias and bottlebrush, and I can hear muted conversation from workmen trimming trees on the other side of the buildings. Beside the soft greens and browns of the flower beds, the tarmac turns copper in the afternoon light. The smell of eucalypts, of growth, is everywhere. I breathe in deeply. I never imagined a prison would be peaceful. I could get used to a place like this. I should have come sooner.

Can you feel me here?

In the rear-view mirror, my eyes are bloodshot, dark circles beneath them. I don't know what I'll say if an official asks what I am doing here. I am so underprepared. But there is sunlight in this car park, and the same sunlight might be dancing across your skin, too. Can you hear that helicopter overhead and see the blue, cloudless sky?

It feels like I'm the stalker now, Ty. I hold the cards. I am the one waiting.

I think of Rose as I park in front of one of the most expensive hotels in Perth, imagining that this is what she would do.

One final trip.

Going all out.

There must be a kind of freedom in being ill, a narrowing of priorities, a focusing of the mind. I should email her; I feel bad about leaving her hanging. I could recommend she come to Perth and stay in this hotel, enjoy the beaches and restaurants. I could live my time here as if I'm living it for her.

At the front desk, an immaculate receptionist asks what sort of room I'd like.

'High up,' I say. 'I want to see as much of the city as I can.'

Then, when she asks, I do something I haven't done for years: I give my old name, my dead name.

'Gemma Toombs,' I say. 'I'll pay for ten days up front.'

She nods, nonplussed. I wait for any sign of recognition. Does she remember the name Gemma Toombs? But she just types it into her system and offers me a smile.

'I'll explain how to reach your room…'

I order room service and crack open one of those tiny whiskies from the mini bar. I raise a toast to Rose, hoping she has people around her who care and won't leave her sick and alone. Soon, I open another tiny whisky and raise it to Sal.

Then I text Mum.

> I'm here! Everyone is very friendly and welcoming, and the sea is so warm. Already been in! Turtle watch starts tomorrow. Exciting! Xx

She'll like my message, it's what she would write. Then I send the same text to Dad and thank him for the money. He replies with a wink emoji—*weirdo*—but it makes me smile anyway. I should go away more often; my relationship with my parents already feels stronger. I feel stronger.

But I don't feel relaxed. My skin is on fire and I can't stay still. I keep pacing, looking out the window, opening drawers. Here I am, so close. I unpack the few clothes I brought, and all of Mum's pills I've been squirrelling away—thirty-three phenergan, forty-six valium, fifty citalopram—then I add my own stash of mirtazapine, propranolol and zopiclone, and spread them across the bed. I could kill myself several times over. I could kill you several times over. My heart races with the thought and, quickly, I push them into a small toiletries bag that I thrust inside my handbag.

I dig fingernails into my palms.

Stop it.

I'm not here to kill you. Or me.

Nothing's going to be fixed if I do that.

But what if things don't turn out the way I've planned? Or you're not who you should be? Sometimes it helps to have a Plan B.

After another couple of vodkas from the minibar, there's nothing else to do but get ready for bed. For the first time in years, I don't take any of my pills. I've been wanting to give them up for a long time anyway, so why not now, when I can feel everything with full force, and see you with the same clear eyes I had when I was sixteen?

I stand at the floor-to-ceiling windows and watch the city darken, wondering if I can get onto the roof. Falling would be quick, a certain death, no mess like there would be with pills. I bite my lip and watch the sky, hot pink now, the shade of one of Mum's lipsticks. The last of the sun turns the Swan River golden, and I scan for dolphins that swim up from the sea. Perhaps I could swim back with them, keeping pace, heading further and further out, until I can't swim any longer. I'd sink, exhausted, to the bottom—a peaceful way to go.

In the street below, ant people scurry to get to dinner or a movie. I still can't help wondering: if I did kill you, would people see me as a hero this time, or forever a victim? Is there anything I can do now to get rid of that label?

Then, as if she knew I'd been thinking of her, the ping of an email.

Dear Kate,

I'm excited to hear more about your trip ideas. Perhaps I could take that direct flight to Perth you mentioned, and then onwards to explore the great country! Let's start with the craziest itinerary you have and work down from there. Sounds mad, but it will make me smile (hospital appointments today, I need something to cheer me up!). Send me the itinerary for your ultimate trip, where would you go if you could go anywhere?

'Rose,' I say out loud. 'Get out of my head. This is my trip, not yours.'

But I'm smiling; I kind of like that Rose is coming with me.

February 7th
Five days.

I don't think I've slept at all. I go back, of course I do. I can't keep away, like you couldn't. I blink and try to force my eyes wide as I drive; I swerve, once, into the other lane. Several times I wonder where I am, what I'm doing. This isn't real, it can't be. But I get to the tree-lined driveway.

In the prison car park, the gums with the swirling pale bark, my old gentleman, are still gossiping. I would like to lean against one of their trunks and listen, but I stay in the car, waiting. Can you hear the magpies' morning song too? Rolling down the window, I hear a child's voice echo around the car park, a woman shushing her. Then a loudspeaker announcing the beginning of visiting hours. There's a buzzing noise. But the sounds of the magpies, wattlebirds and mynahs prevail.

As I rest back in my seat, a prison officer carrying a bundle under his arm emerges from a side entrance to the left of the main doors. Behind him comes a skinny, older guy. The officer stoops to say something to him, gesturing towards the car park, and then puts the bundle into the older guy's hands.

It's a release.

This is what will happen when you come out.

The officer returns through the side entrance alone, and the released guy looks around at the car park, the trees. Soon, a car pulls up and a woman gets out—younger, larger. His wife? She tries to hug him, but the released guy's arms stay wrapped around the bundle. They walk away from the prison together, heads bowed, talking, as if what is happening is nothing out of the ordinary.

Will anyone be here to meet you?

More cars arrive for visiting hours. Everyone knows what to do, which path to follow. There are lots of kids, so many babies, far more women than men. It's louder now, the birds have competition: it's more like a festival than a prison, all these people moving around the car park in the sunshine. It feels almost happy, hopeful. A smartly dressed woman runs to catch up to the family ahead of her, laughing about her high heels. A bird peels like a tiny bell. And then, once they're all inside, it's quiet again. Just me left in the car park. The pounding in my chest is paralysing. I scan the police cars parked to the right of the entrance: have the officers noticed me? The conditions outlined in the victim-notification letter specify *No less than one hundred metres*. But how close could *I* come to you? There is nothing about that. What if I am the one to approach?

But I don't try to find out, not today. I start the car and head back to the hotel.

February 8th
Four days.

Still no sleep. I should have stayed on the pills. A wave of emotions inside me is about to crash hard. I lie on the bed big enough for a family and think about killing you. When I'm angry, I could do it. You should know how much you've hurt me, and how I feels as if I'm still kidnapped, still tied to you. It would be all over if I could do it. I understand when people say revenge is sweet. I curl up, tight as a nut, and cry as if I'm losing something, or it's already lost.

In the afternoon, I walk around this city where I lived for months while Mum and Dad and I waited for your court case. I didn't want to go home then, back to school, even when my parents tried to convince me, not even when Dad had to return so he wouldn't lose his job. It was as if I'd break a spell if I left.

There are more high-rise buildings now, more office workers and tourists. But this time, no one stares at me. In a department store, I study the knives, winking in the artificial lights: *pick me, pick me.* And I do pick them; one by one, I test their weight, how they feel in my hand, how they nick the skin on my arm, how swift and how smooth.

I take one small, very sharp knife, then collect a bedspread, blue as cuckoos' eggs, sheets, a ceramic bowl, a kettle that whistles, the softest mohair rug and an iron. It's fun carrying it all to the cashier.

'New house,' I say. 'Moving in with my fiancé.'

The girl behind the desk smiles like she's happy for me.

'A nice new start,' she says.

It feels right. The word nesting comes to mind. But what exactly am I preparing for? I leave my new purchases in the footwell of the hire car, too embarrassed to take them up in the lift, past the discreet, perfect receptionists.

February 9th

Three days.

I can't sleep, can't eat, can't think. I'm going mad in this hotel room. For a while, I even imagine someone is following me, chasing me. I catch glimpses of someone in the mirror and in the windows at night. A tall, thin, willowy person.

What would you think of this room? Would you lie with me in my ocean-sized bed?

'It'll get better when I see you,' I say to the mirror.

I walk all the way from the hotel to City Beach in thirty-seven-degree heat. For a moment, I think I see Nick in a crowd out the front of a restaurant. It's strange: now that I'm in Perth, it's not your face I see everywhere, it's his. Is that progress?

At the beach, I leave my clothes in a pile and step into the ocean. It's not cold and the waves are rough. I put my head under straightaway, shut my eyes and kick, hoping for a current to carry me out. But I get pummelled into shore, again and again, as if an animal is tossing me back. I keep my eyes open underwater until they sting. I draw patterns with my toes in the sand.

Grow up, I tell myself, as I step back into my shorts.

Soon, I'll see you.

Soon, it'll be easier.

In the late afternoon, I walk back, still wet, then dried by the warm air before I know it. Coloured lights glow in the sky above Kings Park, and I find myself part of a crowd. I move with them, towards some sort of festival. *The trees speak,* a sign tells me—a light show. A kind of fever is building as I sway with the bodies to booms and crashes, a throbbing drumbeat, noises like thunder and lightning, and words rumbling through the trees:

Kambararang.
Wildflower season.
Time of birth and life.

You would like it. This land lit up. This beauty.

Trees flash yellow and red. Tiny glowing flowers of light fall around me, so real I think they might settle on my shoulders. I reach my fingers into the air to catch them, but my hands remain empty.

Birak.
First summer.

Now shadow animals flee across the canopy. Orange light and crackling fire. Colours light me up. You would be smiling. The saltwater I swallowed earlier is still tangy in my throat as I step forward again with the crowd.

Bunuru.
Second summer.
Season of heat and coming of age.

Bunuru is now, I realise.

Then it's *Djilba,* the season I spent with you in the desert.
Season of wetlands and conception.

And maybe something was planted within me back then in that season, something that's still growing ten years later, something you made. Maybe a new you is growing too, inside those bars.

As the show comes to an end, and I breathe in the smell of citronella and hot chips, I wish I could turn to you and ask if you know these words that are new to me. Six seasons for this vast land seems more reasonable than a mere four. Or perhaps these seasons are just for Perth, and there are more than six for that desert.

From the hill of Kings Park, I look across the dark water towards the lights of the city; the buildings that turn west, back to where I've come from. Behind me, the flat, dry land is waiting, silent and powerful, with its fire-red sunset skies, burning rocks, oily sheens of snakes, and glare of salt-pan patchworks. I often wonder what made the first Europeans think they could control it so easily. You're from England too, Ty, originally, whatever you told me about this land being yours and you being of this land. Maybe you would understand the chaos in my mind, the confusion I have about ownership and the power of control; how it feels possible to own and be owned at the same time.

February 10th

Two days.

I blink awake to messages on my phone.

Mum: So glad you're having a wonderful time, darling. Just what you need. Swim in that warm, bright sea and let your worries sink away. Tell me about the other volunteers, the food, the turtles! Xxx

An unknown number: Where are you?

Is this Nick? Or just a slip of someone's fingers? I click out of it before I'm tempted to reply. There is also an email from Rose.

Kate, you write with such passion about a place that sounds so different from London, almost dreamlike. I never realised the Australian desert was so huge! How do you know it so well? Are you planning any more trips there soon? Any guided tours?

I frown. Maybe I shouldn't drain the contents of the mini bar and then answer emails. I test out the thought of taking Rose on a desert trip with me, imaging us like Thelma and

Louise, driving into an escarpment, having a kind of bucolic gap year. Would having Rose with me fill the absence inside? Would it be better to have her than you? I fling my phone away. What is wrong with me?

I get up and cast the curtains wide to watch the dawn come. I'll find you soon. You'll be real. Better than any of this.

February 11th

One day.

I drive around the city for hours, tears on my face, and end up in a car park north of Fremantle. The Swan River is beside me and I have the urge to jump in, swim and swim. I turn away and glance across the lot to the few shops in the corner: Tax Accountants, Cake Shop, Opportunity Shop, a rundown cafe.

What will I do if someone else is there to meet you instead of me?

If you're alone, I could take you for lunch. Afterwards, we could lie in that big bed in my hotel room. We could talk and talk.

Why me?

Why did you do it?

Did we ever...?

I will wait for your apology.

But you won't have any clothes to go out for lunch, not when they release you. I open the car door and slide out. There's a buzzing feeling inside me: a sort of thrill. This is a plan. This is me preparing for you. So I walk towards the shops, remembering that *opportunity shop* is the charming Australian name for a charity shop. Today the name feels entirely right.

In the window is a smart, dark-grey man's suit. When a

woman calls from the back of the shop—'You alright, love?'—I point to it.

'How much?' I take a wad of notes from my pocket.

The woman frowns as she approaches. 'We've only just put that out.'

I'm ruining her display. But it's your size, and you'd look good in it. She tells me the price and I hand over the money. With a suit, we can pretend. We can go somewhere fancier than a rundown cafe, perhaps to one of the beachside restaurants with a view. I'll get you drunk.

'It's a good suit, this,' she says, as she struggles to remove it from the window. 'You want the shirt too?'

I nod and take the pile of clothes from her. I even buy a sequined top for me, and hand over more cash.

February 12th

The day. The release.

No reporters, only a few cars in the prison car park. I blink, check the date on my phone. The pounding in my chest moves into my throat. Things will be different, I remind myself. Seeing you will be a release for me too. Everything will be better after this.

But it's 11.32, and still no sign of movement at the door. Perhaps you're not coming. It's possible that you committed some misconduct in the past few days and they're keeping you longer. Or that the police know I'm here and they're protecting you from me, waiting until I leave before they sneak you out. Glancing at the cameras, and at the lone police car parked near the entrance, I don't get the feeling of being watched. But then I didn't get that feeling before, when you were watching me.

If you're alone, I'll pull up as you start to walk away. I'll invite you into the car and you'll come, won't you? You owe me that much, at least. It's hot, even with the windows down, and I need the toilet. But what if I go looking for one and that's when you appear. I can't miss you after all this.

Then the side door to the left of the main entrance opens. The same prison guard comes out again, and, like the last time, he's carrying a bundle. I stay very still as he turns back to the door, holds it open for someone else. The released! I lean forward, holding my breath. A man appears. Tall and thin. Blond hair.

It's you.

Only it's not you.

You are taller than this. You are blond as the sun and blue-eyed as the sea. You are proud. You are younger.

This guy is pale, hunched, smaller. His hair is long and thin, in a ponytail, scraggly. This guy has a scruffy beard, and his muscles are wasted. His stomach is firm, but not rock, beneath your T-shirt.

Your T-shirt.

The T-shirt you wore that last day in the desert. What's it doing here? The words on the front say *Telder Station*. I used to think those words might be a clue of where we were, a clue I'd need when I escaped.

Your T-shirt on this guy.

But this isn't Ty. This isn't you. I won't let it be.

Only it is, isn't it?

You've split in two,

like me.

You are who you were, and you are also this.

But I am not scared of you like this. I feel almost…sorry… for you.

The prison guard hands over the bundle in the same careless movement he made with the other man, then goes back through the side door, slams it. And you are left alone. Nobody comes to meet you. There is no reporter taking a picture or thrusting a microphone into your face. It is only you. The whole world has shifted, and only I know.

I should be making my move.

You don't look around, not up to see the birds, or across the forecourt to watch the old man gum trees, or even up to me. You just stuff the bundle into a plastic bag you take from your pocket and walk away. Only me and the birds see. As you go, slowly and quietly, it's me I want to cut into now, to punish myself for believing a fantasy.

This isn't fair; it's not what I deserve.

Is this my last view of you, my kidnapper? The end of it— of you, of us? I want to grab you and shout, *No!* This isn't what I need.

But this is a release, if I let it be.

Could I let it be?

I bite the steering wheel in a silent scream, and watch you disappear, walking down the long, eucalyptus-lined driveway, until I can't even see your shadow on the concrete. I am hollow. I can't move. I will be stuck in this car park forever, until Mum comes to fetch me, and I will sob like a child.

You didn't even look at me.

I dig my fingernails so hard into the steering wheel they break open a seam. I pick it open further, then lean my head down and cry.

I don't follow you. I can't.

Motionless, I listen to my breathing, and to the wattle-birds, the mynahs and magpies. Somehow, I am still alive, and somehow you are too. But I don't know how to move again.

I have lost you.

I will go back to my life in Barkingside, without you.

I think of the pills in my handbag—an option.

And then, as if in a dream, I somehow start the car, pull

out of the car park, past the old man gums. I'm still crying as I turn onto the main road and pass cars, houses, a bus stop. There is only one man waiting at the bus stop, head down, hands clasped.

You.

I veer off the road like a hooligan and park on a verge further on. I hunch down in my seat, but I needn't bother; you don't look up. You are like a statue. What's the use of getting out of jail if you're just going to sit still and look at the pavement? I watch you in the rear-view mirror, trying to pick out the traces I once knew. The shape of you is right, more or less, you're still tall, but you've sagged. You're like an old football, kicked in the middle. I could still invite you into my car and take you away to a quiet place.

But would you have anything to say?

A bus comes by fast and hides you from me, and I'm instantly anxious. What if I lose you again? In the rear-view mirror, I see you get on. So, you do have somewhere to go. When the bus pulls out and overtakes my car, I duck down in my seat. Maybe you'll see me, thump the glass to make the bus stop, run back. But the bus carries on, and I follow.

I keep a few cars between us, but I'm not watching the road like I should; all I can do is stare at the bus. I'm not crying anymore, which feels like a victory. Driving at sixty kilometres an hour feels like a good rhythm, too. I'll just see where you go. I'm sure many people would agree that I'm looking after myself, that I have a right to find out. I'll see where you live and that will be enough, the closure I need.

I overtake the bus as it stops again. I think I see you, about halfway down. You still don't look up. How are you allowed to ignore me when I can never ignore you? I grit my teeth, but the fury inside me feels better than fear. I trail you for close to forty minutes, through the suburb of Canning Vale and places I've never been, through the glare of the day, the house windows glinting. I'm a minotaur in these winding suburban streets and you are my prize. I have the urge to flash my lights and beep my horn as I chase you down, but I don't want to alert you, not yet. I pull back, slowing each time the bus makes a stop. Someone is sitting next to you now; they have no idea about you or what you have done.

When you eventually get off, you keep your head down, and your shadow stretches behind as if it's beckoning me along. I oblige, trailing in my car, still finding it hard to believe you haven't noticed me. Or have you? Is this a ruse to get me to approach you?

You walk for twelve minutes—I measure on the dashboard clock. Wherever you're going, you know the route. When was the last time you came here? There was no bail for you ten years ago. As you turn into a smaller street, Banksia Drive, I hang back and park the car. You've led me into an old housing estate: dusty red-brick dwellings, overgrown gardens, sun-stained cars sitting on front lawns next to rusting swing sets. I follow on foot. I like this new, proactive version of me. Crouching behind a bush, I watch you walk all the way to number 31 Banksia Drive, where you stop.

You knock. When no one answers, you knock again on the glass of the front window, and the curtain twitches. You glance back at the street, but not all the way back to where I am hiding. I don't breathe as we wait.

You step away from the front door and run a hand through

your lanky hair—the only sign that you might care about your appearance. I try to imagine your hair cut and washed, try to picture you with your shoulders pulled back, a tan, a smile. I can't, not quite.

A woman appears in the doorway, and then disappears inside again.

A woman?

Denim shorts over pale legs. A pink tank top. Short, black hair. She couldn't be your sister. She's too thin, she's not blonde. She didn't hug you, either. She just left you on the doorstep, your hands held up in a gesture that could mean something like, *See, I told you I'd come.*

So, who is she? Was she expecting you? And if so, why wasn't she at the prison? She can't care about you that much.

One thing's certain: this isn't your house. You don't believe in houses, in owning anything. You once told me that what's yours is everyone's and what's out there is yours, which is ironic, really, when you took me just for yourself. Nevertheless, you walk into this house without hesitation, a vampire over the threshold. Would it have been as easy if it had been my door you'd arrived at? Would I have stepped aside so calmly? I think of Nick with his toe jammed inside the doorway of my flat, that nasty proprietorial glint in his eyes. What if Nick had been you? You'd have sloped in and expected everything to be like it was, and I would have let you in. The Ty I thought you were would have done that, anyway. The Gemma I thought I was...

But this new you? I don't know anything about this version.

I wait to see if either of you comes out again. The dynamic of that house must have shifted now, like I have inside. With hardly a ripple on the surface, a knock on the door, a step, and all our worlds change.

Who is she?

Prisoners often receive letters from admirers, especially if they look like you did when you went inside. Sometimes they even marry their correspondents while they're behind bars— the ceremony takes place in prison. I've seen the documentaries. This woman could be one of your groupies, an opportunist, someone who claims to love you but doesn't really know you. Maybe you need to be protected from her. There's a gnawing feeling inside me now, and I know I can't leave without finding out more. I duck my head, keep my eyes on the pavement and walk up Banksia Drive, my heart about to explode from anxiety. As I glance up at number 31, I both want and don't want you to come out of the front door. I rehearse lines I could say if you do emerge, but nothing sounds quite right.

The house stays silent, so I creep down the side to the bins, listening for your voice, or hers. I open the lid of the recycling bin, reach armpit deep into packaging and pull out a bill.

A name: Louise M. MacFarlane.

That isn't your sister's name. Or your mother's. Who is she? A wife? The name stares brazenly back at me, telling me I'm trespassing. But when did you get a wife? Why? You wanted me. Only me. You said it would never be any different.

I retreat into the shadows, breathing hard. You both lie under the same surname, lie in the same house. I lurch for my car and leave.

Back in my ocean-sized bed, I stare at the pills spread around me, but drink only rum for now. It's cheap and tangy, bought from the 7-Eleven on the corner. You have the release and the wife. What do I get?

After five pills, I reach for the phone by the bed and dial the number that matches her name. A woman's nasal tone:

Hello—

Who is this—

Look, stop playing funny buggers—

I'll call the police—

The phone clicks off.

After ten pills, I slip on the sequin top from the opportunity shop. It feels right. If I'm not going to wear it for you…

Then I take everything out of the mini bar. How much would it cost if I drank the lot? Would it matter? Mum would be disappointed if she could see me now, which must be part of why I'm doing it. And you wouldn't care, wouldn't know.

After fifteen pills, I pick up the first mini whisky, crack the lid. I'm disappointed in myself. Did I really expect you to be released from prison after ten years and look like you did before? Did I expect you'd still be searching for me? That you'd be repentant?

Yes, I did.

I've been stupid.

I swirl a rum and whisky cocktail in my mouth.

I expected you to be better, bigger—to be who you could've always been. A night together and we would've made things good, found answers for what was lost. An ending. But you've moved on. You've walked away and left me behind. You are not who you were.

I've forgotten to count the pills, and lost most of them in the bedsheets. I drink more of my golden elixir rum cocktail. It gets dark, but I don't go searching for the light switch. Objects in the room are morphing into shadow creatures, demons waiting. In the darkness, I dream you come after me. I run on a hot, tarmacked road, and the skin on my feet peels off like snakeskin, until I'm running on bare bones that are crumbling as you come closer. But when you reach me, you speed past. I'm left breathing hard, alone. I can't catch up.

Somewhere between the sweat, the dehydration and the desert you showed me, between when I said I hated you and when you said you loved me, is when I changed. Back then, you were better; you were real. That's when I loved you, or thought I did. You were a magician; you made light appear from darkness, beauty from ugliness. And you were beautiful, Ty. You made me feel beautiful too, in a way nobody else ever has.

Do you remember?

The first time I wanted to touch you, you were on the veranda of your desert den at the end of the afternoon. In the gold-dappled light, your skin was the colour of dark honey. I came out from the darkness of that room you called my bedroom and I sat with you. You didn't say anything, which wasn't unusual, but you gave me one of your faint, crooked smiles. I looked at your mouth properly for the first time.

And I wanted to touch you.

February 13th

My legs are tangled in the sheets and my mouth is dry. In the grey pre-dawn, my heart is racing and I'm gasping with panic. You are so close, but I am letting you go. I try to sit up but can't. Too sick. There are pill packets, still full, stuck to my sweaty cheeks.

I peel them off and throw them aside. I can't do anything right.

I turn over and try to forget.

I dream about driving towards desert rocks, with Rose beside me. I lean over and kiss her on the lips, and she laughs and places her arm across my shoulder. I tap my hand on her thigh to the beat of music and she squeezes me tight. It's nice and it's not you.

When I wake, it's even hotter. I don't get up to turn the air-con on. I want this sweat, want the water inside me to evaporate, want to be left a husk.

Did I imagine you yesterday?

I try to push the sheets back, but everything is spinning, and I am upside down. There is vomit on the sequins of my top.

Dear Rose,

I'm thinking about where I'd go if it was my last trip. My perfect trip would be more than just Perth. I'd hire a 4x4 and head into the Western Deserts. Straight up the Great Northern Highway, past Cue and Marble Bar and Meekatharra, towards Newman, where there's a turn-off onto a track. I'd follow this track for hours, days maybe, until it peters out. Then I'd drive over red-as-blood sand, until I reached a beautiful stretch of land, secret land. The colours here are brighter than anywhere, the horizon bigger, the silence deeper. The perfect place to run to. I wanted to tell you. I don't know why, but you seem like the kind of customer who'd understand.

February 14th

I slump against the bed, shut my eyes and listen to wind on the windows. The building is swaying. There is nowhere else but this hotel room and these thoughts of you.

118

February 15th

Terrified that you've disappeared, or that I only imagined you, I pull on cargo pants and boots, and head back to Banksia Drive. Out the car window on the way, I see galahs in eucalypts, and the Swan River glinting like a fish. It is too beautiful out there for me to fade away in a hotel room alone.

This time, I park at the end of the street. From here, I can see that the curtains on number 31 are still closed. I wind my window down and smell sweet frangipani flowers. After an hour or so, the front door opens to let in a small, tabby-coloured cat. You'd never let a cat in anywhere, so it must have been her, that woman. I think of her skinny legs and wonder whether she shaved them for when you got out, what else she did to prepare for your arrival…My phone beeps.

Miss you darling. How's it going?

Mum would pick now, wouldn't she? There is no kiss after her message this time. She's hurt I haven't contacted her more often, worried I've forgotten her. It's a jolt to remember Greece, and the lies I've told.

Everything is fine. I'm going on a smaller island expedition soon, so I won't be in contact much unfortunately. It's great here. Thanks for encouraging me to come.

She replies immediately:

Proud of you darling. Keep in touch. X

And there it is, the x. The endorsement. I imagine her hovering beside her phone, waiting for me to type the next bit too. So, I do.

Thanks Mum x

Transaction complete. She's put the phone back in her handbag now, satisfied. Her daughter is as she should be. I sigh and rest my head against the window frame, my temples throbbing.

I tried to articulate this to Rhiannon—how I must be grateful for everything Mum has done for me, even grateful for her pride; grateful that she is somehow responsible for all that is good inside me. How it's either that, or Mum withholds her love entirely. There are so many different conditions for love, and loving someone might be the most complicated thing there is—always a transaction of some sort. You're not all that different from Mum. You thought you were making me into what you wanted me to be. You wanted me to be grateful too.

I glance up, put my phone down on the seat. The front door of 31 Banksia Drive is open again, and now you're standing on the threshold, looking out, a cigarette in your fingertips. You haven't given that up, I see. Slowly, you bring it to your mouth and suck its glowing poison inside you. You could be looking at the desert from the veranda of your den, watching the horizon for change. I run my eyes over you: you're wearing a well-worn blue shirt, the sleeves rolled up to reveal your bare arms, scruffy stonewashed jeans, sunglasses perched on your head. You look so ordinary. At least you've trimmed your beard and washed your hair. After flicking the butt into an empty pot plant, you reach back into the doorway and grab a small backpack, shut the door behind you, and you're on the move.

I slink down in the seat as you pass by on the other side of the road. I feel like a crocodile, my eyes above the water, holding my breath. This is the closest I've been to you for over ten years and I'm not sure how to take you in. It would only need a slight turn of your head for you to see me. And why don't you expect me to be here, Ty? Did you think I'd forget so easily?

You're walking faster today, your shoulders pulled back. Your eyes are still blue as jays' wings; but you look so thin, as if there is no muscle left on your body. What happened behind those bars for you to end up so gaunt?

At the end of the road, you turn right, and, after a few minutes, I start the car and follow. I think of the woman you've left in the house, of her lips on your neck, her hand on your hipbone. You've left her behind.

Again, you get on a bus and, again, I follow it down the highway, but in the other direction this time, towards the city. After about twenty minutes, you get off outside a tired-looking shopping centre. It's harder to keep my eyes on you amid the traffic and pedestrians. No one else pays you the slightest bit of attention. It's easy, isn't it, to pass unnoticed, to be a wolf among sheep? I know that feeling of walking along a busy road carrying something dark inside: a secret no one else sees. Watching you weave through the crowd, I almost swerve into a cyclist. I curse and pull myself together, then park the car carefully in a side street. I put on some dark-red lip-gloss and shake my short hair out so that it spikes at the ends like a manga character. I pull my sunglasses down from the top of my head and jam them against my eyes.

A chat. One conversation. It's not much to ask for.

I've come all this way, after all.

I put the small knife inside my cargo pants pocket, just in case. By the time I walk back to the main road, I'm worried I've lost you. My first thought is that you've cottoned onto me and now you're waiting, somewhere further along the street in a doorway, ready to confront me first. I walk faster, my eyes darting everywhere. When I get to an intersection, I stop. On the corner to the left is a police station. Possible? The sign at the entrance is a list of services and when my eyes snag on the words *Community Corrections Centre*, I remember the victim-notification letter. You're meant to check in as a condition of your parole. And here you are, doing it.

A fresh, new start. A fresh, new you.

I haven't given you the benefit of the doubt.

I wait with my back pressed against the wall of a news-agent, opposite the police station, my sunglasses firmly down. Soon enough, I see I'm right. You come out the door and stand on the steps, looking at the road for a moment, before you turn and walk. I move fast to follow. Almost immediately, you take the first entrance into a park. I should run across the road and tap you on the shoulder. But I hang back. Not yet. What is wrong with me? This is what I came here for, isn't it?

I walk along the edge of the park, peering in. Soon, I lose sight of you, and I panic again. Now I have another thought: maybe you didn't go to the police station to check in, but rather, to tell them about me. You've known I've been watching you; now I'll be accused of stalking. I glance behind me—no police cars following.

What are you doing in a park?

I'm tense as I go through the gates, sweating, but I pull my hoodie over my head anyway. I weave between the flowerbeds, past a pond and a big grassy area surrounded by tall trees. There you are, only a couple of metres away on a park bench.

Even with your darker, longer hair, I recognise the back of your head. I take a step to the side so I can see your cheek too, your scar. I haven't forgotten your story about that scar, or when you told it to me—on one calm, warm evening on the veranda of the den. It happened after your dad died, and you were running from men who were trying to catch you, wild boy that you were. They used a net on you, as if they were catching an animal, and it slammed down over your face. Once caught, you were punished, one of the many times you were hit as a child.

I take another small step, angling myself to see better. Now I can see your eyes behind the sunglasses, your lips moving. You're talking to someone? I've been so focused on you I hadn't noticed the second person on the bench. When I move my gaze from you to see who it is, I go very, very still. You're talking to a girl. A teenager. With long dark hair, wearing a school uniform. She must be about sixteen. She looks like me, how I used to look when you took me.

I turn around, looking for someone to tell.

Why are you doing this? Does she realise who you are?

I gasp a breath. This girl is more tanned than I was, and her eyes are brown; she's prettier. Not quite the same as me. But she's smiling at you. Even from here I see she's not scared. You are making her smile, and now laugh. Her laughter is louder than the mynahs and mudlarks, louder than the crying babies or office workers on their phones.

I want to stop her, stop you, SLAP YOU, take you by the hand and lead you far away.

There's blood in my mouth, and, as I run my tongue over my lip, I taste more. My teeth are knives, shredding me.

What are you doing?

And then, it hits me. I *know*.

I step back as I realise: you, me, you watching in a park. You're going to do it all again. Everything you did with me, you're going to do with her.

You make her laugh again, and I falter, stumble in the dirt. You take something from your pocket, a small bag. It all seems so obvious. You're so predictable. Here are the drugs you're going to use. Inside your backpack, you must have everything you need for her disguise and the getaway afterwards. And then? You will go back to your desert den. *Our* den. And you will do all the things you did with me, and all the other things you didn't do. And she will love you.

My fingers clench into fists. I've been an idiot. You haven't changed. You're just like before, only worse. You're going to do it all again with someone else.

But this time, I'm watching. I can stop it.

I step close enough to hear your conversation.

Your voice, for the first time in ten years. That low, soft drawl. If I shut my eyes, I'm back. But I'm so tense with listening, I can't make out what you're saying. All I hear is the blood pounding in my ears.

You can't take someone else.

It can't happen again.

You open your hand and show her the bag, the drugs. She doesn't run scared. She grabs something in the bag and puts

124

it in her mouth. You dig your fingers into the bag too, and something goes into your mouth too. You smile at her. Then she takes the bag and puts it in her pocket. This is different from what you did with me. I didn't take your drugs willingly; I didn't even know about them.

'I'll see you later then,' she says, smiling. 'Thanks.'

As she stands, I step back and find a tree to steady myself against. I hear you laugh and say something else—words I can't quite catch, but I hear your laugh perfectly. It sounds like before. Like you.

But she is walking away, and you're not following. Perhaps this isn't what it seems. Is this girl someone you know, a family friend? But why the packet, whatever she's taken from you?

'Wait!' you call.

You get up and follow. You don't look back to where I am standing, so visible, behind you. I see your real plan now. You are going to follow her to a more secluded location, where you'll wait until whatever she's just taken starts to kick in, then you'll make your move. You are smiling as you walk after her. That broad, easy smile. It's almost beautiful, almost perfect. But there's nothing about what you're doing that's perfect. You are working out how you can grab her, and I won't let you. I can't. I take the small knife from my pocket and follow. The girl walks past the pond, towards the trees and ferns. You trail behind.

'Wait!' you call again.

She doesn't wait, keeps walking. I will her to move faster. Soon you will catch up. I break into a half-run. Only then do you hear me, my steps loud on the track behind you.

'Hey!' I say, and you stop watching her and turn to me.

I keep running, closing the distance between us. You frown

as you see me; I watch your mouth open in surprise. Now you are thinking about me, not her. I've got you. I clamp my hands around your arms. It's surprisingly easy to pull you away, probably because you've just taken something from that little bag too. Your expression is a mess of confusion as your eyes swim into focus. You've recognised me, haven't you? You're not completely sure yet, but you're starting to comprehend.

You know.

I wait for you to say my name.

Gemma,

Gem.

But you just stare, your mouth still open, your eyes wide as lakes.

'Come with me,' I say.

I don't have to use the knife. I just yank you over towards the ferns, pulling you by your shirt. You look shocked, and you don't resist. If anyone sees us, I'll say I'm an old friend, helping you get your head together. My heart is pounding, everything inside me straining for you to say something back to me: my name.

Through your shirt you feel scrawny, all bones. I'm not scared like I thought I'd be. I feel more alive, more real than ever. This feels good. It feels right. In the trees you start mumbling about needing to get somewhere, about being late. You're avoiding eye contact as you pull away from me, but it's only when we're deeper in among the trees that you really start to struggle.

'What is this?' you hiss.

That's when I show you the knife. You reel backwards, but I'm still gripping you hard.

126

'Don't struggle,' I say.

Your eyes are spinning, looking everywhere but at me. I can feel you shaking, like me, as I clasp my hand to your back, steering you to the exit. How dare you be so wasted and useless after all these years I've waited?

'You're pathetic,' I mutter.

I want to say it louder, shout at you until you are cowering beneath me. But shouting at you isn't enough. I drag you through the trees and back towards the exit to my car, keeping a tight hold on your waist. I can't let go, not like I did when I was sixteen years old. Not when, this time, I can do things my way. I push you through the park gates and up the main road. Your eyes flicker and start to focus on me. Surely, out of all the people who've looked at me over the last ten years, it is you who will finally see me: the Gemma behind the Kate. I wait, clasping you, letting you look.

My name.

This is the moment where things turn out alright: your redemption, our release. We'll talk and you'll understand. We'll go back to the ocean-sized bed in my hotel room, and things will be okay. You'll even explain about the girl—that you weren't going to do it again, not with her, or anyone. I loosen my grip, wait. When your lips part, as if to speak, I almost smile, ready. Then your head turns back towards the road, and you run.

You run?

I'm so shocked I just stare after you for a few seconds. Then I lower the knife, tuck it away. This isn't how it was meant to go. I run down the main road after you. And luck is on my side: you head down the side street where my car is parked, and this is a dead end. As you realise and turn back, you see me, and this

127

time you meet my gaze. But there's no relief in your expression, no love. Only fear.

You hold your arms out, a buffer between us, as you look over my shoulder. You'll try to dodge around me, overpower me, throw me to the ground and make your escape. I'm a couple of metres away now, the knife again held out in front of me.

'Hello, Ty,' I say.

Your staring eyes seem as large as planets as you blunder backwards a couple of steps. Surely, you can't still think there's a way out?

'You were stalking her, weren't you?'

When you don't answer, I jam you up against a brick wall, the firm muscles I've made from swimming holding you there. There's a thud as I push you back. Your head? Your eyes flick back to mine. I feel the heat coming off your skin; I hear your breathing.

Bite me, just go on and sink your teeth in. This is what I want to say. *Bite me, and I'll bite you back.*

You push me. I stumble, but reach for the knife again and hold it close to your face. Is this how it's going to end? Me killing you right here? I could say you followed me and that it was self-defence. You did bad things—you were about to do them again.

'I saw you,' I say.

You look over my shoulder as if you're still thinking of making a run for it.

'You were going to take her.'

I feel the anger inside me like a spreading fire. I lean closer, so close I smell your staleness, your sweat. Since when did you smell like this? Since when did you start to look so old? I twist the knife and cut you beneath your jaw, enough to make you

128

still again. You hardly flinch as you stare at me.

'Don't do it,' you whisper.

I wait for you to say it. *My name.* I want to shake you until you do. I want to dig the knife in to force the word out. I want you to stop thinking about the schoolgirl in the park and the woman in that house, and just think about me. *Remember.*

'I'll go to the cops,' I say. 'I'll tell them what I saw, that you were going to do it all again.'

I'm not wary of you anymore; all my fear is gone. But what is left? Anger? And something else fierce. It snakes through my veins, firing me up, filling me with hatred. I wasn't expecting this. I thought I just wanted to talk, just wanted you to understand. One more night together to make things right, find what was lost.

But now I want you to pay.

I thrust my face up closer. 'Apologise.'

I'm so close I could kiss you. Bite you. You could fall on your knees and beg for forgiveness. You should do all this, and more. My heart is a storm as I try to keep steady.

But your scar looks the same.

Your blue eyes, behind your huge pupils, the same.

But you don't look enough like what I want, what I remember.

'You idiot,' you murmur, 'you'll ruin everything.'

A car goes past the end of the alleyway. Police car. We both notice it.

'I can make them come after you,' I say.

The skin around your left eye twitches. You know I could. I like this power I have over you.

'I'll say you were talking to another underage girl. Like you did before, Tyler MacFarlane.'

Your mouth opens at the sound of your full name, which tastes sour in my mouth, but you don't look like Ty right now—not the Ty inside me—and I can't bring myself to use that softer name. With your wide darting eyes, you look barely human. Sweat beads below your hairline, runs down to your jaw. It should be enough, knowing I can make you sweat, feeling my new power. I step close to you again, really take you in—the sweet, stale smell, your dirt-brown lashes, the cracked edge of your lip. My whole body is trembling, but I make myself stay.

'Apologise,' I say.

You stare at me, your lip curling. 'You first.'

And then you shove me harder, and you're running again. I lurch after you, grasp at you, but even with all the swimming, I'm not strong enough to hold you.

'Just leave me the fuck alone!' you shout.

But I'm not going to do that. Not after what you did, what you were about to do again. Besides, you don't get to tell me what to do anymore.

'The hell I will!'

I barrel my body into you, and you stumble into the brick wall, swearing and reeling. As you lift your hand to your head and find blood, I see confusion in your face again, then surprise when you look back at me. Once, you assumed you could do anything to me: you were strong then, and even if you're wasted now, you could be strong again. I slam you backwards before you've got time to react.

'Come with me and I won't tell,' I say quickly.

You just stare at me. Slowly, I reach for your clammy hand and take it in mine. We both watch our hands, as if they are

130

something separate from us, strange objects to be observed and marvelled at.

'Come with me, Ty,' I say, more gently now, starting to lead you to my car. 'We'll work this out.' I use the voice I reserve for reassuring children and animals. 'No more prison, or police. Just a little talk, you and me. Trust me.'

You're shaking your head, but I can also feel the resistance seeping out of your body as you take these steps with me. I open the door and bundle you into the back seat, where you lie sprawling. Leaning over you, I feel your breath on my cheek as I check your jeans pockets—more little bags of white pills and tight bundles of weed, which I immediately toss into the front passenger seat.

'A druggie now?' I ask. 'Want me to go to the police with that, too?'

'But you said no—?'

I pull the knife out from my pocket again and hold it in front of your face, hoping you can't see it shaking. 'You do what I say now.'

We're as close as we've ever been. As you reach for the pills in the front seat, I slap your arm away.

'No more!'

Again, that surprise in your eyes at my tone of voice. But perhaps this is the real me, my true, strong voice, the one Rhiannon always said I'd find one day. Have I found it? When you see the knife, your eyes roll backwards, before I shake you back to me. I have a junkie in my car, the kind of person my mother turns her nose up at.

I have Tyler MacFarlane. And he's doing what I say.

'Gemma,' you whisper.

Just that.

I inhale sharply. Because my name in your mouth doesn't feel like an answer after all. You shut your eyes, and I wonder if you've passed out, but then you make a sound that could be the beginning of a laugh.

'Gemma...' Your voice is soft and slurred. 'Should've known I'd get this kind of luck...not even out a week before you...'

'...find me.' I finish your sentence.

When you open your eyes, the pupils aren't as huge as before, and your eyes are still blue as summer skies, so much deeper and wider than Nick's. Whatever power I thought I had a moment ago evaporates in the heat of the car.

'Open the door, let me go,' you say. 'Don't follow.'

I shake my head. I'm not letting you go anywhere.

'Whatever you think you're doing, Gem'—I flinch at your abbreviation of my dead name—'you know it's stupid for us both.'

Your voice is slow and lazy. You smile, just a little. Do you think you're back in charge, back controlling me?

'No,' I say. 'This time you listen to me.'

Your mouth hardens, but before you can wrench free, I reach down to the footwell and grab the shiny silver iron from the department store. Your eyes widen.

'What the fuck?' you yell, struggling to push me off.

I slam it into your head fast, once, twice, until you crumple back against the seat. I gasp at the sudden blood on my trembling hands, on you. But you're quiet again, eyes closed, compliant. Now we can get on with things. Now it's my turn.

Still shaking, I squeeze into the front seat and drop behind the steering wheel, my hands sticky with your blood as I try to insert the key in the ignition. Thank God there is still nobody else in the side street. Only us. I start the car and drive. I don't want to turn around yet, don't want to look at you, at what I've done.

I watch the car from above, seeing it weave through the city streets, marvelling at how it signals and changes lanes. I've no idea how I'm managing to drive, or where I'm going, but somehow, we're moving forward. All I know is that I can't take you to my hotel room like this.

The pounding in my ears is deafening as I remember how I hurt Nick, and as I realise what I've just done to you is so much worse. I am so much worse. But you deserve this. You were going to do it again. I am a vigilante. I make myself say the words out loud, say them to you in the back seat, even when there's no response.

Eventually, I screech into an empty car park somewhere to the north of Fremantle, familiar somehow. And then I realise: it's the place where I got your suit. Your suit? I almost laugh. What the fuck was I thinking? That I'd pick you up, you'd change into the suit and we'd go for dinner on the beachfront, as if the past ten years never happened, as if you never did what you did?

I breathe into my spine and pull off my hoodie. I need to get a grip.

You still haven't moved. I lean over and check your pulse, my hands shaking so much I can't keep my fingers steady against your neck. I take off my seatbelt and come closer, holding my hand above your mouth.

A breath. You must be concussed, that's all.

I rest my fingers on your arm. You're warm. I want to clean your face, make you better, cut your hair and shave off the rest of your beard.

I am crazy.

Rhiannon told me to bring you back into my life, invite you in, see where it takes me. And where is that? A dead-end car park beside the Swan River. Perhaps I should haul you from the car and tip you in? Could it be that easy?

My vision is blurring, and I have to shut my eyes until I'm steady again. What am I doing? I should be taking you to the hospital, not to the hotel, not into the river. I should be turning myself in.

I take a deep breath. I won't do any of that.

I know where to take you; I know what I have to do.

I crush one of Mum's sleeping pills with the small knife and dissolve it in a bottle of water—ready for later. I cover you with the soft rug from the department store, check my face in the rear-view mirror for blood, and then I start driving again.

I need to put distance between you and the schoolgirl, between you and the woman in Banksia Drive, between us and the city. We should hole up somewhere, wait until it gets dark, but what if you wake up and start struggling? I can't risk that while we're still in the city. I could tie you up, tape up your mouth or put you in the boot, like you did once with me. But I can't carry you to the boot by myself, and I can't exactly ask someone for help. What would I say? *We were out drunk, celebrating. He had a little too much.* It's easier to get away with kidnapping when you are a man, not a woman.

Kidnapping. I say it out loud.

Because this is what I'm doing, isn't it? I'm you now. But I'll finish the job; I'll do it better.

The tears come so gently that I don't realise I'm crying at first. It's only when I'm gasping for air and can't drive straight that I'm aware of my wet cheeks. I remind myself of the schoolgirl in the park, of how you looked at her, how you followed her, of what you could do, of what you did to me. I tell myself that I'm preventing that schoolgirl from being damaged, like I've been all these years. I'm saving her. Maybe I'm saving that woman in 31 Banksia Drive from you too. I glance at your backpack in the footwell, wondering again what's in it. Is it possible you weren't planning to return to her at all?

You make a soft, gurgling sound, and I lean back and touch your boiling skin. I pull over under the shade of some massive she-oaks and sob. I'm making enough noise to wake you, and yet you're motionless. I don't know what to do. It's already the afternoon and I'm out of the city now; the roads are emptier. I take a sip from a fresh water bottle, then crawl into the back seat with the bottle I prepared for you earlier. You must need fluids. I push your shoulder, but you still don't wake up. You're breathing harder now, hot, sticky breath on the back of my hand.

'Come on, Ty.'

I peel back some of your hair and look at the gash on your head, where the blood has congealed. Would brain damage be a fitting punishment for what you did? Is that what I've done?

I shake you again. 'Come on!'

Your eyelids flicker open, focus on me for a second, then

shut again. I hand you the water, but you're too out of it to grip the bottle.

'Open your mouth.'

And you do. I pour the liquid between your lips. You swallow, as if you trust me. You have no idea what I'm doing to you. And yet you must've done all this, once. Did you pull over to the side of the road too? Doubt yourself? Cry? What I'm doing doesn't feel like revenge, not exactly. It feels like something stronger.

I wait until you've had almost half the bottle and your eyes are closing again. I see the sweat and dirt and yellow in your teeth. The possibility of killing you throbs inside me. I have the pills. It could be as painless as taking an extra sip. Death can be a gift. Sometimes it is beautiful—in some of Shakespeare's plays, and in films about love and sacrifice—that last look, the release, knowing there is no more trying. A prize.

On the edge of suburbia, I pull into a petrol station in a small shopping strip. I change into a clean pair of shorts I'd left in the car and stash the bloodstained cargo pants under the seat. You're still sleeping. Your skin is still hot and your hair is drenched in sweat. You stink even worse. I should clean you up properly, pull the rug off, let your skin breathe, tend the wounds on your head, change your shirt. I like the idea of dressing you, fixing you. But it's too risky now. We need to move as fast as we can for as long as we can.

After filling up with petrol, I head to a builders' merchant round the back of an industrial estate and buy rope, gaffer tape and a crate of water bottles. I pick up antiseptic, hand wipes and a packet of trail mix from a display near the tills. I'll stock up on the rest later. I probably look suspicious enough as it is, although I see other people are doing the same, preparing for road trips.

'Hottest time of the year to be travelling,' one man says to another in the queue. 'Are we mad or something?'

I hurry back to the car and keep driving. When I turn on the radio, 'Working Class Man' blares out. Australian cock rock. You'd probably like it. The singer screams about running like a cyclone—just like us, whirring faster and faster. I drive into the sun, everything glinting gold. It's hard to see straight, I'm so hot. Even the four-wheel drive's power air-con can't cope with the punishing heat. You start snoring; at least I know you're alive.

This is what I wanted, isn't it? You, me and this wide empty land. Action, taking a chance. Inviting you in.

I'm squinting, trying to keep my eyes open, when I hit the creature. A soft thud, then the steering goes. I pull the car over, but you don't stir. The sun is everywhere. I know the advice: don't drive at sunset out here, there are too many roos. But I haven't hit a roo, it's something smaller. When I get out, the heat slams into me, pushing me back. It's my mother saying *Stop*. I gasp.

And then I see it, thrown aside like a piece of rubbish.

A fox.

Really? Out here?

I peer at it to make sure. The first one I've seen in Australia. As I approach, my eyes fill with tears, guilt twisting in my gut. This fox is skinnier and browner than the ones in London. Have I killed her? I kneel down. She's panting, eyes closed, one of her legs twisted. I check down her body but can't see any other obvious wounds, just a bit of blood on her forehead. Maybe she's got concussion like you. If I leave her here, she'll get eaten, picked apart by raptors or dingoes. Or run over again.

I stroke the tip of her ear and think of my Sal. Perhaps she has mated now and is back under the bakery shed waiting for her cubs to arrive. Does she remember me? I lift this fox gently and the slit of one eye opens. She doesn't resist as I wrap her in one of the new towels and lay her in the footwell of the back seat beneath you. You keep snoring.

Walebing, Miling, Wubin. The small towns we pass through seem entirely without movement, their houses like stones. The long, straight road continues endlessly past the service stations and memorial parks and grand old gold rush hotels. No huge road trains out in this darkness. Just the stars, the moon. And perhaps cows and roos I could hit at any moment. I keep driving, my eyes so dry and sore it's almost hard to blink.

The dashboard says 1.48 a.m. when I hear you moan. You're awake! I drive off the road and park beside a couple of trees for camouflage, although there's no need to worry in this empty darkness.

'Wha...? What's going...? Where...?'

I lean between the seats, place my hand on your shoulder. 'You're okay,' I say. 'I'm taking you somewhere safe. It's going to be fine.'

Saying it out loud, it seems so easy, so obvious. Maybe revenge is overrated.

I give you more water. Give myself some too.

Sleep.

I jolt awake in my seat to a loud screeching, a commotion in the back seat. You're shouting, arms flailing. Something small and fast is scurrying around. The fox!

Shit.

I look for the other towel to throw over it, but grab the rug instead. You grapple with the door handle, but I switched on the child-safety lock, so you can't escape. You bash at the window.

'Wait!' I scream.

The fox goes wild again, thrashes out from under the rug and scratches your leg. Your shouts turn hysterical. The fox leaps into the front passenger seat, cowering, shaking, and pisses on the seat, next to the pills.

I unlock the doors and you and I tumble out. I trap the fox and then get away from her stench. When I turn back to you, you're stumbling towards a tree. You steady yourself and piss long and hard, before collapsing against the trunk.

'Better?' I say.

You shake your head, blinking.

We sit against the car in the dark. I attempt a smile, but things aren't right—*you're* not right. You told me before that you'd find me, that we'd meet again, and things would be better. But I found you, and here you are, and nothing feels better.

'You okay?' I whisper.

You crash backwards onto the ground, your eyes open, as if you're looking up at the stars. The gash on your head is bleeding again. I pass you more of your water, and you drink it down. It's not long before you're asleep beside me. I retrieve the rug from the car; it's colder under the clear dark sky. I tuck you up, pushing the yellow tassels beneath your chin. It stinks like fox, but everything stinks now.

Carefully avoiding the shaking fox in the footwell, I also retrieve the tube of antiseptic, a new water bottle and the ceramic bowl, which I fill with water and place next to your head. I scooch my legs under your shoulders and pull your head up until it rests in my lap.

I watch you as you sleep, note the wrinkles on your forehead, around your eyes and mouth, your longer, thinner hair.

How did you get so old? Did you look so much older to me when I was sixteen, too? You're sleeping deeply, evenly, Mum's tablets working a treat. It wouldn't be hard to hold my hand across your mouth, use the fingers on my other hand to pinch your nose shut. Or I could get the pile of towels, bundle them and press. Why shouldn't I, after all you've done? But there's something else. I'm thinking about what you promised when I was sixteen. How you said we'd return.

I use one of the towels to dab your head wound, wipe away the dried blood, then I smear on antiseptic cream. I must keep the wound clean, can't let the flies get in. They'll be back in force when the sun comes up. Your head in my lap, I study you, my fingertips grazing your scar as lightly as a butterfly. You're not frowning now. No longer a kidnapper or a jailbird. Almost beautiful. Almost.

The fox bares her teeth when she sees me, crouching and shaking under the front passenger seat. She's made the car smell so putrid I gag. I pour water into an empty takeaway coffee cup and hold it out for her. I want to touch her, help her, but as I get closer, she lunges at me.

'You're not really like my Sal, are you?' I whisper. 'C'mon, just drink and rest.'

When she finally starts to drink, I pour a little of your tainted water into her cup. Soon enough, it's easy to wrap her up and lay her in the boot.

The sun's already hot when your eyes open. I've been sleeping too, beside you, my head resting near yours. I don't know for how long.

141

'Come on,' I say. 'We better get going.'

You let me pull you to your feet, calling me by another name. Marie. Your sister's. You must be delirious. You follow me, murmuring something about your dad, how he won't be home for another hour, and I take the opportunity to force some trail mix into your mouth. You look at me, clear-eyed for a moment, as you chew.

'Where we going?' you mumble.

'Somewhere safer.'

Perhaps I'm delirious too. This is a dream. I'm not doing this at all. I'm in my hot flat above the Barkingside bakery, about to wake up. Or I'm sleeping on a beach in Greece.

'We can't stay here,' I say.

You reach up and touch your head, then turn and look at the flat dirt behind and the empty road in front. 'Ow,' you say. 'What did you do to me?'

I drive for hours on the Great Northern Highway, the windows down and the air-con blasting too. Soon everything is soft with pink sunrise. It's not long before the day turns bolder, half-orange, half-blue, and everything splits, half the world land, half sky. I'd forgotten how big a sky can be, how much land there is beneath, how the world is made of opposites.

When I stop for petrol again in Mount Magnet, you are sitting up in the back seat. I hand you more of your adulterated water, hoping it kicks in before you realise it's what's making you sleepy. I feel a twinge of guilt, until I remember that you must have given me more drugs than I've given you. But I'm still nervous about you being awake while there are people around. Before I get out, I turn in the seat and glare at you.

142

'If you try to make a run for it,' I say, 'if you do anything, I'll say you kidnapped me. That you broke parole. The police will believe me. And there's a station in this town. I've checked.'

I haven't, but you don't know that. Your eyes narrow, but you stay silent. Me against you? In this, at least, I'll be the one believed. You know it too.

You look away. Embarrassed? Ashamed? It's hard to tell, but that hint of admission feels good. You glug down the water and it's not long before you're slumped in the seat. I prop your sunglasses over your eyes.

When I return to the car, you've been sick down your shirt. You look disgusting, your head lolling, stringy vomit through the loose hair of your ponytail. How is this possible when you haven't eaten anything but trail mix for, how long has it been now? I'm running on empty too.

Your eyes are slits and your mouth twitches, as if you're trying to smile, as if you're happy about what you've done.

'Bastard!'

As if the car didn't stink enough already!

You look like you're going to lurch towards me and out of the car. A spewed-up, messed-up Ty could be a giveaway. I push you back across the seat, away from me and out of the sightlines of the shop.

'Did you do this on purpose?'

You give me the leery smile again. Who am I kidding? I did this to you. My heart thuds as I realise how completely out of it you are. Am I slowly killing you? When the odour of your vomit hits me again, I slam the door on you. Back in the driver's seat, I wind the window down and try not to gag, try to

143

look casual as I drive out of Mount Magnet with my face set, sunglasses down. I even manage to open a muesli bar and chuck it at you.

'Eat it!'

When the stink makes me too lightheaded, I turn off into a dirt road, slowing down immediately so I don't skid. There is no one around, nothing but a single bird of prey far above. You're mumbling, off your rocker. As I pull in behind an abandoned farm building, out of sight from the road, I notice the rest of the packet of sleeping pills is now on the centre console. A whole strip is empty.

I twist in my seat to face you. One of your eyes is open, watching me. You are sly and hopeless; you know exactly what you're doing.

'I hate you,' I say slowly. It feels good to put those words into the space between us. Finally. You don't react.

I get out, open your door, grab your shoulders and drag you onto the hot, gravelly land. I push you, and you fall on your shoulder with a grunt, then face-plant. As you right yourself, I see gravel stuck to the blood on your head, to the vomit on your face. You dab at it, study your finger, then sit in the dirt, watching me, laughing, slow, deep, malicious laughter—your way of telling me you're winning.

'You're filthy,' I say.

'And you're a cunt.'

You laugh and laugh.

I want to return you to the prison.

But it's too late to go back.

I'm shaking uncontrollably again as I grab one of the litre-bottles of water I bought in the petrol station, open the lid and tip it over you. You gasp and laugh, and I keep tipping. I grab another bottle and tip that too, until you're soaking and bleeding and laughing, and vomiting in the dirt. When you still don't shut up, I hit you, an open-palm slap across your face. It sends you spinning; I half-expect teeth to fly out in an arc.

I stand in shock. I did that? I didn't even think about it before my hand flew out. You stay face-down for a second, then another, until…you laugh again.

'Just shut up!' I yell.

You smile through bloodied teeth. 'Righto, Gem, righto.' You mime zipping your lips.

I wipe sweat from my eyes. There is saliva and vomit hanging from your lips, sticking to your mousy-blond beard.

'You need a razor,' I say. 'You need to shave all that off.'

I'm scared and thrilled by how much I want to keep hurting you. I could hit you until you finally apologise. I could damage you, ruin what ruined me.

'You took those pills,' I say. 'Didn't you?'

Your head lolls, somewhere between a nod and a shake, then you smile again. You probably know about the adulterated water, too. You lean onto your elbow, grin up at me, before turning your face to the dirt and vomiting again, convulsing into racking coughs, your shoulders shaking. But I don't feel sorry for you. You don't care about me. There really is nothing left of the Ty you made me believe in: the wild boy who saved me from the city and showed me the land. Even so, I can't forget those promises you made all those years ago about us being together again. Your naked body in the pool. The art you made. The way you looked at me as if I was a new, special creature, yours. I have to bite hard into the inside of my cheek

145

to stop the memories overwhelming me.

'Would you rather I left you here?' I say, as I help you lean against the side of the hot car.

Maybe it's what you want. But if I leave you here in the dust, you will have won again. And killing you now would be like killing a half-dead dog; it would be more like mercy.

'We're going to the den,' I say.

Half your face is smiling as you shake your head. *The fuck we are,* your eyes say.

I kick your legs. 'You'll help me find it.'

The smile creeps to the other half of your face as you peer at me, your head tilted back.

'Believe it,' I growl.

I reach into the car and throw the opportunity-shop suit pants and new shirt at you. 'You may as well put these on now.'

The fox's eyes are open but glazed. It's too hot for healing. I give her more water in the same coffee cup, then run my fingers down her leg. It doesn't seem broken, just a little swollen around the ankle joint. She stinks, like you do. I shouldn't have taken her, but if I'd left her on the side of the road, she would have died for certain, picked off by another animal or human. And I was the one who hurt her, after all; she's my responsibility.

I make her a bed inside the cardboard box that contained the ceramic bowl and leave her to it. I'll find more food for us all in the next town. I'll start making things better.

I give you back one of your bags of weed and watch you fossick in your backpack for rolling papers to make a joint. If you've got drugs, you'll keep doing what I say. You smoke out the window.

If you're scared of me, you're not saying it.

If you feel regret, you're not saying it either.

If you're going to apologise…

As I drive, I gaze out at the flat, brown land, the trees spindly and brittle—as if they'd snap from the slightest breath.

'Why didn't you ever tell anyone about the den?' I say. 'All these years you said nothing?'

I watch you in the mirror, running your tongue over your teeth, taking another toke.

''Cos it's mine,' you say. 'Why should I?' When you look back, your eyes are hard. 'Only thing that ever fucking was.'

I press my foot down more firmly on the accelerator. Here's a bit of the old Ty, though not the nice Ty. The sudden fear inside me is a bit of the old Gemma too. I've forgotten key parts of how you were; I've landscaped you into a view I like better. You stare at me, unblinking in the rear-view mirror.

'Everyone left me. Everything. Then you fucked off and all,' you say. 'Back to London.'

Meekatharra is orange: the dust, the heat, the men in mining vests, the sun on the melting tarmac. Burning hot light has oozed into everything: the town is slow and shimmering.

I don't remember any of the places from the first time we made this trip, and Meekatharra is no exception, but I suspect little has changed in these dust-bowl towns. This one has a church, several general stores and three pubs, one with an adjoining motel. A metropolis. There is even a small park with yellow grass, a slide and swing set, and a statue of a soldier.

In the pub we choose, a couple of miners are playing pool. Orange fish and orange chips are the daily special. I ask the server—the first woman I've seen all day—to wrap them and we eat in the car like wolves, teeth bared, sunglasses down. In the rear-view mirror, I watch you lick the grease from your fingers, lips smacking, until it looks like the sun has oozed out over your shiny, hot face too.

'Better food than prison?' I say.

'Why should I tell you anything?'

But this time, you can't keep my gaze. I reckon you must know by now that you owe me everything—everything and anything I ask you for.

When you pass out again, I check my emails. Nothing urgent from work, nothing panicky from Mum. I check the news sites. Nothing. Nobody cares about us. You and I are not such a big thing after all. I email Mum and tell her I'm going on another trip to another island. Then I email Charli to say I have the flu and need time off from work. As I scroll down, I see an email from Rose. I stare at the subject line: *Are you okay?*

I feel guilty; in all the excitement of taking you, I'd forgotten about her. And here she is, waiting—*dying*.

> Dear Kate,
>
> Maybe I'm reading between the lines, but are you okay? You sounded upset in your last email. Let me know. Your wellbeing is more important than planning my silly old trip. Though, have to say, the stuff you wrote about the desert does sound great and I'd love to know more, love to go exactly there on my trip too!

I look over at you, your eyes shut, your chest rising and falling. I have time to respond; it's the least Rose deserves before I disappear from her life. What have I got to lose now?

Dear Rose,

You're right, I'm not myself. So, I'm going away for a bit, somewhere quiet, where I can get my head together. I'm going to find things I've been missing. I'm sorry to leave you, though. I know how important your trip is, and I so wanted to help. But I'm worried about that, too—I've let my own thoughts take over.

I'm going to pass on your details to one of my colleagues. Charli will be able to help you better than me. Like I said, I'm going away, and I don't know when I'll be back. There are things I need to do to find closure. I hope you'll understand.

But my advice if you do still want to see this land is to learn about it first. The Australian desert isn't what you think—not the images Qantas and Tourism Australia show us. The land is more than this, and it's less too. In some ways, it'd be better if you didn't come and explore it—if no tourists did. The land can heal then, grow, away from the pressures of having to be entertainment, make money. But if you do come, be respectful. I'm beginning to think the tour operators are not helping anyone. They make tourists fall in love with a fantasy, not the real desert.

Your head is resting on the sill of the open car window, the sun on your eyelids. What would you think of my words? You told me once that you knew this desert land better than anyone, but now it seems you don't care about it at all. You said this land was your lifeblood, that you measured yourself against it. And I came to measure my feelings for you against it, too. When I started to love the land, I started to love you. Without it, there would never have been an us.

149

February 17th

I see the turn-off for Newman well before any evidence of the town. I want to go and see the place properly this time. We could get a coffee and talk about when I arrived here from your den, after I'd been bitten by the snake. You could look at me over your beer glass and explain that decision, your choice to save me, even when it meant sacrificing yourself, getting arrested, abandoning your well-planned fantasy and leaving your dream place. Do you hate Newman now because this is where it all ended for us? I'm sure the town must have grown and changed since, but we don't stop to find out: the turn-off to the den can't be much further, and anyway, I don't want us to be noticed. Even if the locals don't know The Story of Gemma and Ty, we'll look different from them. We'll stand out.

Your eyes are on the glovebox. I see you've moved your backpack closer to you. I should've looked inside it when I had the chance, checked whether you packed the same sort of equipment to kidnap that schoolgirl as you did when you kidnapped me.

'You're coming with me, remember?' I say.

When you don't respond, I feel the urge to slam on the brake and jolt you. You should be excited to be here again: I

150

am doing what you should be doing, bringing us back. But it's so obvious that you don't care. You want the first bus out. You want Perth and that woman in Banksia Drive. And who knows, if you get back soon enough, she won't even notice you were gone.

You want escape from me.

There's more traffic now, cars and mine trucks, as well as the road trains. Some of the drivers raise a hand in greeting as we pass. Somewhere, not too far on, is the turn-off to the den. I've been counting on the fact that you remember; my ten years of Google Earth scanning and researching won't be enough.

'Pull over,' you say.

'But we're not at the turn-off yet.' I pull the car to the side of the road anyway. 'This isn't far enough.'

I peer out the window at a sign on a dirt road: *BHP Access Track*. A wide, graded road. Staring into the distance, I can see it crosses the rail track. If your turn-off was only this far out of Newman, anyone could have found us last time. From here, a person could walk or hitch back along the highway, a person could get back to Newman before dark. You take the hire-car map from the pouch at the back of the passenger seat, open it for me.

'This is the place,' you say. 'Here, look. My den.'

You stab at the map, at a spot near a mine site on the Fortescue River. Then you gesture to the BHP Access Track again. The fire-red road winds on towards a mountain range, towards the Fortescue River. It's all wrong. But you're hardly looking; you don't care whether I believe you, you just want to get your drugs and go. Do you really think I'm stupid enough to trust you?

I take the map. 'I thought the den was out here,' I say, pointing near Karlamilyi National Park, over past Telfer Mine.

You flinch. It's barely noticeable, but it's your Tell. I'm onto you.

'No,' you say, with that same vague hand gesture to the track on our left. 'It's that way.'

I oblige you and peer again out the dusty car window. There's an old, faded coke can, discarded below the sign. Again, you grab the map and point at a squiggle that could be a creek, or anything, really. 'The den's up there.'

You're lying. This time I'm certain. There was no creek near our den, our water supply came from an underground spring that bubbled up into a rock pool. The den is definitely further along the highway, where I will need to turn off to the right and head towards Karlamilyi.

'So, give me my stuff,' you say, menace in your voice. 'I've shown you where it is.'

'But I don't believe you.' I wait, watching.

You lunge for the glove box, but I intercept and push you back between the seats. You should try to overpower me; it would be the sensible option for you. But you tumble out of the car and stagger down the middle of the highway, stumbling and swaying. *Stupid!* A road train won't be able to stop in time to avoid you. I start up the car and come after you, sidling along beside you, but you keep your face forward, squinting into the sun as you limp on.

'Get in.' I say.

When I lean over and open the passenger door, you turn to me, furious.

'FUCK OFF!'

I tilt my head at you. I'm not going anywhere.

'Fuck off! You're a fucking bitch!'

I jolt the accelerator in anger. I despise the way you're looking at me. The car clips your hip, and you collapse onto the tarmac, hitting your head again. Did I do that intentionally?

I jump out and grab the rope from the boot. The fox barks at me when I bump her box.

'Soon,' I say. 'I'll get you better too.'

I move her box back to the front passenger seat. She'll be safer there, and I'll be able to keep a better watch. But I need to get you off the road before there's any traffic, or you'll become roadkill too. You've rolled onto your back and you're blinking at the sky, stupid. Bending over you, I truss you up as best I can, winding the rope across your shoulders and under your armpits. Then, from the back seat, I lever myself against the middle console and haul you in, my muscles on fire and sweat running down my arms. After you oblige me by pulling your legs in, I slam the door shut. When you start to moan, I clamber back in and gaffer-tape your mouth, throw the rug on top of you, and drive off before another truck comes.

After a last stop for supplies at a welcome petrol station, I drive to Skull Springs Road, where I take a right. Google Earth has shown me that the Telfer Mine access track comes off here. I've spent hours on my laptop tracing this track, zooming in until another smaller track intersects, tracing that one in turn, until it peters out into blank space, untracked land marked by crosshatches. No matter how much I zoomed in, my laptop never revealed anything different. This is where your den must be—deep in this unmapped place.

You see, Ty, I paid attention, and I did my research. I knew all along where it was; I knew better than you. But it'll take hours to get to the next turn-off, where the land will be denser with vegetation, the sands softer, more difficult for the car. I don't know if I've got the skills to drive there, or if this car is up to it. But by then we'll be back in your country, and surely then you'll be tempted to help.

When the sandy track begins, it's impossible to drive above forty kilometres, although is it in better condition than I'd assumed. Someone has been down it with a grader recently. I always thought nobody went anywhere near your den, not even miners; I thought it was the most remote place on earth. Things have changed in the years we've been away, more mine sites, more prospectors.

By sunset, I can't stop blinking and yawning, and I'm starting to swerve. I've got a headache. Sometimes I peer out, hoping to find camels, but, for hours, I've only seen roos, waiting on the side of the track, watching us curiously, like hitchhikers waiting for a ride. We haven't passed a single vehicle, of course, and no cattle either.

'Just mine sites,' I murmur aloud, because the silence is getting to me, especially yours. 'No one to find us.'

I feel as if I'm spinning, as if I'm on drugs too. My hands are shaking again, although that could be from gripping the steering wheel as the car judders over the uneven ground. Everything inside me feels shaken and fragile. I glance over at the sleeping fox; she's juddering too, water spilt in her box.

Before it gets dark, I pull over, not that it matters out here if I park in the middle of the track. I get out and go around to the other side of the car, fling open the door, push down the rug and pull off the gaffer tape. I press another tablet to your gums before you can say anything.

'How you feeling?' I say brightly, as if I'm some sort of nurse and I didn't just run you over.

You spit at me and the pill pops straight out.

I hand you a bottle of water, calculating how much we have left. It's only enough for us both for a few days, which isn't smart, but I also remember the water pipe that you rigged to your den, and that there is fresh water in the middle of those strange golden rocks you called the Separates. Soon, we could bathe in that freshwater spring. I smile as I realise how close it all is. You strain against the ropes I've tied around you.

'It's strange you being the one tied up, isn't it?' I say. 'This time around.'

You glare, daggers in your eyes.

'Do you want to come out of the car?'

Nothing.

'Don't want a pee?'

Before I loosen your ropes, I stroke the blond hairs on your arms. They look the same as before now, your skin browner like before, too. All these tiny pieces of you, returning. We just have to keep finding more, keep looking. But, unlike you, I'm not being put together out here: I'm shedding a skin. Here, I'm peeling away cold London and finding bone underneath, muscle too. I'm becoming less of a victim, as you become more of one. I untie the rope around your chest so that you can sit up, but I keep the one around your legs wound firm.

Leaving you and the fox in the car, I lie on the hot sand in the middle of the orange track, staring at the stars. The constellations are upside down, and there are so many more than in

155

London. I gaze at the ones I recognise. There are more stars here than there are streetlights, candles or flickers of flames in the wotld. More stars than the thoughts in my head, or in yours, or in our heads combined. It's all becoming more familiar: the dusty lemon scent of the plants, the sand stirred by night-time breezes. It's all seeping inside me.

February 18th

A few hours later, I get back into the car. In the inky dawn light, I turn off the track and spot the shadowy Separates in the distance. I aim for them, taking narrower and narrower tracks, animal trails now. The sun falls on these rocks before anything else in the land, igniting them into giant, golden marbles. They could be something from a fairytale, strange and otherworldly. I didn't think they looked real the first time I saw them; it was easy to believe a powerful spirit of the Dreamtime created them into being. They must have an Indigenous name; it's odd you never told me. Now, it seems wrong.

As we get closer, it all looks more familiar, but with more vegetation, dominated by stringy paperbacks and various acacia trees. Ahead, I see the sand dunes. I thought they were mountains once, my ticket out of here, but now I know that we'd get bogged there almost immediately.

I'm still looking for camels—for the one we left behind when we came out from the desert, the one you trained and who became almost a friend. Although, if she did cross my path, I'm not sure I would know how to recognise her now, and she wouldn't know me. Besides, she's probably dead. I watch a couple of huge roos lounging in the shadows of a patch of spindly trees, and a flock of zebra finches zip and squeak past the open window, overtaking the car.

We're no longer on any sort of track; we must have reached the unmapped area. There are wings in my chest, fluttering faster than the finches. The car is going more slowly than it's gone all trip, but we might as well be flying. We're close. I feel it in my skin. Can you feel it too? We bump and sway, swerve and jolt, until my head's out the window, panting for the first taste. I feel like singing.

'Aren't you excited at all?' I say.

In the mirror, you glare at me again.

Soon, I see something different in this red land of rocks and rickety trees. Something man-made. Made by this man. You. Your house.

But it doesn't look the way I remember. It's trashed, like you are.

I drive closer, the car revving and struggling in the softer sand. In the back seat, you remain silent. This is the den. *Your* den. But it's more a pile of rubbish than a home.

'We've found it.'

You keep watching me in the mirror. Feigning indifference?

'Sit up. Look!' I try to contain my frustration, but really, I want to shake you.

You don't look, though. You lounge on the back seat, lazy as the roos.

As we edge closer through the soft sand, I see graffiti on the walls: huge, scrawling black letters, spelling hate. Someone has found this place before us. I put my foot flat to the pedal, even though the car is screaming.

Cunt. Fucker. Devil house.

It does look like a devil house now, like a snake pit, a hell hole.

'Well, shit,' you say finally.

Your dream house, where we'd live for always: ruined. You must be feeling something.

I try to keep my breath steady. Maybe it won't be so bad, close up. But I can see that the roof has fallen in at one corner and the solar panels you set up are smashed and lying in pieces on the ground. Branches and debris cover the veranda; nothing is neat or organised the way you left it. The pen you made for animals has been blown down too, fence posts buried in the sand. Bits of the blue plastic water pipe that ran from the spring in the Separates back to the house are scattered across the sand. Ruined too? The fluttering in my chest is no longer from excitement: I want to cry, drive us back, start again.

I stop the car.

Your smile is a wild, desperate baring of your teeth, how a wolf would smile. Or a fox, backed against the wall.

'Well, shit, Gem,' you say again.

I don't know how long we stay staring at your house. Eventually, I turn off the engine, and the car shudders and sinks. An immense quiet settles around us.

'Shouldn't do that,' you say.

It takes me a moment to come back to you. You mean the car. It's probably going to bog. I don't tell you I haven't planned on driving it anywhere else. Looking at the wreck of the house in front of us, maybe that was the wrong decision. There's nothing here, after all. I feel a well of sadness inside as I run my eyes over the house again. I knew it wouldn't be perfect, but this? The worst thing is knowing that it's not just nature that has eroded your house, but that people have done it too.

'I don't understand,' I murmur. 'You never told anyone where this place was. I was there in the courtroom—you never said...'

You turn away from me and stare at the upholstery of the car seat, then reach forward and pick out a thread. 'It's a free country,' you say. 'Anyone could find it.'

This is the most we've said to each other in a long while; a conversation of sorts. An olive branch? When it gets too hot to stay in the car, I open the door and lurch out.

'What about me?' you say, pointing at your legs, at the tight knots I've made around you.

I suppose it doesn't matter if I untie you now—where can you go? Unless you found the strength to push the car back out of the sand...I appraise you through the window. Once I wouldn't have put anything past you.

'Soon,' I say.

I duck into the driver's seat and take the key from the ignition. When I look back at you, you're as still as a snake, your eyes darting to the glovebox. It's obvious what you want, what you're still planning. I open it and take out the drugs.

I go straight past the house—there'll be time enough to explore that later. Here, on the other side of the building, there's an unobstructed view of the Separates. I have a sudden urge to make sure they're all here, all real. I've thought about these rocks so often—dreamt about them too—but it's still a shock to see them again, rising magnificent from the scrappy scrub and flat land all around, as if someone had dropped them there by accident. I hope whoever ruined your den hasn't ruined these too, defaced them with scrawled, horrible words.

I pull off a small dry branch from one of the mulga trees growing near the side of the den and walk over to where two termite mounds stand erect, exclamation marks in the sand. I dig, deep as I can with only the branch, my small knife, and my hands, and put the car key and the pills in the hole. I drop the bags of weed in too, then remove them. You probably need something to help with the withdrawal from the other drugs I've forced into you.

You see, Ty, I do care.

I fill in the hole with sand and stick the mulga branch in upright, burying the base to mark the spot and leaning the top of the branch against a termite mound. Then I kick more sand over the spot to disguise my digging.

Satisfied with my handiwork, I come back to untie you. You've managed to tip yourself out of the car onto the dirt and are now leaning against a tyre, but your attempt to pull your feet from the ropes is not going well. I take my little knife and slit through them. Now you're free and you watch me, gimlet-eyed. I don't doubt that you could overpower me if you wanted. I should have thought this through. Bringing you here is like bringing a wild animal out from a cage; I should have taken more precautions, kept the ropes around you for longer. When you took me, you had prepared this place for months, years, and I was a teenage girl, not a fully grown man. You could torture me, get me to give you the key and pills, make me take you back. Or worse. It's just you and me out here alone, after all. But you just keep looking at me, as you move your legs out from the rope. Maybe you feel as if you've ruined me enough. I swallow and tighten my grip on the knife all the same.

'Where'd you put everything?' you say, your eyes darting to somewhere behind me.

'Somewhere you can't find.'

The sand in my fingernails stains my skin. I'm hiding things in your land. Once, you would have got angry about me touching your space, changing it. You turn back to face me, as if you're considering all the things you could do to me. I keep your gaze; I won't show any weakness. I'll be like the Separates, immovable.

'How long you going to do this stupid game?'

I shrug. We will stay until you apologise, until you give me something back.

And there we are, a plan.

It feels easier now, doesn't it?

I imagine my skin turning into smooth, hard rock, my emotions and resolve solid. I'm the one in charge.

'If you're good, I'll give you some weed later.'

I don't know whether you believe me, or care, but you look away. You glance towards your den. If you're sad about what you see, your face doesn't show it. Maybe you're thinking that, if you're going to die anywhere, this is as good a place as any. Maybe I should be thinking like that too.

'This place ruined my life,' you say very softly. 'You must know that.'

I didn't expect these words from you. They hurt. There's a whole heap I could tell you about feeling ruined.

'You don't know shit about having your life ruined!'

'Yeah? You reckon?' You turn quickly and spit.

The gob lands near my shoes. I repress the urge to spit back. I take a step towards you, crunching dry leaves.

'Did you try to kill yourself?' I say. 'In prison? People do, I hear. Did you feel so bad that you tried?'

'None of your fucking business.'

But how dare you? Everything about you is my business, just as everything about me was yours.

'Maybe you should've,' I say.

The sun is searing my shoulders, the backs of my legs—it feels like a challenge. Am I tough enough to bear it?

You look at me, one eyebrow raised. 'Beginning to wish I had. Just to escape this nonsense.'

I'm about to unleash the anger inside me, when I remember the fox. The inside of the car must be like a furnace.

I throw open the passenger door and pull the cardboard box out and into the shade by the side of the car. Her eyes are closed, but she's panting hard. Too hard. I find a bottle of un-drugged water and pour some into her cardboard coffee cup, but she doesn't drink. I tempt her with the cat biscuits I bought on one of the fuel stops, but she doesn't react to those either. You watch, shaking your head, eyebrows raised.

'She was hurt,' I say.

'You hit it, you mean.'

So, you do remember. You weren't that out of it after all. You turn back towards the den.

'Do you think she'll be okay?' I ask, then feel stupid for giving you any sort of power in knowing an answer.

You shrug. 'Fucking stupid to bring that here.'

'I couldn't leave her.'

'Bitch is better off dead. Reckon we all are.'

✧

163

You stay slumped in the shade of the car, and I leave the fox with you. She isn't going anywhere either, and I don't think you'll hurt her.

'I'm going to have a look,' I say. 'Sure you don't want to come?'

Your head lolls back, eyes closed against the sun, your suit shirt open. I toss you one of your baggies of weed in case you think about leaving, and walk across the sand. This isn't how I imagined our return to the den.

The wooden slats on the veranda feel rickety under my feet, as if I could fall right through. I tremble as I think about the dark space I'd land in—the snakes, spiders and God knows what else. The front door opens easily, but the contrast with the glare from outside means I can't see for a moment as I step in. The heat inside is heavier, older somehow. Dust hangs in the shafts of light as if waiting, expectant.

In the kitchen, the cupboards are open, messy, empty of food, though I find a few bowls and plates, some cutlery. There are shards of wood where the kitchen table used to be. Beyond, in the living room, the couch is still there, but it's been ripped open, the guts spilling out. The floor is littered with leaves, sand piled in the corners of the room. Part of the roof is hanging down, corru-gated-iron roof panels leaning against the far wall. In one corner of the living room, blackened floorboards suggest someone has tried to make a fire. Either that or the sun has burnt them. It is so much hotter here than I remember; sweat is running down the insides of my thighs. I can't hear anything scuttling, rustling, but it's daytime: sleep-time in the desert. My chest is tight as I breathe the dry air, watching, waiting. What is left in a place where some-thing bad has happened? Do particles of it remain?

I enter the room you called my bedroom, where you tied me to the bedposts. I should do the same to you, see how you like it. There's still a mattress on the bed, still sheets; the room isn't as ruined as the rest, despite the cobwebs on the pillows, and the sand across the floor. Fear of finding a nest, or worse, stops me from opening the chest of drawers to see if my clothes are still there.

Whoever found this house couldn't have known it was yours, could they? But then I remember the words scrawled on the front.

Devil house.

What would they do if they found you here now? Found me?

The bathroom is like the living room, half-falling in, sand everywhere. We can't sleep in this house. Not yet, anyway.

There's only one room left for me to inspect.

The camp bed is still there, in your room. Like the other bed, it looks to be in decent condition. I grab one metal end and drag it across the floor. Nothing scuttles out from underneath it. I manage to fold it up and brush off a few cobwebs, checking first for spiders.

I'm about to back out with it when I spot a brown shadow in the far corner. Perhaps it's just my dry, tired eyes, or a trick of the light through the torn curtains, but it also feels like something is watching. I stay there, checking to see whether it moves. The extreme heat is making me uneasy. Too anxious. I try to close the door when I leave, but the wood is warped and I can't shut it properly. I manoeuvre the half-folded camp bed back through the corridor, avoiding looking into any more corners.

✧

165

I push the ripped flyscreen and step onto the veranda, gasping, the air cool compared to the stifling den. You are still slumped against the car, the sun directly above now. Your face stays impassive as I haul out the camp bed. When I get up close, I see your eyes are half-closed. You've got into the weed.

'You don't have to smoke all of it,' I say, dumping the bed beside you. 'Anyway, aren't you getting burnt?'

I squint at the sun, shielding my eyes. I've only been out of the house a minute and I feel as if I'm turning red raw. Flies buzz around my ears and settle on my sweaty neck. You don't bother shooing them off your face.

'I said, aren't you—'

'I heard.'

You slide down the car and sprawl in the dirt, shuffling backwards, until your head is underneath the car.

'Happy now?' you call back.

'Don't get bitten.'

I'm still thinking of the spiders in your den, the possibility of a creature in your bedroom. I glance back. The house now looks the way people probably imagined it during the court case—a house out of a horror film. I guess nobody, apart from you, will ever know it the way I did. Already the old images are getting replaced, ruined, by what's here now.

'Think we can fix it up?' I say.

'Reckon we'll die first.'

I kick sand at the car, at you.

I set up the camp bed, then secure the rug to the top of the car with rocks and drape it over an acacia to make a slanted roof—a sort of tent, some shade. I drag the camp bed underneath, avoiding your legs sticking out from under the car. If we

166

can't live inside the house yet, this will have to do. Inside our new shade, I sit beside the fox, who is breathing heavily. I try to force her to swallow water, but it just trickles into her fur. I shouldn't waste the water if she's not going to drink.

'It's hotter than last time,' I say. When you don't respond, I prod your thigh. 'It's hotter!'

'I know!' Your voice is muffled. 'It's summer.'

Bunuru, I think, remembering the light show in Perth, *wildfire season*. Out here we could burn to death. *Season of coming of age.*

'Is it cooler under there?'

I should crawl in with you, or at least put the fox under there. I make a mental inventory of everything we have in the car: six bottles of water, maybe seven; bread; apples; muesli bars; a box of cereal; antiseptic that should go on your head; one of my spare T-shirts; towels; an almost full box of cat biscuits.

I lift the rug to peer across at the sheds, at the padlocks on the doors. Whoever came here obviously didn't bother going in there, and I'm surprised. Other folk might've wanted to burn this whole place down if they'd known it was yours. I remember the name the tabloids gave you—*Desert Devil*. But there will be supplies in those sheds. You had everything. *Enough gear for the rest of our lives.*

'What are the codes for the locks?' I say. 'On the sheds?'

You say something I can't hear, so I lie on my back and wriggle under the car too. The sand is cooler here, and you're so much closer. The space feels too intimate. When you turn to me, your face is less than a metre away. My breath falters.

'You remember those numbers.' Your eyes swivel to meet mine.

I shake my head. 'You never told me.'

'Sure you do.' You look back at the underside of the car, then stick your tongue out as if you're trying to touch the tangle of metal above you, trying to taste it, before popping it back in your mouth with a snap. 'The date I took you. Same for any code out here.'

Your high-pitched burst of laughter makes me jump. Maybe it's your head wound talking, you've turned septic and unhinged.

'The codes are the date you kidnapped me?'

'You call it kidnapped now...' You give another burst of laughter.

I remember: your catchphrase from last time. *I'm saving you, Gem. Saving, not kidnapping. Remember that.* I called it saving too, for a time, back in London, when I would lie awake at night with memories of resting against your warm, tanned chest, tasting the dusty tang of your skin, feeling the brush of your lips in my hair. We'd said I was being saved from my parents, from meaningless city life, from school that only indoctrinated me. You were taking me back to nature, back to what was real and beautiful. You said all that, and more, and I believed you. It took years for me to believe anything else, that it was all a fantasy. Looking at you and this place now, I wonder: has it finally sunk in?

There's a glint in your eyes. 'Why don't you try the numbers and see?'

You're daring me. I edge away as far as I can without my legs pressing against a hot tyre. We stare at each other. If I only look at your eyes, you could be the Ty in my head. Once I thought I could thaw your cold, blue eyes, warm you up. But it's

168

warm enough here now under the steaming bowels of the car, and those eyes are still piercing me.

'You're worse than before,' I say. 'You know that?'

'You any better?'

Something is stinging behind my ribs, like a wasp has got inside me. I won't let you see my tears, so I peer at the undercarriage. I'm no better than you; I've done the same terrible things.

'You're still a little kid,' you say.

'You're a shit.'

Like my mother always told me you were.

After I slither out from the under the car, I almost run to the outbuildings, glad to get away from you. Of course I know the code: the numbers that started everything.

The padlock on the closest shed clicks opens easily. It's so much cooler inside that I wonder immediately if I should sleep in here instead of beside the car. I leave the door wide behind me for light, then I step in and see it all again, these rows of supplies, the tins and boxes and bottles, all this organisation and control. There is a bad smell, of things old and forgotten, and of something dead too, and there's dust over everything, thick as fur. I tread softly down the middle of the aisle of shelves. There are cobwebs over some of the tins, and some boxes and containers are open, some eaten, as if they've been ravaged by rats or something worse. Tins of chickpeas, lentils, beans, peaches, all out of date. Not for the first time, I wonder how long you expected to keep me here, whether we'd have ever gone back to a town if there'd been no other way to keep me alive. Could we really have lived out here alone forever? Would we still be here now? Perhaps nobody in the outside world, apart from me, was ever enough for you. The smell gets stronger as I go further in, clogging my nostrils.

When I see the glass enclosures at the back of the shed, I freeze, remembering. Strange to have forgotten something so terrifying. My body goes still with the effort of listening for rustling, scuttling, the noises that used to be here. But now everything is quiet. I walk slowly, glancing behind for the quickest exit back if I need it. It's so much darker, even with the door open. Inside the tanks it is even blacker. I squint at them, heart pounding. The first thing I make out is a pale snake-skin. Where is its inhabitant? I take another couple of steps, watching and waiting. But, still, nothing moves inside the glass, no flicking, no skittering. As I bend down to the enclosures, I see the skeletons. Snakes curled up, decomposing. Desiccated spiders. All that is left of the scorpions are their tails. It all stinks like death. I know there is no longer anything here that can kill me. Still, I tiptoe backwards, watching for movement.

You kept these creatures for anti-venom, that's what you told me. You were going to inject me, and you, with their poison, make us immune. But a snake got me first. Thinking now about your plan, it seems insane. Was it only ever about collecting, keeping everything under your control, but saying later that it was for safety?

When I pull back the rug, you're out from under the car, leaning against it. I smell weed and sweat. I wince as I look down at you. The heat will make sloughed skins of us, like the graveyard of snakes in the shed. Are you ashamed of leaving these creatures like that, of that needless death?

'I found this,' I say, sighing. You squint, and I hold the box closer to your glazed eyes. 'A water purifying straw.'

You should know what it is, you bought it. The box is soft from age, but inside the straw-tube looks brand new.

'We can use it in the spring in the Separates,' I say.

'*You* can.'

I dump some tins of food next to the tyres. 'Plenty more in the shed. See if you can work out a way to open them. Do something useful.' Near the camp bed, on the ground next to you, is one of the bigger bottles of water I'd been keeping for emergencies. Empty. 'You drank all that?'

You smile slyly, nod. Your eyes close against the sun as you try to swat at flies settling on your bloodied head wound.

'You didn't ask my permission.'

You blink once slowly, and I kick my boots into your legs.

'I said, you didn't ask my—'

'What are you now, my prison officer?'

I grab your arm and try to yank you to your feet, but you're like a sack of stones. 'Come to the Separates with me,' I say. 'You need a wash.'

'I'm staying here.'

At least I think that's what you say through the slurring. Beneath the flies on your wound, there is pus, yellow as dried egg yolk. I drop you back on the ground, then realise you've moved the fox into the shade under the camp bed. I go towards her to check.

'How is she?'

'Going to die.'

You crawl across the sand, away from the car and the tins of food, and towards the bed, looking like a drunken gorilla. You heave yourself up, sighing as you rest your head on the dusty canvas.

'I remember this bed,' you say. 'It's your turn to nurse me now?' Again, that bark of a laugh. Those bright eyes that won't stay still.

I can't drag you to the Separates like this, but it doesn't look like you're going anywhere else, either. Like the creatures in the shed, your venom has gone.

'Fine,' I say.

February 19th

You stare at me through slits. It's a miracle, isn't it, that we're still here, still alive. You should be proud of me, or at least grateful. I watch you on the camp bed, and the fox underneath. When I get up from the sand, my stomach's rumbling; I'm lightheaded. I walk to the car as if I'm floating. I open the boot and get two muesli bars and another bottle of water. Five bottles left after this, not enough. I take one sip, pour more for the fox, and leave the rest with you, along with a muesli bar.

Then I crawl under the camp bed to get closer to the fox, to stroke her. She still looks so sick. I try to force a cat biscuit through her sharp, white teeth, but she spits it out and hisses. A wild animal shouldn't let me touch her like this, Sal wouldn't.

'Bloody stupid thing,' you murmur. 'Shouldn't be here. None of us should.'

'I thought you'd be glad I brought you,' I say. 'Grateful.'

You grunt.

Surely being here is better than being in prison, better than being with a woman who didn't even pick you up on your release day. I rub water into the fox's ears to cool her and she doesn't object. Everything about her behaviour, and yours, is wrong, but all I can do is wait. I crawl out from under the camp

173

bed and look at the wound on your head, the flies circling: an infection could be contributing to your lethargy.

'I'll dress your wound later,' I say. 'It looks like shit.'

'Don't bother.'

On the way out, I kick the camp bed, enjoying how your body judders and how you moan from the impact. Maybe I should leave you to die.

I set off for the Separates, the straw purifier in my hand, kicking the sand with each step. I'm a moody kid again, just like you said. But what did I expect? That by bringing us back, everything would be alright? That you'd turn into the Ty I dreamt of in Barkingside?

In the full sun, I keep my head down, my body wet with sweat. I don't think I'm walking straight. I hold my arms out to stop swaying. I should dig up the pills and we could overdose together, fry ourselves in the heat and let the wild dogs find us. But what about the fox? Maybe she could she join us, a group suicide. Only she didn't choose any of this.

As I get closer to the rocks, I could be sixteen again, approaching for the first time, marvelling at their huge size and smooth exterior. Above, I see the fissures, the gills. When I hold out my hand and touch the rock surface, it feels like skin and muscle, a version of my own skin. I lean my cheek against them and feel them breathe. I listen. You said these rocks were swept here by a huge flood, long ago: they made a path through the land, and the path filled with water and formed a river behind them. Like that, these rocks made life. I know this is just another of your stories, but still I stay, listening to the rustle of birds above. I prefer to imagine these rocks being sung into creation, by some long-ago being. Returning to these rocks, I feel myself shifting too, sung open by the birds, altered.

As if it was only yesterday when I last saw it, I find the path in easily and follow the broken water pipe. No graffiti, no rubbish. Everything is calmer here than in the heat with you. I stick the water straw in my back pocket, scramble deep in between the rocks like a spider, legs and arms spread wide. The leaves on the bushes are greener here, juicier, I almost pop them in my mouth and chew. Maybe they'd help my headache.

Soon the path peters out and I'm back on sand, walking into the atrium of the Separates. Colours everywhere: browns and oranges, whites, greys, greens. And swirls in the sand. Snake tracks, I think, tangled as if they've been dancing. I move more slowly, more carefully. Everything is silent, not a breath of wind to gossip with the leaves. I come across the cages where you kept your chickens and expect to see more carcasses. But the grasses are so thick inside and around them, there is no way of knowing what's inside. I walk on. Far above, in the dust-covered branches of a gum tree, I think I see the bright-green wing feathers of a parrot.

As I approach the pool, I feel almost as anxious as I felt outside the prison. I'm scared the pool will be changed, too, dried up and useless. I am desperate for this water now; my sweat has even crystallised into salt; all of me longing for moisture.

I pick my way round the last corner and there it is, waiting, cool and deep between the fire-red boulders. Something welcome out here, finally. I stop myself from charging through the high grasses around the edge, and pick up a stick to bash them, alerting any snakes of my presence. *Bunuru*, wildfire season, is also snake season.

Under the huge gum tree, I take off my stinking clothes

and walk in naked. Even in the shelter of the tree and the boulders, the sun sears me.

And then relief, the water a balm on my scorching skin. Achingly cool.

I sigh. It doesn't matter that the pool is no longer clear as glass, or that there is algae at its edges. This is what I've returned for. I paddle to the edge, retrieve the straw from my shorts and suck as I swim. The water tastes like pondweed, but I gulp it down. Then I float on my back and stare at the blue, blue sky, at a kite circling far above. You need this too, to make you well again, so we can start to staunch the wound of everything gone wrong, before it all runs away from us.

I duck and dive, again and again, further down each time. I was scared the first time here, anxious about what might be lurking underneath, but now when I open my eyes underwater I see fish and weed and the fathomless blackness between the rocks at the bottom. I touch the ledge above the dark space below. An underwater cave—the source of the spring water? The home of a mythical creature? Strange, but I don't remember it being there before. It could be a place to hide something never to be found. It could be the place to hide you.

I need salt for your wounds, so I walk back towards the supply shed, ignoring the shed that contains your paintings, the installation work you made from, and about, the land. I would like to see your work again, feel its effect on me, although I don't know how I'd react if it's as ruined as you and the den. Those landscapes you made from ochre and plants and sand were vivid and alive. They were part of what made me love this place.

I told Mum about your paintings, explaining how you used

elements and colours from the land to create them. I told her they'd look good in her gallery in London, that we should go back for them.

'You'd make a fortune,' I said, 'selling the work of a kidnapper. And if it's us selling them,' I continued, 'we'd be getting our own back.'

I wanted to take your precious things and control them myself, make them my own. But Mum didn't agree. She didn't even want to talk about it, and certainly didn't want to look at anything artistic you might have made.

'He's no kind of artist,' she said. 'There's no worth in anything he does.'

She never wanted anything to do with you. She barely listened when you spoke in court. She certainly never believed me when I said you could make art, beautiful art that even she would like. She was mistaken: if she was scared of it, she should have tried to understand it. Once you understand something, the fear diminishes. You have a better chance of controlling what you understand. Haven't I told that to Rhiannon enough times? But what happens when what you thought you understood has changed?

Between the dark aisles of the shed, I search for salt, more food and a can opener. I do not go near the enclosures of the dead creatures. I rub my finger across dusty labels on a few glass jars until I uncover the word SALT and then OATS. Mum went through a phase of soaking oats in cold water before she went to bed, claiming it was more nutritional that way. This is what you need: nutritional food and the land. And me.

You're asleep when I get back, breathing deeply. I kneel beside your bed and check the fox too, try her with a little more water, which, this time, she drinks. When I touch your skin, it's still hot and you murmur. When your eyes flicker open, they're glazed. Could the infection have gone to your brain?

After soaking the oats for later, I tip salt and water into the ceramic bowl and unwrap a fresh pillowcase to bathe your wound. I clean the pus from it and, still, you don't wake. Scabs are forming. Should I pick them off and clean underneath or leave them? I want to check my phone for information, but, of course, it's run out of battery and my charger is in the hotel room.

Lying on your back, the lines on your face are almost smooth. Your parched lips are parted, a tiny hole in the middle. Very slowly, I undo the remaining buttons of your shirt. If you are so hot and clammy, you need more air. You might get another infection if I don't wash you properly. And I want to see all of you again, all this skin that's been hidden from me for years.

I pull the shirt open. Your body once had contours, ridges and hills of its own, but now it is milk-pale and full of scars. You're Nick's colour now, sallow in comparison to everything here, no longer infused with sun or dirt or life.

'I'm going to wash you,' I say.

Your head moves slightly as you murmur again. An acceptance? You don't resist as I fold the shirt back. You even seem to help, moving a little to free it. I place my fingertips on your belly and touch a trail of hairs that lead down to the suit pants. I empty the old water from the bowl into one of the plastic bottles in case we get desperate, and pour in more salt and water to clean your body. When I return, you're snoring softly, head lolling, chest exposed. Again, I think: I could do anything I want to you.

So I do. I take my small knife and hover above your head. I grab your ponytail of hair with my left hand and, holding it steady, I saw straight through. Now you have shorter hair, like before. I drop the chopped hair to the sand and pocket the hair tie, and you sleep on.

Avoiding my guilty thoughts, I dip the other side of the pillowcase into the water and bathe your chest, rinse it and do it again. I am healing you. I am changing you back to what I want, cleansing away all that I hate about you. It feels a little like a sacred ceremony. You moan when the water touches your stomach. I unbutton your suit pants, slide them down your sweaty legs. It's easier than getting your shirt off, and again you help me, moving your feet as I pull.

You are naked now. It feels wrong to be staring, but I need to do this, to see you properly. *You.* So vulnerable. So mine. And besides, you did this to me once. It's only fair.

Isn't it?

I start to sponge, then rinse, and sponge again. I examine all of you as if you're a piece of art. I wash your legs, your chest. Carefully, I wash the hairs around your penis. It stays still, unthreatening. I imagine chopping that off too, the scream you'd give. Then I imagine carving into your body, making patterns in you, the way you made art in the sand.

I wring your sweat into the bowl, then drown it with salt-water. When I wipe away the dried saliva at the edges of your parted lips, I hold my hand above your mouth and feel your breath. I want to breathe into you, put the Ty in my head inside you. I lean closer, so close that your face blurs beneath me. Your eyes remain closed.

The old you wanted to kiss me. Do you remember? Would

it be wrong, then, for me to do it now? Does it make me as bad as you were? Does it make me worse? I watch for a sign, but you sleep on.

I don't touch you with my lips, but I do with my hands. I press my right index finger to your hipbone, and trace below and around, to all the places I never touched before. You are new territory, something to be conquered. I am placing my hands on it all. It is my right.

After I have inspected your whole body, I take one of the crisp new Egyptian cotton sheets out of its packet and lay it over you, then cover your head wound with the other pillowcase to protect it from flies. Now that you are wrapped in a shroud, I can wait for your resurrection. I tie your legs to the camp bed, just in case.

I soak the shirt in the left-over water and hang it across the roof of the car to dry. You'll be better tomorrow; your skin is already cooler. Everything will be better tomorrow.

I bathe the fox too. Like you, she doesn't open her eyes, doesn't make much sound. You're right: I should have left her at the side of the road. I shouldn't have extended her agony.

I return to watch you sleep.

February 20th

At dawn, your eyes are open and steady, watching me.

'You survived then?' I say.

Second night and neither of us died: a victory. In the early-morning softness, your hand reaches down to the dirt. You must be thirsty, but your fingers skim over the bottle and keep scrabbling. The baggie of weed.

'I put it somewhere safe,' I say. 'You can have more when you get better.'

Now I'm glad I tied you to the camp bed. You try to lurch towards me, straining, then slam back when you discover the ropes. I sigh. It's going to take more than a bit of sponging to exorcise this new you.

'You'll stay tied up until you stop being such a dick.'

I should have tied your arms as well. You could still grab me, choke me. It looks like you want to do that, and more. Perhaps I took the weed away too soon, had too much faith in your resilience.

'Besides, you still haven't apologised,' I say. 'Hard to know where to start with apologies, though, isn't it? I'll help. For talking to that girl in the park, for taking me in the first place. Should I go on?'

181

You glare at me. I should have let you stay infected, let the flies lay their eggs in your open wound.

'I'm waiting,' I prompt.

'I'm naked,' you say.

'What did you expect? I washed you. Yeah, you're welcome.'

You look away, and I smile. But your eyes fall on the ponytail in the sand, and you reach up to your head and touch your shorter hair.

'This is sick,' you say. 'Breach of basic rights! You should be apologising to me.'

Your speech is no longer slurred. I've brought your voice back; it's a start. You glance down at your body under the sheet.

'I should've killed you while I had the chance?' I say. 'That what you're thinking?'

You slam your head back down onto the camp bed. 'You wouldn't. You don't have the balls.'

'If you try too hard, that'll tip over,' I say, indicating the camp bed. 'You'll be face first in the dirt. Easy to kill you then. Just a quick stab in the back of your neck.'

'Where'd you put the stuff?'

'In the sand.'

'You buried it?' You roll your eyes. 'Out here? You know you're crazy?'

'Learnt from the best.'

Another glare. Now your clear blue eyes are sharp.

'You want to torture me?' you say. 'Want your own back? That what this is?'

I like this fire inside you. We can work with fire.

'I want you to go back to who you were,' I say. 'The good parts.'

Again, you slam your head into the camp bed. 'That's bullshit.'

'Aren't you glad I cleaned you up?'

'I'm naked,' you repeat.

I shrug. 'You made me naked too.'

'That was different.'

'Really?' I almost laugh. 'What makes this any worse? Because I'm a woman?' I shake my head slowly, but perhaps this isn't the time to lecture you on the gender equality issues of being kidnapped.

'Because you're insane.'

'You weren't?'

'I was different then,' you say. 'I was vulnerable.'

I snort, incredulous. 'More vulnerable than a sixteen-year-old girl? One you kidnapped from the other side of the world? One you held against her will?'

You look at the dirt. 'Fine. You were different too,' you say. 'You weren't...*this*.'

I wait for more, for answers about myself. I'm not that old Gemma, you're right, but now I don't feel quite like the Kate back in London either. I feel infused with fire.

'I changed my name,' I tell you. 'I'm Kate now. Perhaps you should use it.'

You shrug. You won't.

'You know, these past years I've changed for the better,' I say. 'I've tried, at least. Whereas you've just got worse. I'm doing you a favour this time around, bringing you here, helping you.'

But I know our crimes are different. You took a sapling and tried to turn it into a twisted tree. I'm taking a twisted tree and righting it. You hoist yourself onto your elbows, no longer flinching from pain. You see, I made you well enough for that, even if you choose not to notice.

'I don't understand you,' you say. 'You know they'll put me back inside if they catch me with you, if I don't report in…That what you want?'

'No one will catch you,' I say. 'You're staying here. They don't know about this place.'

Your eyes widen as you make a strangled sort of laugh. 'So, you don't care about me at all now?' you ask, holding my gaze. 'You did once.'

And here you go with your emotional manipulation, your charm. I brace myself for more, but you stay quiet.

'I don't care about *this* version of you!'

'But this is me.'

'It's not.'

You sigh and lie back down on the camp bed.

'What do you think'll happen when I don't show? They'll go looking, that's what.'

I shake my head. 'And they're not going to find us out here, are they? Because you didn't tell anyone where this place is.'

You look away, but don't say anything to the contrary.

'So we're safe here,' I say.

Alone.

February 21st

It's cooler today, clouds dimming the sun. It even looks like it might rain. When we were here before, the skies were blue and endless, at least that's how I remember them. I pull down our rug shade to get some air, then stare across at your den. You look across too.

'We should start to fix it up,' I say.

'Sure.'

You say it too easily, too quickly. You even smile, but not with your eyes. You just want to be untied so you can go looking for those drugs, find the car-key and leave me here.

'Who do you think wrote those words on the den?' I ask.

'Land's land. Anyone's free to find it.'

'But it's private property, *your* property.'

The edge of your mouth curls up. 'You still think that? How'd you reckon I got away with not revealing anything about it in the trial? No one found this place by going through my stuff, no one found any deeds.' You shake your head. 'It's not mine.'

I go very still. Did I just hear you right?

'Not yours?'

'I mean, I built it, but...'

185

'Whose is it then?' I say. 'This land?' Unsteady, I sit down by the camp bed.

You bark a laugh. 'Officially, fuck knows. Mining land probably. Most of it's mining land, now. *Unofficially...*'

Were you going to say that this land belongs to the Indigenous people, the traditional owners, that all of this place did or should belong to them? I remember how you used to align yourself with them. Do you still think you're entitled to what was and still is theirs?

I glance over to the Separates. 'Will miners come?'

'How'd I know? Probably. Reckon there's more development here now.'

Nothing, it seems, belongs to you.

My head is spinning so much I have to close my eyes, squeeze them shut. You laugh.

'You never thought I actually owned the place, did you?' I hear you shift on the camp bed, hear the disdain in your silence. 'Out here, you take what you come across.'

'Like you did with me?' I whisper.

You laugh again, just once, and the sound is like gunshot. 'Yeah, like you.'

You said I was the only one who ever saw you as you truly were, the only one who ever noticed you in that London park. You said I was the only one you ever truly loved. Was it all a lie? I shake my head, hard. *No.* The old you was different, the old you would never speak like this.

'You're a shit now,' I say, opening my eyes to scowl at you.

'Ah, well, that makes two of us.' You don't look away from me as you sneer, your face shiny with sweat and smugness.

186

'Also, I'm gonna need a piss.'

'I'll bring you a bucket.'

I cup my hands around a pale brown cricket I find on the bark of a mulga tree and put it in one of the empty water bottles to bring back for the fox. I wonder if I should kill it before I drop it into her box, or whether she'd wake up from just knowing there's an insect next to her; maybe it'd be good for her to hunt.

When I lay my fingers on her fur, I feel little warmth, and when I press my fingertips to her black lips and try to open her mouth, she doesn't flinch. She's almost dead. I feel awful and glance across to see if you've noticed.

'Bloody stupid bringing a fox out here,' you say. 'Even if it gets better, it'll only kill the other animals. Why'd you think there are fences? What the hell else they trying to stop?'

Ignoring you, I pick up her box and walk around to the other side of the car. I'm crying, but I sure as hell don't want you to see.

'Yeah, that's right! Go and release it, make everything worse!'

I take the fox out and lay her on the ground near a clump of saltbush. She will die here, away and alone, and it'll be because of me. I'm making a mess of everything. I walk back with the empty cardboard box.

'You were a while,' you say, looking at the empty box as you smile. 'She dead then?'

You are glad she's dying, and you are glad something's dying in me now too.

'You should dig the grave,' I say, as I stride over to the shed.

I find a spade in a dusty pile of rusting gardening tools,

along with a rake and some shears, though God knows what they're for out here. I imagine chopping the shears through your neck, cutting strips from your arms. I return with only the spade and chuck it next to the camp bed.

'Bloody stupid idea,' you say. 'Leave it for the vultures. Only thing it's good for.'

I start to untie you. I don't care if the first thing you do is pick up the spade and bash me with it. Why not do it and bury me with the fox?

'Do what the fuck you like,' I say.

'Righto. I'll take the car and go.'

I look at you, rage pulsing inside me. Do you really mean that? 'I was stupid to think you'd be grateful for what I've done for you, for bringing you here...'

The laugh explodes out of you. 'Grateful? For this?'

You turn onto your back and rest your arms behind your head. I stop untying. You still don't care, don't get it. I step back, away from the loose ropes on your legs.

'You said you'd find me, wherever I went, whenever you got out.'

Your mouth curls into that sly smile I'm getting used to. 'You still thought that?'

'Why shouldn't I?'

'That was a long time ago, Gem. Before prison. Anyway, you said it yourself, we're both different now.'

I fold my arms. 'When did you get to be such a shit?'

'Wasn't I always?' You turn to stare at me intently. 'No, seriously. Wasn't I?'

I blink at you. The Ty in my head wasn't a shit. That Ty would've come back for me. He might've stalked me again, but

188

I would've been important to him. I would've mattered more than this.

'I thought you'd at least feel remorse.'

'Then what, we'd start over?'

I want to pull the sheet from you so that you are naked and vulnerable again. I want you to know how inferior you made me feel back then. I sigh hard and look away, because I have no answers for you, and because, you are right: starting over is exactly what I wanted. You're meant to be so glad to see me again that you'd do anything I want, fix me however I want. Otherwise, what's the point of all this?

'You promised,' I say. 'You made me believe it all.'

I wait for you to say you remember—every single moment when we walked together in this land, when you showed me the beauty in it and the beauty in you, the beauty in me. Here is why I can't let you go, why we're here. I want that fantasy; I've been hanging on to it for ten years. It didn't matter that I was a mess in London, or never had friends, or a boyfriend, or fun. I had you. I had this in my future.

'Didn't you want it too?'

I hate this shell of you that shrugs so easily, as if none of it matters, as if you can't remember what I'm talking about.

'This isn't you,' I snap.

Because *this* isn't what we had, and you aren't him. Him? It's strange thinking of you as separate, like an ordinary *him* and not as something inside me. I glower at you lounging, so casually, on the camp bed. You raise your eyebrows.

'You know, I'm flattered, Gem,' you say slowly. 'But I think the person you want ain't here.'

'He is.'

Playing the fool, you make a show of looking under the sheet, behind you at the scrub, then across at the Separates.

'Nope, can't see him. Reckon you might've killed him.'

My fingers clench into fists. I want to punch this Ty out of you, this part I never bargained for. I shouldn't have had to wait ten years for this.

'You're not the same person either, if you really want to know,' you say, more quietly now. 'You're kind of a bitch.'

I kick the camp bed. 'I'm trying to help you.'

'Right, but you kidnapped me. Or have you forgotten that?'

'I just wanted to talk, understand.'

You snort. 'Well, Gem, seems only one of us has grown up. Seems one of us is still a little kid.'

You suck your teeth as you watch me, and I remember how you used to chew on native tobacco leaves for hours, sometimes mixing them with ash from the fire first, how I thought then that it suited you, that you looked like a cowboy.

'No point remembering all those crap parts of life, is there?' you say. 'You have to move on, Gem. Forget.'

A hot breeze tickles the backs of my legs, then whips sharp bits of sand against my skin. 'Prison hasn't helped you at all.'

'You have no idea about me,' you say with a shrug. 'Not now. Not ever.'

'I do. I'm the one who remembers.'

Your eyes hold mine, softer for a second, before you grin again. 'Can't step into the same river twice, Gem. The river's older and dirtier and full of shit.'

I shake my head. 'You said you loved the land, wanted to save it. You wanted to be authentic.'

'See my words got you hot and sweaty, at least.'

The twinkle in your eyes says you're still laughing at me. I approach the camp bed again and want to kick, kick, kick, until your insides are so shaken up that when they reassemble you are you, not him. I lean down to grab your shoulders, ready to shake. But when I get close, I stop. Your face is calmer now, expectant—you're daring me to lose it, to hurt you. I don't want to give you what you want.

'Do you think you deserve it then?' I say. 'You want me to punish you?'

Another shrug. 'Once you get it out of your system, maybe you'll see sense. You'll see you have to take me back.'

Is that some sort of apology? A shred of remorse, of humanity, left in you after all?

'So, you know you did wrong?' I say, my fingers clenching your shoulders. 'Know you fucked me up?'

That curl of your lip. 'Reckon that's pretty obvious.'

I grip my hands tight enough to hurt you, but I stop myself from squeezing any tighter. Your hold on me changing my hold on you.

'You don't care at all,' I say.

Your caring is the least I deserve. You don't blink as I stare at you, waiting for your words of apology. My face is so close to yours, I could bite you. Instead, I lean down closer and press my lips to yours.

I kiss you.

Your lips are softer than I expected. When you don't kiss back, I press harder, angry, as you freeze beneath me. I push my tongue into your mouth, slamming into your teeth. My hands are on you, moving down, pressing and pushing at you, willing

191

you to respond. And you do. With a roar, you push me from you, shoving so hard that I stumble back into the dirt. I look up at you, my breath gone. So, there is strength left in you.

'No,' you say.

Your eyes are glinting with fury. You wrench your legs away from the camp bed, straining the rope ties. They hold, and you arch your back against the bed.

'Thought you wanted to kill me! Thought you wanted your revenge, but this?' Your mouth twists.

You look so disgusted by me that I turn away. 'I've been trying to help you!'

'Help me do what?' You make that sound again, guttural, more animal than human.

I step backwards, licking my lips, tasting your sweat. Once, this was all you wanted: me wanting you, me wanting this place.

'Just be grateful!' I shout. 'I came back!'

'What the hell's wrong with you?'

You lurch towards me so violently the camp bed tips. You go over like a mountain falling, fumbling in the dirt, trying to right yourself, wrestling yourself away from the bed, but your ankles are still tied to it.

'Fuck you!' you shout. You reach for me, try to grab my legs. 'Bitch! I never did nothing like this to you. I never did nothing so sick!'

I stumble to my feet, away from you, panting. I've unleashed a demon.

'You're the sick one!' I shout back, kicking dirt in your face. 'The whole world thought that! You're the twisted fuck who went to prison!'

You're screaming too, words and noise, but all I hear is
You're sick.
You're sick.
You're sick.

Like a wildfire, you're still coming for me, grabbing bits of vegetation and water bottles, throwing them at me. I stagger away, turn towards the house. But I can't lock myself in, because there're no locks on your falling-down shithouse doors.

'Just stay away!' I scream. 'Stay away, you fuck!'

I felt so certain that you wouldn't hurt me, not after everything you put me through. I felt sure you'd feel too much remorse, accept your punishment, let me do the things I needed to do. I leave you scrambling in the dirt. As I go, I see myself from above: a person not quite me, and not quite anyone else, screaming harsh ugly words back at you.

You'll come around. You'll see what I've been trying to do and then you'll understand. Then you'll come back. Or maybe I'm not thinking straight. Maybe I'm the one who needs locking up.

Inside the den, I shut the door and lean against the soft wood, breathing hard. When I can no longer hear you hollering, I find a broom in the pantry and start sweeping furiously, pushing the leaves and sand, branches and insects towards the wider veranda on the other side of the living room. I open the curtains and the Separates appear through the cracked windowpanes. Insects drop on me and I brush them off and carry on. I'm the whirling wildfire now.

As I sweep bigger and bigger mountains of sand onto the veranda, sweat trickles down my back and legs. It settles in the corners of my eyes, clouding my vision. You should be doing this; we should be doing it together. I grip the broom, so full of rage I could snap it. I shake off a spider, brush it outside too.

When I step back to survey my handiwork, I want to scream. It hardly looks any different. I sweep harder, trying to get every bit of filth out the doorway and onto the veranda. I shove the couch out from the wall and bash it, clouds of dust choking me. I wipe the curtains across the windows to let light in through the glass, then yank them from their rails, ball them up and chuck them onto the load of debris on the veranda. I move faster and faster.

I must be crying as I shove the broom down the corridor; my face is itchy, and I keep wiping my eyes to see. It's darker here, the meagre light from the windows doesn't reach this far, and the dust seems thick as mud, up to my ankles in places. I stab at it with the broom, scream at it to go away. All I know is that I have to keep moving, keep sweeping, keep trying to push things back to where they were.

And then, in the doorway, slithering out from your old bedroom—a snake, wrapped around the corner of the door, in the gap I couldn't close yesterday.

'How dare you!' I shriek at it.

Its head curls around the door, resting on the floor, watching me sweep. What right does it have to make its home here, in our place, when it has the whole desert? I feel nothing but fury at it. No fear at all. All I can think is that it shouldn't be here, just one more thing ruining this house.

I grab onto the door and slam it as hard as I can against the snake's body. When it hisses, I do it again. When it raises its head, I bash the broom down too, pinning it between the door and the frame, smashing it over and over. When its tongue darts out, I thud the door against it again.

It's you I'm bashing. I see your head on top of its body, your unblinking blue eyes, your tongue flashing. You're laughing at me, low and nasty, mocking me. Any moment now, you will rise and strike. You will latch onto my ankle and you will not let go. Your venom will spread before I can stem it. The pain will never end. I hit you harder and harder, until the snake's body goes limp.

When I finally stop, there's blood on the doorframe. My hands are shaking and red. I steady myself against the wall of the corridor. As I shut my eyes, everything spins. I hear racking sobs. Mine, I guess.

'Just shut up!' I shout. 'SHUT UP!'

No one shouts back. If you have untangled yourself from the camp bed, you're not coming to find me. I kick the snake with the tip of my boot, but it doesn't move. It's a brown snake with a pale underbelly, not all that big. I don't know if it's venomous. But I didn't kill it because I was scared. I wanted it to die.

I remember how careful you were with snakes, how you treated them like precious cargo, animals to be admired as much as feared. Despite the dead creatures in the storage shed, you would never kill a snake unless there was no other option. Once, you wouldn't have. I look down at the dead snake and swallow shame. That's two deaths now: a snake and a fox. Who's next? Me or you?

I drop the broom in the corridor and slope back to the living room. It's hopeless trying to fix this house. The floor may be swept, but the windows are still smashed, and the roof is still falling down; there are cobwebs across the ceiling. Like you, it's never going to be what it was. You're right: we should never have come back. I slam the wall with my fist and more dust billows out. I crumple in the doorway of the living room and let more sobs come. What have I done?

I lean my head against the wall and shut my eyes, my whole body aching with tension. Even now, I listen for the rusty squeak of the screen door opening. But you won't come in here. You won't do anything for me. You hate me now. That much is obvious. So, do I take you back to Perth? Be done with this?

I'm breathing hard as I consider it: driving you back down that long, straight road and returning you to the woman in Banksia Drive, or to the teenage girl in the city park. And what then? You tell your parole officers about the things I've done to you. After that, it won't be you going back to prison, it will be me. And if you got more than ten years for the things you did…

I imagine Mum's face if she finds out, realises who I've become. She wouldn't start a charitable fund to help me this time. And Dad would retreat even further into the cave he's made, die a little more. Nick would find out too, he'd know about all my secrets then. Even Rose, my sick hopeful client, even she would find out. Strangely, her knowing about me feels most shameful. She doesn't deserve that shock; she's suffering enough as it is. But I'd be front-page news again, and it would be more than embarrassing and regressive; it would keep me tethered to you.

No.

If I took you back and you told the police, this time the world would think I was the sick one. No more *poor little Gemma*. They'd say *Poor Ty, just when he was trying to rehabilitate, too.* They wouldn't know about the girl in the park, or your addictions, or your smug, nasty smile. They wouldn't know that you don't care about me at all now. You would win, and I would lose. You could do whatever you wanted, without me. I would be the one stuck, still with no release.

The tears come again, and I slam my fists onto the floorboards. I've made a mess out of everything. But is there another option?

If I kill you, neither of us is a victim anymore.

If I kill you, I go back down that long, flat road alone, return to Perth, then to London, as if nothing has ever happened. I even get the last night of my hotel booking.

If I kill you, I still tell Mum that I helped the turtles.

If I kill you, I tell Mum I'm better from my time away, and, who knows, maybe I will be.

If I kill you, I will have the release and you will not. You won't go back to prison, and neither will I.

We will both be free.

I stand and walk out of the house, letting the screen slam behind me and head back to you, of course I fucking do. Where else? But you're not where I left you. The camp bed is still tipped to the side in the dirt, but you're not tied to it. I bend down and pull the rope away from the bed, wind it up and pile it next to the car; I shouldn't have started untying you, making it easier for you.

The spade's gone too. Did you bury the fox, after all? Somehow, I doubt it. But she's not where I left her either. I look for disturbances in the earth, evidence of a grave. Nothing. What have you done with her? I haven't seen any raptors, or dingoes sniffing around, and she couldn't have survived and crawled away. Could she?

When I look more closely, I make out faint footprints in the sand, heading towards the side of the house closest to the Separates. Of course, you've gone searching for your drugs.

I start to run, following your footprints as they veer close to the house at one point. Did you hear me screaming inside, killing the snake? Did you stop and wonder about helping? I clench my fists: you were so close to me and you didn't come to help. That snake could have killed me, and you wouldn't have done a thing. I round the corner near the mulga scrub and termite mounds and see your back, the skin around your spine stretched and white under the blazing sun, like a pearly-pale grub. You're bent over, digging. You throw sand behind you in a red arc.

You chuck the spade to one side and get onto your hands and knees, scooping the dirt away furiously. Then you filter it between your fingers, searching. There are other piles of dirt around you, aborted attempts. You must have been at it a while. I didn't know you had the energy. All this time, you would've heard me bashing and screaming and crying inside the house, but you just kept digging.

Perhaps you think I've died inside the house, now that it's quieter. Or perhaps you think I'll emerge at any moment; that's why you're moving fast, hoping to find the drugs before I find you. You're digging in the right place. At your side is the discarded mulga branch I planted as a marker.

As I approach, I have the urge to tip your hunched body head-first into the hole. It wouldn't take much. But I stop quietly behind you, the spade between us, less than a metre from my feet. You grunt as you dig, sweat running in rivers from your hair and down your back. The dirt has stained your

198

legs rust-red and your feet are as pink as galah feathers. But you haven't found anything yet.

I wait like the snake in the doorway.

Then, that increasingly familiar gunshot laughter rings out. You have seen something.

I step forward fast. If it's the bag of pills, you might swallow them right away. You must hear me because you stand and turn to face me. You hold up your right hand, a triumphant grin on your face. I stare at your pale, naked body and your scrawl of pubic hair, your wild expression. But it's not a bag of drugs in your right hand, it's the car key. You're laughing again as you see me staring. You against me? Right now, you are scoring the points.

'Bloody stupid hiding place,' you say. 'Why'd a bit of mulga be sticking up here if you hadn't put it there?'

You've come back, your knowledge of the land saving you again. And me, still the loser. I'll never know enough.

'Knew where you'd buried it,' you continue. 'Just had to keep digging to find it.'

You look at the key as if it's a prize, a reward for having to endure me for so long.

'Well, that's it then,' you say. 'I'll be off now.'

You're not staying to search for the drugs, or to search for us. You're already striding away, the key ring slipped over your index finger and the key clasped inside your right palm, your naked body straight and tall, walking across the burning sand as if your feet were made for this. You're going to leave me behind. No one will know what I did, or where I ended up. My disappearance will be a bigger mystery than it was the first time round. This time, however, no one will be held accountable.

'Have a good life, Kate,' you say over your shoulder.

This is wrong, wrong, WRONG. And how can you call me Kate, now?

You walk towards the car, away from me, away from your home. And I am no longer Kate, or Gemma, or anyone. You've won.

So, I do the only thing I can do to stop you.

I grab the spade and swing.

February 21st, later

My knuckles are white as I grip the steering wheel, driving fast, the car bumping and lurching over the rough ground, my body jerking, my head hitting the roof. My skin is on fire, sweat all over. The red warning light on the petrol gauge came on a while back, but the air conditioning is off and the windows open; I'm even talking to the car.

'Keep going,' I say, over and over.

Maybe I'm talking to myself. The car rumbles over softer sand, sputtering. A tyre will blow. The fuel will run out. I'll break down here and that will be it. But I don't want to die on a mining access road. I have to live. I have to get far away.

Your face appears in front of me, smeared across the windscreen, your skin covered in blood and sand. No, I can't think about you right now. I shake the sweat from my eyes. I need to keep driving. The car moans and I stroke the steering wheel, will it on.

'Good car,' I say. 'Hang on.'

The last bottle of water is rolling around on the passenger seat. Not enough to get me through the next hour, let alone beyond that.

'I'm thirsty too, my friend,' I say to the car, as I rattle

headlong down the dirt track.

Again and again, I flick sticky hair from my face. The ache in my right shoulder is spasming all the way to my forehead, my head pulsing with pain, but I grit my teeth and keep my foot down on the accelerator. Perhaps the real story of me starts here, driving fast with the engine screaming. This is my real release.

Soon the car is sputtering harder, moving more slowly through the sand. The wheels grind and spin as I manage to swerve off the track and under some trees. Then with a shudder, the car stops. I gulp hot, dry air. What now? Gum trees and scrub. Roo shit. Huge silhouettes of birds against the massive sky. No water. No petrol. No you. I topple out of the car into a blast of steam coming from under the hood, then leap away fast. I try to shelter under the scraggly trees, slouching down in the dirt, eyes on the car in case the smoke turns to flames. The sand on this part of the track seems more compact. Does that mean I'm not far from the tarmacked road, after all?

'You did your best,' I tell the car. 'You did all you could.'

I murmur sweet nothings about the car's bravery and ability to cope in a crisis, then stop when I realise how nuts I sound. But it's miraculous the car and I got this far; that it wasn't bogged when I started it up; that I could drive after what I did. In the footwell is the scrunched receipt from when I bought us fish and chips in that mining town. I remember you sucked the grease off your fingers and gnawed bits of batter from the wrapping. I blink sweat from my eyes as I see you again, sprawled across the dirt, blood all over you. When I blink again, there's only red sand in front of me, swaying and dancing in the heat. I rub the heels of my hands into my eyes. Your feet and your toes must be cool, deep in the earth, even if your face and shoulders

202

are sizzling hot. Could I go back to you? Is it a sign that the car broke down before I reached the road? I could walk back to where I left you.

When I push away from the car, I'm no longer sure which way I'm facing. Everything is spinning, the trees are on top, the earth is blue, not red. My hand flies out to the car to steady myself, and I scream from its sudden heat against my skin. Again, I shelter under the trees; I'm going to be sick. But when I retch, nothing comes up. Heat stroke? Or guilt? I deserve this. Dehydrating on a miner's track after what I've done would be a fitting end. But if I die now, what would be the point of any of this? I don't trust myself right now: if someone stopped to pick me up, I'd start babbling, revealing everything. I'm still too close to you.

I pinch the skin on my arms. *Just get the fuck together.*

I grab the last bottle of water and start to walk; I'll keep going as long as I can. This time you won't rescue me. And Mum doesn't know where I am. There's no worldwide manhunt paid for by government funds. It's up to me.

I walk with my head down. Close up, I see how well maintained the track is. We couldn't have lived our days out here in blissful isolation; someone would have found us eventually. And maybe, not too long from now, someone will find you. Will they recognise you? Will they frame what happened as a revenge killing?

As I walk, I try to formulate a plan. Once I get to the main road, I'll flag down a car, hitch a ride back to the petrol station where we filled up for the last time. I'll drink cool, clean water, and hitch back with water for the car to drink, before driving it back to Perth. After I've cleaned it up and got my money back,

I'll ring Mum and say the island trip was amazing.

Then I'll forget this whole experience. I'll forget you.

I won't drive past 31 Banksia Drive and check what that woman is doing, and I won't look for that teenager in the park. I'll just get on the plane I'm booked on and leave.

I put one foot in front of the other and keep going.

Then, like a mirage, the bitumen road.

I go close enough to touch it. Flinch. The tar is glistening in the sun, melting from the heat, but it's real. Ten years ago, it took longer than this to reach a proper road. The land is changing.

I shelter beside a termite mound at the side of the road, checking both ways. No vehicles, just the trembling movement of a heat haze. I sit in the dust and wait, ants crawling over my legs immediately. I'm burnt and sore, like you must be now. And I've almost finished the water. I peer down the road. The heat haze is playing tricks: I see trucks that aren't there, camels and horses. When I stare across the glistening road and see dead, blackened trees, they look like hunched shadow-men, surreal sculptures. Far away, dust moves through the land, wound in a dark tornado. Everything else is still. Everything is dead.

One last mouthful of water. I'd be stupid to save it. What if a car came by and saw me like this? I use it to wash your blood from my hands, clean my face.

There's movement down the road, a vehicle approaching. I sweep the wet hair from my face and stand, my fingers holding me steady against the termite mound. No flag on the hood, not a mine vehicle. As it nears, I see it's a white transit van with a logo on the side. *Desert Dreaming Journeys*. This is going to look weird, me being here.

The van stops close to me, too close. The window goes down and a man's face appears. He is round and red-cheeked and clean-shaven, so different from you.

'Where've you come from?' he says.

I feel the tickle of a nervous cough, but swallow it down.

'I've been travelling,' I say, my voice steadier than I feel. 'Hitching.'

He raises his eyebrows. 'Why'd you get off here?'

I point vaguely in the direction of the access track. 'Got a lift with a miner.'

He snorts. 'Pretty foolish place to leave you.'

Fear roars inside me now, the fear I thought I'd left behind. This man doesn't believe me. A stranded girl on the side of the road, looking like I do? It's suspicious. He's frowning.

'My car broke down,' I stammer. 'I ran out of fuel. I just need to get some more, that's all.'

He nods, a smile creeping lazily over his wide face. 'Why didn't you say that, instead of pretending? Tourists are always running out of juice up here, always getting into strife. I got a couple of jerry cans in the boot, always carry them. Where's your car?'

Something inside me unwinds a little. 'You'll help?'

As I look at his eyes, diluted grey and watery, he gives me a wink.

'Always help a damsel in distress,' he says. 'That's what I'm here for. *Aww*, don't be embarrassed, love.'

I nod. I know how to play this. I need to be the stupid young girl who doesn't know what she's doing. I stare at the ground, feigning embarrassment. I know the role well enough, but this time it's less comfortable to slip inside.

'Wanna hop in then, love?'

I glance back to the company name on his van, the logo a cartoon camel in a sombrero galloping across the sand.

'You're a tour operator?'

'Not yet.' He grins. 'Starting up soon, though. It's just so underexplored out here, you know? Well, I guess you do know now!' He laughs through his teeth, a kind of whistling. 'Anyway, you getting in or not? It's hot with the window down.'

I toss the empty water bottle in the footwell and jump into the passenger seat. I hope I don't stink too much or look too weird. I hope this man doesn't realise how out of it I really am. I hope he doesn't murder me.

'Just take me to the petrol station down the highway,' I say. 'I'll sort it out from there.'

After he puts his van into gear, he turns and looks at me, crossing his arms and making a face as if he's offended.

'*Aww,* what kind of bloke would I be if I just left you there? Nah, I'll help you out.'

'Honestly, I'll be fine. I'll—'

'Don't you worry, I got the jerry cans in the back. I'll get you going again, missy.'

The car moves off before I can say anything else. It's clear I can't argue with him. He wants to play the hero, and I don't want to make a scene.

The whole way, he talks about how stupid I am. 'What on earth were you doing out here anyway?' he says, enjoying himself a little too much.

I shrug. I may as well indulge him; I need his petrol, after all.

'Taking photos,' I say, sighing. 'It's so beautiful up here, don't you think? So...*spiritual*.'

I don't know where I pull this lie from, and I don't know if he believes me, but he doesn't ask about my camera or where it is. He nods and makes a clicking noise as if he's communicating with a horse.

'You one of them godly types? We get a few of them up these parts too.'

I nod and smile. Maybe if he thinks I'm religious he'll pull fewer moves on me.

'You're so lucky being up here,' I say quickly. 'You must have a lot of material for your publicity shots, for your new tour business?'

And that's all he needs. He's off again, talking about the places he's going to take tourists. I resist the urge to tell him how I could run his business for him without even trying. I tell him I'm a gap-year student and talk about hitchhiking around Australia. I play the clueless young blonde.

'I'm Tony, by the way,' he says. 'At your service.'

I smile thinly, then lean my head against the cool glass of the window and bask in his air-conditioning. I'm not sure I'm ready to give him a name. I watch termite mound after termite mound flash past, blurs of orange and brown, as he drones on about the website he's building and how much he's going to charge for each trip.

'What do you reckon? You'd pay a hundred bucks to see a cool sunset, right, like with roos and birds and shit? Bit of sparkling wine thrown in?'

'Sure,' I murmur.

He grins, satisfied. 'Could even do a bit of stargazing after.

You ever had anyone show you the stars out here?'

I nod. 'Car won't be too much further,' I say, hoping.

He tells me about a road trip he's planning with some mates. Just as I'm convinced he's about to invite me as part of my gap trip, my dirty, dusty car finally comes into view.

'Blimey,' he says, when he sees it. 'You really did need my help!'

He lifts the jerry cans from the boot and uses a funnel to get the lifeblood inside the car. I watch, guzzling the water Tony gives me. Predictably, he brushes away my offer of assistance, so I just sit in the shade. Soon enough he's writing his mobile number on the back of one of his new tour brochures and handing it to me.

'That's my personal number,' he says, winking at me again. 'Anything at all, just call! Always here to help a lady.'

He waits until I start the car, and I watch him wave at me in the rear-view mirror as I pull away. When dust finally obliterates my vision of him, I exhale loudly.

In the dusky forecourt of the petrol station, I fill the car up properly, then fill myself up with water too, before buying a phone charger for the journey back to Perth. The man behind the counter studies me. I think he might be smelling me, wanting me out of his establishment.

Before he can say anything, I get a cup of coffee from a nearby machine and sit at one of his tables, plugging my phone into a nearby socket. As I wait for it to switch on, I scratch a mosquito bite on my leg until the skin runs red with blood, until there's blood under my fingernails. I pull my fingers away, even though I want to scratch all my skin off now. As I gasp down the coffee, my phone starts pinging. I read the email from Rose first.

Dear Kate,

I pause. The name looks strange, after my time with you. It's like thinking of a season I'm not in, imagining myself in different clothes, my skin a different shade. I feel a twist of guilt as I read her words: I've let her down, worried her.

> Hope you don't think I'm being nosy, but I had to reach out one last time. You must be about to have your big adventure, but I wanted to say before you go: if you need an ear to chew, I'm here and I'm sending you all the best, wherever you are. I'll go on planning my own holiday in the meantime. Keep in touch, I'd love to know when you're back in London, what you're up to.

Sent earlier today.

I picture her, with a cup of tea and a tabby cat beside her. Will she ever get to go on her trip? I scroll back through what I wrote when I told her I was going into the desert. It was only a few days ago, yet it feels like a lifetime. I reply, because there is something I can tell her now.

Dear Rose,

I'm sitting in a petrol station. Seems my adventure wasn't such an answer, after all. Nothing turns out as you expect, right? But, even so, I saw what I needed to for the last time. Out here, it's not how it was. There's more development. Mining is destroying the land. Whatever it was I needed to find is dead, gone.

> I don't advise you make your last trip here. Think about another type of wilderness. Or spend your last holiday with family and friends? I've come to

think people are the biggest wildernesses of all.

Thank you for your concern about my wellbeing. I'm fine. I'll come back to London soon, and I'll start over.

I'm surprised by what I write. Why am I saying all these things to a stranger I'll never meet? Because I can be whoever I like with her. Rose thinks I'm knowledgeable and in control, and maybe that's what I need to think too.

I look out at the car, almost pink now from the dust. I should burn it, get rid of the evidence. Your old jeans and blue shirt are on the back seat; I hope Tony didn't notice. I might as well incinerate myself while I'm at it. I scratch the mosquito bite, check the charge on my phone. Half-full. Any moment now, I will drive away. I will turn right and head back down the Great Northern Highway all the way to Perth. And that will be it. The end.

But I can't move yet.

I imagine your skin burning under the sun, your pain. Then I think of the endless red dirt and scrub, the zebra finches in the mulga trees. I remember what you told me once, that zebra finches recognise each other's voices, that they have individual calls for their mates and remember those unique songs for as long as they're alive.

I don't know if I can do this.

Supreme Court of Western Australia
PERTH

October 15th

Mr Lowe, the barrister for the prosecution team, begins his opening speech, reminding the jury of everything I'm accused of. The courtroom is quiet. Although I'm staring straight ahead, I can tell that Jodie is watching me. Is she checking if I'm alright with all these words that define me now?

Kidnap.

Torture.

Perversion of justice.

Murder.

The jury are watching me too. Does my face fit these crimes? Jodie told me they tried to find jurors who wouldn't remember me from your trial all those years ago, but she also said that being remembered may play into our favour.

I want to turn my head to see the gallery, see who's here, but if I do, I'll get another scowl from the judge. So I imagine them: friends of Louise MacFarlane from 31 Banksia Drive, front row, centre. Even if she's not here yet herself, I feel her eyes on me. Her hate has the same force as the heat in the desert. Mum should be up there, Dad too, and the Perth detectives. It's quite the reunion. Could Nick be there too? I listen as Mr Lowe sets out his argument to the jury, and tells them who will be called by the prosecution team to give evidence over the next few days.

First, the guy in the garage, then the tour operator, then Nick.

Three confident, respectable-looking men—against me.

But there's no body, and no murder weapon, and I note with interest that Mr Lowe doesn't mention either of those facts. Jodie told me that this lack of crucial evidence helps our case, but she also said that, because I lied to the police, I will seem like an unreliable witness. Mr Lowe has already mentioned my lying at least twice.

I turn my eyes to the deep brown on the wooden table beneath my fingers. I imagine my nails sinking into it, touching sand, digging and digging, my skin staining red. I see blood seeping under my fingernails, moving up my arm. I could scream the truth right now, make everyone listen. But would anyone really hear?

Eight months earlier
GREAT NORTHERN HIGHWAY

February 22nd

The rust-red land is covered in shadows as I drive. In the moonlight, occasional scatterings of shrubs appear, dark stubble on the flat skin of this country. In the distance, hills, or clouds. When I flip on the radio, late-night Aussie rock blares out, and I think of you. Bon Scott has your voice, and you're screaming at me about *a one-way ride…No stop signs…*I shake my head to banish you, change the channel, but you are still here in the car.

I open the window and let in the dust. Outside, a sign warns of flooding, which is difficult to imagine in this snap-dry night, but then the road crosses a sandy creek bed at least ten metres wide, so I guess, in a different season…water and change and new life. Everything shifts, becomes new again. What was the beautiful name for the wet season I learnt at the Kings Park lightshow? My memory is trembling, so much forgetting, and so much withholding. And I feel so scared.

There is no release. There is only this road.

Supreme Court of Western Australia
PERTH

October 15th

The first witness for the prosecution is called. The man from the garage. The clerk makes him swear on the Bible and state his name.

'Eric Symonds,' he says, his voice softer than I remember.

He says he lives in a trailer behind the petrol station: it makes sense that he remembers me. What else is there to do in a place like that but watch the occasional customer come and go? Of course he noticed me. And I remember him too, how he wrinkled his nose as he served me. I thought it was because I smelled bad, but perhaps he saw some evidence of you on me—blood on my forehead or on my T-shirt.

'Mr Symonds,' Mr Lowe begins, 'can you tell me if you've seen the defendant before?'

'I have,' Eric Symonds replies. 'I saw the defendant twice in February this year. Those times were five days apart from each other, February seventeenth and February twenty-second.'

He sounds so stilted; I suppose he's learnt the words by heart from a statement. All the time he speaks, he keeps his eyes fixed on Mr Lowe.

'Would you tell the jury, Mr Symonds, if there were any differences you noticed between when you saw the defendant on the first occasion and when you saw her on the second?'

'Yes, there was one major difference between the two times,' Eric Symonds replies. 'The defendant was alone on the second occasion she visited my garage.'

'The defendant wasn't alone the first time she used your petrol station?'

Eric Symonds shakes his head. 'No. She was not alone on that first time.'

Jodie warned me about Eric Symonds, what he would say. She'd told me he'd be a strong witness. I may be wrong, but I think I see a glimmer of a smile on Mr Lowe's face as he glances my way. Smug bastard. But he turns back to his witness instantly and assumes his manner of quiet authority. Some of the jurors lean forward attentively.

'So, Mr Symonds,' he continues, glancing down at his notes, 'how are you certain the defendant was not alone the first time she used your petrol station?'

'Because she had a man in the back seat.'

Mr Lowe nods. 'How are you certain of this?'

'I saw him. Clear as day.'

The atmosphere in the court room changes subtly. People shifting in their seats, and a faint collective intake of breath. It's as if there is less air in the room now.

'So, the defendant had a man in the back seat of her car the first time she used your petrol station,' Mr Lowe continues, 'and then, five days later, when she returned, she did not have a man with her. She was by herself.'

'Yes,' Mr Symonds says. 'That's correct.'

Mr Lowe asks the clerk to show the jury a photo. A screen is turned on and an old photo of you appears, in which you are young and handsome, the *old Ty*. You didn't look like that in the back seat of the hire car that day. But

222

maybe there are no more recent photos of you, or only ones of you in prison uniform—not a good look.

Mr Lowe turns to Mr Symonds. 'Can you confirm that this was the man you saw that day?'

'Yes, that was the man in the back seat.'

Mr Lowe angles himself towards the jury. 'So, it would seem that something happened to that man in the intervening period.' He lingers on the word *intervening*, as if it has a nasty taste he's trying to expel. I can feel Jodie stiffen beside me. 'Perhaps the defendant left him somewhere, if he didn't come back with her.'

'Objection, your honour!' Jody shouts. 'Conjecture.'

Once again, I can't help glancing around the courtroom. If you were here, if you could only show up...I feel the judge's eyes on me and turn back swiftly. I tell myself to stop going mad.

'Continue with the questioning,' the judge says to Mr Lowe.

Some members of the jury scrutinise me now. Am I capable of all that's being said and implied? I don't want to see their faces; I want to see Mum and Dad's faces in the gallery. I need to know how they're looking at me, who they think I am, what *they* think I'm capable of.

Eight months earlier
GREAT NORTHERN HIGHWAY

At a sign announcing *Malgi Rocks Picnic Ground*, a dirt track leads off the highway to the left. The car shudders over gravel as I make the turn, travelling too fast towards a jumble of big boulders. In the rear-view mirror, I watch dust lit up from the brake lights, suspended in an orange cloud. There won't be anybody here at this hour. I pull into the car park near the rocks, where old oil drums masquerade as rubbish bins, their blackened insides evidence they have been used for burning. One of them will be fine for what I need.

In between the gunshot holes on the faded sign I park next to, there's text about local Indigenous history, stories about the rocks, and something else about stockmen. When I fling open the back door and reach for your things, your clothes go flying into the dirt. I leave them for now, and return for your backpack. Why didn't I ever look inside it? When you spoke to that girl in the park, I imagined ropes and drugs and even a gun zipped within, more dangerous evidence I'd need to get rid of.

I take the backpack and lean against one of the oil drums, but the mosquitos and night-time insects are too persistent, so I return to huddle against the car, sitting in the dirt. I unzip the backpack and pull out a water bottle—half-full—and I am angry, again, for not checking earlier. I also find a baseball cap, embroidered with a cartoon character of a chicken in a chef's hat; I stick it on my head for now. Then an apple, soft and bruised. The fox might've liked that.

And then, papers. Only papers.

I pull them out and dump them in the dirt beside me, turn the backpack upside down and shake.

Half a pack of Extra chewing gum tumbles out, along with a paperclip, a screwed-up receipt for a bucket of chicken, and a lighter, which I palm.

Nothing else. No gun. No knife.

I check the pockets. No more baggies of weed or pills. No wig or disguises to put on the girl in the park. I sit back onto my heels. What does this mean? You were never going to take her, just like you said? I swallow slowly, nauseous now, and focus back on the papers—a document about rehabilitation after prison, a page of phone numbers and websites titled *If you need to reach out*, a pizza delivery brochure, and your CV. I smooth it across my legs and read.

Your full name, your birthdate. Thirty-nine years old. Not as old as you look.

Under *Skills and Experience* you list a woodwork course in prison, fifteen years' of welding and fixing cars, a job in a mine camp, a forklift licence and a few computer courses. But my eyes snag on the final line: *Winner of the Hakea Prison Life Drawing Award.* I feel a smile twitching at the corners of my mouth. So you didn't give up your art. But life drawing? Who have you been drawing? It was always the land.

I rifle through the rest of the papers, desperate to find something I can hate you for, something about that woman

228

in 31 Banksia Drive, or details of another crime I don't know about. But there's only a letter from Medicare, a leaflet about a back-to-work scheme, and another letter about getting help for drug and alcohol addictions. Perhaps you read that one; it's more crumpled than the rest. I pull it from the pile and read about a Narcotics Anonymous meeting in South Perth. I trace my fingers over a coffee ring in one corner, imagining you pausing your reading to take a sip, remembering that first coffee we shared, the one that started it all. When I turn over the page, I find black-and-white swirls, circles, faces, a whole tapestry, your mind laid out, a hidden part of you.

It's hard to make sense of it at first, the drawings are so tiny, but I hold the paper closer and eventually decipher dogs running, eyes in each corner of the page, a mountain range, and a house that looks like your den. I search for a sketch of me. Along one side of the page is a mermaid arching her back like an ocean wave, long dark hair down her spine. On the other side of the page, I recognise a constellation, Pleiades. The seven sisters chased eternally by the hunter's star, Orion. You showed me those stars once, one hot night when I lay against you. The memory of it brings hot, scratchy tears to my eyes. There is beauty and talent in these lines you've drawn, in the patterns and chaos. You should have been an artist. You should've been so much more than what you turned yourself into.

I shove the documents, backpack and our bloodied clothes into the blackest drum I can find, then ignite the lot with your lighter. The flames flare immediately, and I worry that someone will see, or that the fire will leap and spread to the scrub and set the whole place on fire. It's probably illegal to light a fire here at this time of year: another crime to add to my list. But the flames die down and settle below the rim of the drum.

I wait until everything has turned to ash, until embers of what was once yours catch the wind and float like fireflies into the night. I wait for them to kindle the scrub, for the wildfire to start. But the embers go cold, and so does the night as it draws in.

In the windless evening, I walk up to the biggest of the boulders, where I crouch, my back against it, and shut my eyes. The rock is still warm and the heat radiates along my spine. No sound of birds or bats. I imagine the rock as a body pressing against me, a belly against my shoulders. The rock doesn't care what I have done. The rock has seen worse, seen everything. It still welcomes me, gives me a home I don't deserve.

I open my eyes when I hear a rustling, then a soft, rhythmic chewing. Eyes in the scrubland are watching me, shadows darting along the ground. Roos. They're not scared of me.

'You should be,' I whisper, as tears run down my face again.

I don't think I can do this. I can't leave this place, can't leave you. Because leaving you is leaving me too.

Supreme Court of Western Australia
PERTH

October 15th

When Jodie gets up to cross-examine, she returns to what Eric Symonds said about you not being in the car the second time he saw me.

'But is this proof that something happened to Tyler MacFarlane?' She glances towards the jury before turning back to the witness.

Mr Symonds shakes his head. 'No.' He shifts in his seat as Jodie stares at him. He looks over at Mr Lowe.

'Think carefully, Mr Symonds.' Jodie lowers her voice. 'The items the defendant bought from you do not suggest she had just killed a man. Do they? A twelve-pack of water bottles, a phone charger, petrol. No cleaning products here, no bleach. Would you agree with that?'

Eric Symonds frowns, then he glances at me. 'Yes,' he finally admits. 'She didn't buy anything that proved she'd killed him.'

I watch the prosecution team sit up straighter and I feel a small sense of satisfaction.

'Exactly,' Jodie says. 'So let me present an alternative situation. You could also say that Kate Stone left your petrol station that day and returned to Tyler MacFarlane. You could say there was nothing untoward going on when you first saw Tyler MacFarlane in the back seat of the hire car on February seventeenth. You could say they were just driving together on a trip, having fun. And why was Tyler MacFarlane in the back seat, and not the front, as Mr Lowe pointed out? There could be any number of reasons. He was tired, sleeping. Maybe he was even hiding. Neither of them wanted Tyler to be seen by the authorities, after all.'

'Objection!' says Mr Lowe.

Eric Symonds looks thoroughly confused. Jodie reminds him and the jury of the arguments she set out in her opening speech. That you and I were on a road-trip, returning to a place important to us both, reconnecting with each other after years apart.

In her account, we are more like Romeo and Juliet than Bonnie and Clyde. Both you and I, misguided and damaged, but not dangerous. Her opening speech, when she laid everything out for the jury, was a thing of beauty. Her voice was heavy with emotion when she told the court, with care and sensitivity, about how I'd been diagnosed with Stockholm syndrome after your trial for my kidnap, how confused I'd become in the following years. With utmost respect, she asked the jury if anyone could blame me for getting confused afterwards, for believing the lies you fed me. She didn't say you were on drugs when I saw you in that park; she told the jury that you came with me willingly. She explained that a part of you even wanted to atone for all the hurt you had done.

'They both had a naive dream that, together, they could be something more,' she said.

Expertly, she spun our story as if she was creating a beautiful Chagall painting, full of longing and sweeping emotions.

234

'Though it may be hard for us to understand,' she said, 'they did, and do, love each other. Like ill-fated lovers, they are never able to be together, because of what society might think of their relationship, because of how they'd be treated for it. They had to love each other in private, and then try to escape to the place they thought no one would find them. *Their* place.'

Two weeks ago, Jodie and Mikael, my defence team, sat with me for hours in the remand centre and discussed this part of my case. 'We can show the jury how your relationship was different from what they might think,' Jodie said. 'Is that how you want your story shown?'

I never did ask Jodie if she believed all the things I told her.

Now, in this cold, cavernous courtroom, I stare at the photograph of you still up on the screen above Eric Symonds. The image of you as a younger, tanned, fitter man might help my case. This time, the jury might believe I ran away with you, that I wanted to. Who wouldn't want to run away with you when you look like that? You're so damn beautiful. Too beautiful. But will they believe that you wanted to run away with me?

Eight months earlier
GREAT NORTHERN HIGHWAY

February 23rd

I try to sleep against the rock, let it comfort me, but, before long, the rock, like the night, grows cold, and I retreat to the car. I still can't sleep, but I can't leave either. I never told you all the things I needed to tell you. I shut my eyes tight, but it's no good: the images force themselves in.

Swinging the spade.

You going down.

Blood on the sand.

And then, digging, making the hole bigger. Tucking you inside. A bug in a rug of red. But was it enough? Will your body become soil nutrients?

I think of the beautiful faces you drew on the back of the piece of paper, the constellation of Pleiades. The mermaid.

You did remember me when you were inside. I'm there.

It's still dark when I start the car again. If an animal smashes through my windscreen while I'm driving, that seems about fair. I reverse, skidding in the dirt, and immediately something clunks against the undercarriage. A rock. I'm stuck, suspended on it. As I rev harder, there's a horrible scraping sound and the smell of burning rubber, which reminds me of the smell of your burning clothes and backpack. I push my foot flat, forcing away the images flooding my mind, willing the car forwards, away from these boulders that are cold now, away from this place. The ashes of your clothes, your CV, the words about the prize—I need to leave it all behind me.

The car screams, protesting, but finally judders off the rock to swerve along the track back to the highway.

I squint in the darkness: no roos or cattle on the side of the road. Nothing there. But in my mind I can see camels, far away, loping across the sand. And lights that might be mine sites, or even stars, twinkling in the distance. Final images to take with me on this black night, on this long, straight road back to you.

It feels right, doesn't it, what I'm doing?

It has to feel right.

Supreme Court of Western Australia
PERTH

October 15th

The tour operator is the prosecution's second witness. I can tell by Mr Lowe's second smug smile of the day that he thinks Tony Kowalski is rock solid. Mr Lowe takes his time, getting Mr Kowalski to explain in detail how he found me at the side of the road in a dishevelled state.

'Yes, Ms Stone was extremely hot and bothered that afternoon,' Tony Kowalski says. 'Dehydrated, I thought it at the time. She smelled pretty bad too.'

I run my hands over my belly, smoothing my top. Thanks for that one, Tony. Nothing like the revelation of bad personal hygiene to turn the jury against me. Enthusiastically, Tony recounts the conversation we had in his tour van, his voice swelling with confidence as he speaks.

'She said she was a gap-year student,' he says. 'And who am I to argue? I mean, she only looks like she's fresh out of school, doesn't she? Slip of a thing! Well, not now obviously!'

He describes taking me back to the hire car, how he filled up the car with his jerry can. He sounds pleased with himself, clearly thinking he was my white knight.

'She didn't say nothing about Tyler MacFarlane,' he says to Mr Lowe. 'Not once the whole time we were together.'

He glances over at me, and I hold his gaze. *Together,* Tony, really?

243

He looks away, back to Mr Lowe, and I resist the urge to smile. Not such an innocent gap-year student now, am I, Tony? You just didn't look hard enough on the day, did you, just saw what you wanted?

Jodie begins her cross-examination gently, smiling at Tony Kowalski encouragingly.

'I'm wondering, Mr Kowalski,' she says, 'did you ever think that Ms Stone might not have told you about Tyler MacFarlane because she didn't want to get him into trouble? Because she didn't want him to go back to prison? Ms Stone and Mr MacFarlane knew very well that he was breaking the conditions of his parole by their being together.'

'Objection!' Mr Lowe shouts.

Tony Kowalski shrugs.

Jodie's good, I've got to hand it to her. She may even get me off. But the twelve people to my right are the real ones who decide. And do they believe my story? Do they think I'm a reliable narrator? And where's your voice in all this, Ty? Have I rendered you dumb?

Louise MacFarlane will be a witness tomorrow. She'll say that you never came home after you left on the fifteenth of February. She'll say she knew there was something suspicious going on, even in those first few days after you were released from prison. She'll say she saw me there, watching you. Mostly, though, what she will say will be her word against mine.

After her story, the blood-spatter expert and the lab techs will give evidence about your DNA found all over the car and at the den. Jodie said it's that evidence we need to be most concerned about.

But there is someone else missing from the entrances

and the exits in this court, isn't there, Ty? Are you as pleased as I am not to see her? Nobody except you and me knows about her. That teenage girl from the park. I never told anyone about her, not even Jodie or Mikael. I often wondered if she'd come forward of her own volition, especially after your photographs were shown on the evening news. She's probably the only one who saw me take you that day. But maybe she was only a random girl, just like you'd told me. Maybe she didn't know you at all and, more importantly, didn't want her parents to know that she was buying your drugs.

'Ms Stone...'

As I continue to stare blankly at the jury again, a prison officer at my side gestures for me to face the front. I look at Tony Kowalski, still getting grilled by Jodie. You know, Ty, I might win this. Will you be happy if I do? These days I'm finding it harder to tell what you might like. You're still there in my head, of course—you've been part of me for so long, and I have such a sense of loyalty—but something is shifting inside. Because what if this is it, and you really are gone? Then Rhiannon might ask what it would feel like to take you out from that space in my brain, to move on. Am I ready? But if I'm locked in a cell for decades, will I be able to forget you?

Did you manage to forget me for a time?

You tried to.

Eight months earlier
GREAT NORTHERN HIGHWAY

February 23rd, later

I keep driving, even when I hear a rattling sound—something must be hanging from the underside of the car, scraping and bumping against the bitumen. I imagine metal sparking, flames, incinerating me and the car.

Not yet, please.

I turn the radio up, but loud music doesn't mask the racket. When I skid back onto the access track, the noise is accompanied by a growling.

Can you hear it?

Can you hear me coming?

By late afternoon, the car limps off the track and onto the rougher ground, smoke seeping from the hood. Seems I'm good at destroying things—this car is no exception.

But I'm here. Back.

The car splutters to a stop beneath the spindly trees near the den. Dead. I turn the ignition again, just to check, but the engine whines then goes silent.

'Sorry,' I whisper.

I get out, trembling all over.

You may be dead, too. The first dead body I will see in my life will be yours. I swallow bile at the realisation that I am worse than you. A murderer. I have destroyed something I might have saved. Destroyed you. It feels nothing like what I imagined.

Even after two days, my footprints are still in the sand. Yours too, leading around the side of the den. Before I follow them, movement in the scrub catches my eye. An animal darts away from behind a clump of tea-tree. A dingo? I squint. No, a fox.

My fox. Sal.

But I am seeing things. And I'm being stupid. It's the fox I rescued from the road. But how is she still alive? Could it mean you might be too? I squint at the scrub again, but now see only shades of brown, no bright fur of a fox. Fact and fiction are blurring. I start walking, placing my feet inside your flattened footprints, dread settling over me.

I wipe sweat from my face and neck as I get to the spot. The mulga branches are still lying across the dirt. But you are not here, not in the hole where I buried you. I spin around, scan the land, my chest pounding. Has an animal dug you up? That fox? A person? Did I not bury you, after all?

I look at my nails, now clean. I did do it, didn't I? I try to will the shaking in my hands to stop before it moves across my body. I remember the spade in my palms, the digging. The blood running down the side of your face. I remember making the hole bigger, rolling you in. You weren't dead then, just unconscious, but after I finished, your exposed face and shoulders were directly under the sun. That's how I left you; I wanted you to be able to breathe. Which is crazy, really. Perhaps I didn't really want to kill you—or at least, not be fully responsible. I wanted the land to do it for me. Death by desert.

But you always surprise me, don't you?

I step backwards and trip over the spade, which is covered in flies, settling on what must be your dried blood. There are tracks in the sand as if a huge snake has wound its way across it. But no snake is this big, even out here. I almost look towards the Separates to check they haven't moved and somehow made these marks, but no, they are human drag marks. And they lead straight to your den.

It must have taken some strength to crawl out from the holes and pull yourself along the dirt towards shelter. I follow the marks like a thread, until, at the door to your den, I stop, breathing deeply. Could someone have helped you escape? If you've been found, I'll be caught. Then I remind myself why I came back—how none of that matters now—and I step inside. Everything is as I left it, the floors swept, the roof tiles piled in the corner. The Separates stare back through the cracked window pane, watchful, reproachful. *He's in there*, they whisper, sending shivers over the land towards me.

I follow a trail of bloodied sand down the corridor, past the dead snake in the doorway, and into the room that used to be mine, the one you said we'd share one day. You are on the double bed, splayed across the sheets, face-down in the cobwebs and dust. You are completely red, from the sand, from your blood, from the sun. Your skin has come away and left bleeding raw muscles. You could be one of your art installations. You do not look entirely human.

Trembling, I step towards you, reach out my hand. You said you never wanted to go back into this house. You said our time here was finished, that this place should burn. And yet here you are, waiting. What have I done, and how have you survived it, survived me?

Supreme Court of Western Australia
PERTH

October 15th

When Nick takes the stand, the stiffness in his shoulders and the angle of his body make it clear that he's avoiding looking at me, which only makes me stare all the harder at him.

The Judas, the betrayer.

After insisting so many times that he wanted to get to know me, make something of us, care for me, it seems he was pretending the whole time. There are two pieces of evidence the prosecution will ask him to address, but which one will they start with?

I listen as he begins talking about me, telling the world who he thinks I am. It's obvious from Mr Lowe's questions that the prosecution is presenting me to the jury as a wild woman, full of furious rage and burning for revenge. Like Jodie, the prosecution team have been using my original diagnosis of Stockholm syndrome for their case, but in their version I'm not a victim, far from it. I'm a perpetrator, damaged yet dangerous. A madwoman getting her own back.

'It's all understandable, given her tragic circumstances,' Nick tells the jury. 'But just because she had a tough past, doesn't make it right, what she did, all the crimes she committed, the pain she inflicted on a man only trying to get his life back together...'

And I wonder, Ty, when did you and Nick team up together?

'No man deserves her treatment,' Nick says.

There was a push to televise the case, you know. That's how big the story of you and me has become. Or always was, I guess. That's how much people care. Even without the livestream, we are on the news most nights, photos of you and me beamed into other people's living rooms once again.

Do you like that photo they're using of you? Younger and beautiful, such a handsome antihero. Their favourite picture of me is my schoolgirl shot from ten years ago. Sweet, blameless Gemma Toombs. The public never want to forget her.

'It's fine if they use that old shot,' Mikael said, when he saw me wincing at it. 'It actually helps you. Makes people remember your innocence.'

Now, in this trial, I notice Jodie is also playing on every bit of sympathy people felt for the innocent, impressionable schoolgirl. How affected I was by the experience, how changed, how blameless I was then and still am. Interestingly, she has said that you were also a victim. In her opening statement, she told the jury you were *chewed out by the system, not too bright when it came to life choices, impressionable.* I'm not sure you'd like that being said about you, but I don't deny there's truth there. Strange, isn't it, that it wasn't until the end that I saw you in this way: weak and vulnerable, too. Ten years ago, I thought you were strong, in control, unbeatable. You were my whole world, once.

'All they wanted,' Jodie told the jury, 'was to live out on the land they both loved, with the person they thought they loved, the person their individual life circumstances led them to believe they loved.'

Is that the truth?

I close my eyes to get rid of an image of the two of us at the waterhole, me touching your back, you holding my waist, so close. I scratch the skin of my arms and remind myself I am here, in this courtroom. The zoning out is happening too easily now. I try to focus.

Mr Lowe has an expression of compassion as he listens to Nick's testimony, an expression likely put on for the jury because there's nothing much to feel sorry for when it comes to Nick. And what exactly is the Judas saying now? I try to pay attention as he recounts how we met online and how I was different from the other girls he found on the dating app. It's not long before he gets to that night, the last night we were together, and then the morning after, when it all went wrong.

'I was trying to be nice, give her a chance,' he says. 'I was going to get us breakfast! But when I looked for her keys to get out of the flat, I found a letter from Hakea Prison about the release of Tyler MacFarlane, and I wondered who that was. Wondered what this girl I was seeing had to do with him.'

'What was the defendant's general state of mind that morning, would you say?' Mr Lowe asks.

'Different,' says Nick. 'I'd never seen her so happy, at first.'

I try not to cringe as he tells the jury about the roleplay the night before.

'I went along with it for her,' he says. 'Even though I didn't particularly want to. She wanted me to become

257

someone else. Become like *him*.'

I look down at the table, pick at the skin around my nails. He's right, I had wanted that. But Nick is lying when he says he didn't enjoy it. Anyway, he wasn't like you, not at all. I can see that now.

'And when did you start to put it all together?' Mr Lowe asks. 'That the name on the letter—Gemma Toombs—was also the woman you were seeing?'

'I didn't know what it meant,' the Judas says. 'Not at first. I thought the letter related to a family member. I didn't know her real name then. But I saw the prison logo, and...'

'And you were curious...?' Mr Lowe prods.

'Sure.'

'Because here was the girl you liked, maybe loved, and she had a secret, something she didn't want you to see?'

Jodie stands. 'Leading question, Your Honour.'

I study Nick carefully. I'm sure he never loved me, not really, despite what he's saying now, or what the newspaper reports have said about me and him. But he glances at me anyway, and I see his cheeks flush.

'Continue,' Judge Reece says.

'Yes, I thought she had a secret,' Nick admits. 'And I wanted to know it. I thought it was a game at first. I teased her by holding the letter out of her grasp, just a bit of fun, like the night before...'

I can't help rolling my eyes. A game? Perhaps I have always been a game for Nick. A game he didn't realise I'd stopped playing, and when I backed off, he just ramped up his gameplay. I glance at his neck, where I kissed it, bit it. It all seems so long ago.

258

'I was angry she didn't tell me,' he adds.

Here's some truth. Will he be brave enough to tell it all, how he came to my house at night, stalked me?

'But my anger was nothing compared to hers,' he says. 'I learned that pretty fast.'

He tells the court how I flipped. Of course, he does. I watch the jury as he describes how I threatened him with the kitchen knife, how I used it on him. I see the sympathy on their faces. But when he says he was scared for his life, I see a glimmer of truth in his expression. Now I feel bad. Nick was never the root of the problem—I understand that more clearly now. Even what he did next, well, I suppose someone had to expose me. I couldn't hide forever.

A photograph appears on the screen behind him, one Nick took on his phone, of the scratch I made on his cheek. I force myself to stare at it: the mark doesn't seem particularly big. And when I look at Nick now, I can't see a scar.

'This was just another way in which Kate was trying to make me like Tyler MacFarlane,' Nick says. 'Cutting me, putting his scar onto, *into*, me. She was branding me.'

He gestures to his cheek, to his non-existent scar. If I'd really wanted Nick to look like you, I would have pressed harder.

Another picture appears, this time of you, old you. Mr Lowe zooms in on the scar on your cheek: the scar you told me had come from when you were chased into the desert, and you ran and fell, and then you were punished. A technician adjusts the images until they sit side by side, the two scars side by side, both left cheeks, you and Nick a couple now. Nick, the fancy banker. You, the dirtbag. You, who wanted the good life, to touch the land each morning and night. And Nick, living the fantasy of money and deals in the city. Maybe we are all fantasists of one sort or another.

The picture of you snaps off, and only Nick is left on the screen. As Mr Lowe keeps prodding, Nick talks about the violence within me, what I am capable of, what the act of knifing him suggests I could also do. I wait for Nick to glance my way again. But he doesn't. Does he feel any guilt towards me, or does he simply not care anymore? He's in the spotlight now, being heard, and maybe a part of him likes it.

During your trial all those years ago, you looked at me the whole time. Do you remember? Which is why, of course, it felt so awful when I told the court what the police and my parents expected to hear, that you kidnapped me and held me by force, that you drugged me. When I told them we hadn't run away together, that I hadn't been compliant— not in the way you described me in your story. It felt like I was killing you in that courtroom. And here I am, being accused of killing you again.

Eight months earlier
UNMAPPED

February 23rd, later

I step closer, the stench of your sweat and blood thick in my nostrils. Is this what death smells like? I try to keep my hand steady as I reach forward and touch your skin. It is on fire. But you are alive.

'Ty?' I whisper.

You don't stir. I feel for the pulse in your neck and find it easily, racing, on fire too.

'I'll get water,' I say.

I run back to the car, grab a couple of the bottles I bought from the petrol station. When I return, you haven't moved. I am scared to turn you over. Shaking hard, I reach my fingers to your matted, bloodied hair. I did that. I did all this to you. I feel tears welling as I look.

'Ty, I…I didn't mean…' I whisper again.

You remain motionless. I slip my fingers underneath your head to find your face. I feel for your breath, my fingertips brushing your blistered lips.

'Can you turn?'

When I grip your shoulders to push you, you moan in pain, so I stop. But I've seen enough to know your front is much redder, much worse. I drip some water onto my fingertips and press them to your lips. You close your mouth when I try to give you more. The weeping blisters across your shoulders need water too. I go back to the car for the cotton sheet, shake out the dust, then soak it. I don't care if I'm using too much water. I return to lay it across your shoulders, down over your back and legs.

In the kitchen, I find a bucket and bowl under the sink. After sprinkling salt from the jar I brought in from the shed, and pouring in more of our precious water, I return to you. I try to dab away the blood dried down one side of your body, but there is so much of it. The water turns pink, then red, then brown.

'Stop,' you hiss.

At least, I think that's what you say. I step away from you, and lean in the doorway. I wouldn't want me helping either. If I can do all this to you, what else am I capable of? Soon, your breathing gets heavier, and I know you are sleeping. Is this where our story ends? You sleeping here, slipping away from me, burnt from the land and from what I did. I can't deny that a part of me feels satisfied: I wanted to hurt you. And like this, you don't talk back, no nasty comments, you're not craving drugs. I can imagine you however I like.

But I almost killed you. And the feeling I have as I look at you is not relief or release. It's fear. And it still isn't enough.

February 24th

You stare at me as you take sips of water.

'Do you want food?' I say.

You blink. Has your tongue dried up? You have turned into the land, metamorphosing into rock. Like the Separates, you seem unreal, but here.

264

I sit all day, watching you sleep, watching you wake and stare at me, watching you sleep again. It wouldn't take much to smother you, a pillow over your face as you slept: gone. But I don't feel the raging urge to hurt you that I felt before.

I find some old clothes of mine in the drawers of the room and soak them with water. As it gets darker, I tentatively press them onto your burning skin. When it gets too dark to see properly, I return to the kitchen, darting my hand into the space in the pantry where I'd seen the candles. I fumble about until I touch the sticks of wax, then a box of matches, still full, amazingly. As I pull them out, I imagine the damage that a little box like this could do out here in this tinder land.

I place the lit candles on the bedside table while you sleep. Every sound I couldn't hear, or didn't notice in the daylight, is amplified now, instantly terrifying. Wind spits sand at the roof, the walls creak, there is rustling in the corners. I imagine the snake in the hallway coming back to life. How many of the creatures sharing this room could kill me? Could you, still?

I don't sleep as I sit beside you. I'm guarding against the creatures and keeping an eye on the candles, and I am willing you not to die. I change the wet clothes across your body, and you moan like the wind around the house. I am glad to hear your voice. I drip water on your lips and watch you lick the drops away. Soon your breath is even, your sleep deeper. But if your breath stopped, what then? What sort of person would I be to have killed you like this?

When I have cooled you as much as I can, I lean my head and arms on the mattress carefully, in the same hesitant way I approach Sal. Your breath falters, but you don't shift away. Are you scared of me now? You've realised I can do anything at all to you. I think I might be scared of me.

Your smell is fiercer this close, burnt and damp at the same time, like musty socks too close to a fire. If I were strong enough, I'd carry you to the pool in the Separates and lower you into the water.

'Imagine the relief of that, Ty.'

It's strange to hear my voice in the darkness. But as the wood expands and the creaks in the walls get louder, I keep talking. Maybe you'll feel comforted hearing my voice, not just the den wailing; maybe I'll feel comforted.

'I swam in the pool,' I say. 'It was almost as clear as last time. It'd be good for you, too. I heard honeyeaters calling from the trees.'

What I don't tell you about is the cave at the bottom of the pool, under the rock ledge—the source of the spring. If you do die tonight, or tomorrow, that's where I will put your body. I will find a way to drag you to the Separates, fill your pockets with stones, then slide you under the lip of the rock, secure you with branches, safe and cool and hidden.

I turn over, resting the back of my head against the mattress, staring at the metal ridges of the ceiling. Finally, I tell you about my life in London, about the letters I wrote to you in the beginning.

'If I had sent them,' I say, 'would you still have forgotten me as easily as you did?'

Your breathing is feather-light; you could be sleeping or awake and listening. It doesn't matter if you hear my words or not. The act of speaking them into this space—this house we used to share—is enough. I'll give the words somewhere to rest.

So I bring you right inside my world in London: I tell you about my flat and my plants. I even tell you about Nick. Rhiannon might be proud.

'Maybe it's all like a kidnap,' I say. 'Being taken, having to trust, giving away freedom. Even the good relationships, if there are any…It's all a negotiation. What you can bear, or not.'

Maybe Nick wanted to own a part of me too. Maybe Mum still does. Perhaps it's only ever about power, who holds it, who feels comfortable letting it go and when. It's a balance: how much you give, and how much you take. How much you are happy for someone else to have. I watch your face, the tiny movements around your eyes and lips. Something inside me relaxes.

'I saw the fox when I returned,' I say. 'She'd been waiting, alive after all. She looks like my Sal.'

I tell you about Sal, about how beautiful she is, how wild, and how she comes to me sometimes. How I fed her as a cub, and how she has the biggest, most blazing eyes of all the foxes.

'Like burning amber,' I say. 'She's wise, that fox—those eyes reveal her wisdom. She's found a way to live between two worlds: the wild world and the world of the city.'

I realise how much I miss her, as I talk her into being, right here in the space between you and me in the bed. I curl her up between us.

February 25th

When I wake, still leaning across the mattress beside you, your face is turned towards me. You're peering at me, as if you're trying to work out who I am. Could the sun and the sand have turned you blind?

'Gem,' I say.

'Yes.' Your voice cracks.

'Can you see me?'

You blink, but don't answer. I have let the sun take your sight. You have nothing left but me.

'I'll find some food.'

I change into more of my old clothes: faded green shorts, a brown tank top. They are tighter on me than before; I am taller and more muscular now. I am also beginning to smell like everything else here, neglected and dusty. I make the short hot walk to the supply shed and look for more tins. There are out-of-date sweetcorn kernels with labels that haven't faded too much, so I take them, along with a hammer. I bash them open in the shade beside the veranda and curse when corn juice spills to the sand. A waste. Then I go back to the bedroom with my prize. Gently, I place the tin of kernels beside you.

'Is that not delicious?' I say.

You give me a sidelong glance. So you can see. Your nose wrinkles as you smell the old corn.

'Could've been worse,' I say. 'Could've been the herrings.'

You shut your eyes. This is not the time to joke. You push the sheet down away from you and turn your head towards the window.

But when I return, you have eaten the corn.

I take the tin away and wait in the kitchen, looking out at where you once tried to grow vegetables. Now, it seems impossible that you even attempted it—in this heat! Was there ever any chance you'd make it work?

The day turns to afternoon as I investigate the other bedroom, tracing lines through thick dust across the board games and the books you once thought I'd enjoy. Kids' books mostly. It all seems so simple, so naive, as if the only way you ever thought we'd grow was backwards. I find a small, illustrated book called *Dreamtime Stories*, well-thumbed, and read an inscription in the front: *To Tyler, love Mummy*. The date underneath reveals you were only four: before she left you; before your dad turned to drink and you got taken by the authorities. Perhaps this is where you got stuck all those years back. Flicking through the pages, I find a child's pencil drawings alongside the book's illustrations: small human figures crouching beside dreamtime spirits. Crudely done, but completely you.

This time when I return, you are up, hunched against the window frame, pissing on the floor. When you stumble back to the bed, you don't meet my eyes. Again, I reach for more precious water to clean up your mess.

February 26th

I choose a can of peaches for you next, and when I watch you from the doorway, I see you lick your lips for all the syrup.

When you sleep, I wonder what you're dreaming about. Your eyes move beneath your eyelids and your body twitches every now and then. You remind me of a dog, dreaming of chasing sticks, paws pattering. If I lie beside you, could we run together? I once thought we'd run to where nobody could find us. But we are there now, and it seems we are still running. People like us aren't allowed to run forever.

I come closer as you sleep on, and lean down to feel your warm, even breath against my face. I breathe it inside me, then brush my lips against yours, tasting peach juice. You do not open your eyes. You do not get angry like last time; you do not throw me off. You are too weak to hurt me now: this kiss is just for me. Sleep and I have paired up, won. Only, I feel more hollow than ever.

February 27th

Your eyes are open when I wake.

'Hey,' I say.

We're close, I've been resting my head and arms on your mattress again. I wonder if you feel the ghost of me still on your lips.

'How are you?'

You grunt.

'A bit better then.'

Your eyes narrow as you study me. 'The car?'

'It's dying, or already dead.'

You grunt again. Your lips part as you gather your breath,

270

your strength. 'Why'd you come back?'

I watch your tired face. There are a hundred reasons I could tell you. That I couldn't leave you, that there was no release, that by killing you like that I killed myself too.

'It didn't feel right,' I say. 'I got as far as the petrol station, a bit further. Then I had to return. There was no resolution in how I left you. I couldn't do it.'

I want to say *I'm sorry*. I want to say I read about your art prize, and that I always knew you could do something like that. I want to say I kissed you in the night and then felt guilty afterwards. Instead, I rest my fingertips against yours, and this time neither of us flinches. I'm touching a felon—my kidnapper—and it feels almost okay.

You're quiet for a long time, just watching me, not the way Nick looked at me, or even how you looked at me before. There is no hunger or anger in your expression, only acceptance, maybe even resignation, as if you are waiting for me to do what I need. Have you been waiting all along?

You make that grunting noise again. 'I thought I was going to die,' you say. 'And you know what? I was fine with that.'

'I thought you'd die too. I wasn't.'

You shut your eyes, and I wonder if you're going back to sleep. But then you pull your fingers away from me and close them in a fist. 'You think we'll just live out here?'

'You thought so once.'

'The mine sites…the roads…people will come…'

I think about the unanswered emails in my inbox. Yes, people will come eventually. Perhaps it really is impossible to be hidden forever. But, for a little while longer, emails and other people belong to another world that seems very far away.

February 28th

'You said about the pool,' you say, as the relentless heat of the day starts to withdraw.

So, you do hear what I tell you at night. Some of it, at least. You are improving. Your lips curl into the shadow of a smile. 'I want to go.'

I'm even more surprised when you sit up in bed.

'I'll have the sheet.'

I pass you the sheet from the Perth department store, and you wrap it around yourself, standing hesitantly.

'I'm like Jesus,' you say, 'in my shroud, just woken up in that cave. Resurrected!'

You're like the old Ty, wisecracking—what I thought I wanted. But perhaps you are playing with me, putting on an act: you are waiting until we're outside before you get your own back and run. When we walk through the kitchen, you will see the cutlery, utensils—all things you could hurt me with. You will see the car key.

In the cool of the late afternoon, we make it as far as the veranda, where you stop and lean against one of the posts, breathing hard, sweat beading on your forehead.

'Not yet,' you murmur.

You go back to bed. And I wait.

The fox peers from between the clump of trees where the car died. Can she see me? I bring my hand up to shield my eyes from the setting sun and watch her. She is perfectly still, almost the same colour as the glowing sand behind her. Even so, she doesn't fit. Like me, she is an outsider; she'd destroy others to stay alive.

I hear a thud from inside the house, you must have tipped

272

something off the bedside table. When I look back, the fox has gone. I scan the sand all the way across to the Separates. Perhaps she is imaginary, come to lead you down into the underworld. She is biding her time.

March 1st

I wake with a start and feel across the bed. You're not here! I sit up fast when a sputtering sound reaches me. Now I know exactly where you are.

I jog down the corridor and into the kitchen. The car key isn't here. Of course, you haven't given up. It's a furnace outside, the boiling brightness a shock after being indoors for so many days: I gasp, unable to breathe, looking across to where you'll be. The car door is open and, wrapped again in the sheet-shroud, you're turning the key in the ignition.

Sputter, sputter, sputter, then the car goes dead.

As I get closer, you stop trying and rest your forehead against the steering wheel. Then you sit back up, frowning at me.

'Well, you've fucked this,' you say, sweat running down your cheeks.

You leave the key in the ignition and heave yourself out. I'm pleased you can't go anywhere, but now I'm worried that I can't either. You wipe sweat from your forehead, then curse as you rest your hand on the hot metal of the car's roof and stagger away.

'Here,' I say, giving you my arm as support.

'That car's fucked,' you say again. 'You've fucked us!'

I shut the car door, leaving the key inside, and we trudge back together to the house. I don't mind you leaning on me, your weight against mine.

'What the hell did you do to it anyway?' you say. 'Won't even turn over.'

'I wanted to get back,' I remind you.

'Might as well have killed me the first time!'

I almost drop you in the sand. Even now, I want you to be grateful. Not this. But as you shake your head at me, angry, you look at me for longer: you see me now, even if you don't exactly like me.

March 2nd

I stand beside the bed, surveying you.

'Well, if you're well enough to try the car...' I say.

The sheet-shroud isn't the most practical of outfits for clambering over rocks, and the suit I bought you is still lying in the dirt, so I dig out more of my old clothes from the drawers. You've lost weight since you've been here; your belly is now taut skin; even so, the biggest T-shirt is still small on you and none of the shorts fit. I remember you put skirts for me in the other bedroom, so I get those and we each pull one on. Now you don't look like Ty the kidnapper; now you are me when I was sixteen. As I step towards you and brush dust from the T-shirt, I feel as if I'm brushing it off me.

We wait until evening before we set off across the sand, which is still warm from the day. I watch you from the corner of my eye and reach out to grab you when it looks like you might stumble. You are hot and clammy and I wonder how much

275

better you really are. Soon, we are in the shadows below the Separates. It's cooler, and quieter too, as if the desert has gone silent at our approach.

'Are the rocks like you remember?' I ask, as we start on the uneven path.

'I don't remember.'

You step ahead of me, walking more confidently, your hands outstretched to balance on the rocks. You still know the route.

'I thought you'd die in prison without this.'

'I thought I'd die in the hole you dug for me!'

We're both quiet as we navigate the boulder section. The moon is rising, illuminating the smooth giant rocks around us, making them glow like huge salt lamps. The heat hasn't gone from them yet either. When I leant against the boulders at Malgi Rocks, after burning your papers and clothes, the heat disappeared quickly. How many nights ago was that? Time has become something strange: maybe it's stopped, maybe we've found a bubble we can live inside and not grow any older.

'Do you think we eventually get used to whatever place we're in?' I say. 'Even prison?'

Once, I got used to being out here with you. I got used to thinking I was never going back to England, or to my parents. I got used to you. Maybe you got used to jail, and now everything else seems wrong. Your feet slide out from under you, and you hiss with pain as you reach to right yourself, your fingers scraping rock.

'Want to stop?' I say.

'What do you reckon?'

Despite your dirty look, I hold your right elbow as you steady yourself. I can tell you are feeling something, now you're back here. I can see memories hiding inside you. As we walk on, I hear the flap of wings above: bats emerging from their roosts, or perhaps an elusive night parrot, flying home.

'I've been wondering something, Ty,' I say. 'Do you think it's possible to have Stockholm syndrome for a place, like the psychs say you can have it for a person?'

The psychiatrists told me that Stockholm syndrome was a survival mechanism, a tool to help someone adapt to their circumstances. A strategy that allows a person to feel safer, satisfied, even happy. Did jail change you, make you forget all that was once so important to you? Did you get too used to those bars because you had to survive inside them?

'Stockholm whatsit's a pile of quacks' nonsense. Something they pulled out of their arses to use against me in court. It's made-up bullshit!'

I shrug. I don't disagree with you. Even so, I've often wondered if it was this place that changed me more than you did, shaped our relationship. Maybe the desert is changing me again, making me want to be nice. My toes curl around pebbles on the path as I study your face in the moonlight. I want to touch it. Is it only because I'm back here, in this place, that I want that?

At the pool, you stop and stare into its depths. Does it feel like you're seeing an old friend, the way it felt for me? Tonight, our inky-black pool has its party clothes on, glimmering, a whole galaxy of upside-down stars pinned to its cape. When we slip inside, we'll be stepping into the sky.

'You still want to swim?' I say. 'It'll be soothing on your burns.'

An antidote for that pain I inflicted. You nod, your back

still to me. I could be reaching for a rock, plotting even now to inflict more pain. So maybe you do trust me. Or else you think this is as good a place as any to die.

'It looks shallower,' you murmur.

Can you see the rock ledge? The cave beneath?

'The plants are still here,' I say. 'More of them now, and plenty of wildlife.'

As if on cue, the frogs start up. You smile. They do sound ridiculous, like a chorus of rusty car brakes. You struggle to take the T-shirt off, so I move closer and help pull it over your head.

'Thanks,' you mutter.

'I'll come with you,' I say, 'into the pool.'

'Free country.'

I grit my teeth. Maybe we'll never forget what's gone before, never really start again.

'I had a therapist,' I tell you, as I look about in the dirt for a stick, 'who said we could reinvent ourselves each day if we chose.'

'They obviously never went to jail. Can't wipe that smear off so easy.'

You pull a long bit of corkwood from the scrub next to you and hand it to me: a perfect bashing branch.

'So, if not that, you must believe we're the product of the bad things that have happened to us, that all that stuff moulds and changes us...'

'Who the fuck cares? We're here, wherever we've come from.'

I start bashing the grasses for snakes. After a few seconds, you grab the stick from me and sling it into the scrub.

'You've made enough noise! Snakes have long packed up.'

'Yeah, alright,' I say, stepping past you. 'Just making sure.'

I peel off my T-shirt and skirt, and slip into the water, picking carefully over the sharper rocks at the edge. Are you looking at me? And what do you feel about my new adult body? I feel a strange sort of power as I turn, let you see. Sinking until the cool water covers my shoulders, I look up to find your eyes still on me.

'Do you need help getting in?'

You don't make a move, staring at me, my old skirt still round your waist and your burnt chest shining bare in the moonlight. Is this when you leave me and run? Perhaps I'll let you. Then I'll walk out into the desert and lie down in the sand, let the land do with me as it will, let it consume me. At least there's no cruel intention in death by nature. But you must know there's no point running, not when the car is dead and the summer desert so hot. You pull the skirt down over your legs and slide in, gasping as the water cools your skin.

'See?' I say. 'Better.'

You float on your back, face up to the myriad stars. I drink you in like I drank this water. Then I turn onto my back too and stare up; no light pollution here. I can't tell where the reflection in the water ends and where the real sky begins. Floating, dizzy, I try to anchor myself by finding the constellations, naming them out loud. I thought you'd be proud that I'd learnt the names, but you don't respond. I swim over to you, but you're still as a corpse.

'Can you see them?' I say.

'Hard to avoid.' The water ripples as you turn your head.

'Remember how you taught me all the patterns.'

'Nah, I didn't. I don't know them all.'

'You do.'

You turn back to the sky. 'You're remembering all this shit wrong, Gemma.'

I shake my head. I'm not. And why now: *Gemma?* The name my parents called me, the name you refused to call me by. You told me that I'd only ever be Gem to you; you said I was your sparkling-bright thing and could never be anything else.

You tip upright and frown. Your feet must be touching the ground because you seem steadier than me. I think of that cave beneath us, somewhere to my right, the spring deep inside, bubbling new energy towards us. You said we couldn't step into the same river twice, yet here we are in the pool we were in a hundred times back then—and nothing terrible has happened.

'Are you really trying to go back there?' you say. 'Still? My life was ruined because I took you. Don't you get that?'

'Course I get it!'

You wade away from me, heaving yourself onto the bank.

'You think my life wasn't ruined too?' I say. 'By you?'

'It's obvious it was.' You shake your head, shove on the skirt. 'But it seems as if you want to do it again. Which is all kinds of fucked up!'

You turn to go. Something contracts inside me. This isn't the way it should be.

'I don't want it like before,' I snap.

'Then what?' You fling the shirt across your wet shoulder.

My legs move in circles as I stare back at you. When I stretch down, I can just touch the rock shelf and I balance there.

'I want it to be better,' I say. 'Doesn't everyone deserve a second chance?'

'That's not what this is,' you say. 'This is insane. *You're* insane.' Your eyes roll skyward.

'You're the insane one! You got ten years for what you did.'

'And I did my time!' Your eyes are blazing. 'Just let me the fuck go.'

'No! You don't get to decide that!'

My hand punches out at the bank. I find a fistful of mud and hurl it at you. You step back, avoiding it easily. I find another and hurl that too. You shake your head at me, curling your lip.

'You almost killed me, and that isn't enough for you?'

'No!'

And it seems it's not. I wade through the pool, then haul myself out fast. I stride towards you, not stopping for my clothes. Your eyes widen as I keep coming for you.

'Jeez, Gemma! It's a real shame, alright, what I did to make you crazy like this, but I can't go back, can't make anything better...'

I shove the palms of my hands hard into your chest, pushing you backwards. I have no words that make sense, and I want to scream. Because this isn't enough. You aren't enough. You are meant to make everything better, but I feel worse. I am worse.

'You ruined me more than I ever ruined you!' I shout.

You grab me at the wrists, and I wait for you to twist my arms. Wet and naked, I have no defence. Your eyes bore into my face, but they do not roam across me. You look confused.

'You ruined me too,' you say. 'How d'you think I can go back to Perth now? How d'you think I can do anything? You've fucked it.'

'You don't go back to Perth,' I say, sliding my wrists in your hands. 'You just do this. You let me decide.'

'And then? What you want is a fantasy.'

You release me, and I want to spit at you. You, the great fantasist! You, who never wanted us to grow up out here! You, who pretended you were different! You, the fake.

'You took everything!' I shout. 'My life, my relationships, my mind! Sometimes I feel I am nothing apart from you!'

You open your arms wide, walking backwards. 'And what can I do now to give it back? What the hell can I do to make anything better?'

'You can apologise like you mean it!'

You laugh, mouth open, your teeth white and lovely. 'Okay, Gem,' you say. 'I'm sorry. There. That do it? You happy now?'

As if you'd just forgotten to post a letter, or water the plants. As if it were so easy.

I shake my head. 'Like you mean it,' I repeat.

You sigh. After a moment, you get down on your knees and look up at me. 'I am sorry, Gem,' you say, quieter now.

I wait for the words to sink in. I wait to feel better. To be better. I wait to be more me and less you. I wait to be...different. And even though I can see something more honest in your eyes this time, your smile is still mocking. I thought I wanted you to squirm, grovel. I thought I wanted to be the one in control. But I've tried everything and I still feel so unsatisfied.

You get up off your knees.

'You don't need me, Gemma,' you say. 'You need the opposite of me. And thanks, you know, for fucking up my life too, making everything worse.'

282

You turn and leave me.

I wait inside the rocks, alone, for a long time.

You're lying across the bed, still damp from the pool, as I crawl up next to you.

'This is how you ruined me,' I say. And I tell you about the men, and how I lost myself even more. 'I tried them out. Or they tried me. People called me a slut, but I never felt like I was the one using anyone.'

I talk fast, half of me not caring if you're listening, the other half desperate for you to stay beside me.

'I looked up the definition of slut,' I say. 'A woman with many sexual partners but no emotional involvement. But it never felt unemotional to me. You made sure of that. You took away any ability I'd ever have of being normal with men. With anyone.'

I remember what Nick said that last night: *You can't love, you can't do it. You've lost whatever it takes.* But you were the one who drugged me with fantasy, who made me perpetually unsatisfied, never able to appreciate reality.

'I can't love since you,' I say. 'That's how you ruined me.'

You don't say anything. Eventually, you move your arm across the mattress towards me and keep it there, next to me but not touching. At some point, we sleep.

March 3rd

I can't find you. You're not in the house, or the car, not even in the Separates. I wonder if you have walked away from me, saved yourself. There is panic and sadness inside me, but I do not cry or scream. I keep looking all day, walking further out across the sand until I am closer to the dunes. And there, in the late afternoon, I find you, cross-legged like a buddha, staring up to the sky. As I get closer, I see there are marks in the sand beside you and I wonder if you have been making your art.

You lean away when I sit beside you. I look up too. I wonder if the stars are the same as they were ten years ago, maybe millions have died and millions more have been born.

'Pleaides,' you say, raising your arm abruptly. 'Or, if you prefer, the Napaljarri sisters being chased by the hunter. You remember him?'

'Yes. Orion in the North.' I trace the line between the bright hunter's star and the tight cluster of Pleiades. 'But he's never going to catch those sisters.'

You nod. I'm expecting you to say that the hunter will always be following the sisters, never giving up on them, like you used to say, but instead you ask, 'That because he's too slow, you reckon?'

I smile in surprise. 'Maybe because he's a star!'

Which makes you smile too. You rest back onto the heels of your hands, looking at me now. This isn't how it was before. You're right, it can't be. It must be something new.

'Thought I'd go mad not seeing the horizon,' you say eventually. 'But turns out you can get used to anything.'

'My world shrank too,' I say.

Then finally you tell me something: about how you were only allowed to talk to one or two people a day for all those years, and how you ate the same food every day, and how the same sense of unease followed you everywhere.

'Sounds like me,' I say. 'We've been living the same life. You made both of us shrink.'

'I know.'

Returning to the house, you stare at the dirt all the way. I notice that your back is so much better: there will be scars, but your skin is no longer angry and red.

'You want to go somewhere else? Just us?' you call back. 'That what you really want?'

I can't answer. I don't know anymore.

I'm letting this place take over, seeing what might happen.

I bring in another can of sweetcorn from the shed. I even bring back one of the precious muesli bars I bought from the petrol station. I've been saving it. We eat it together on the veranda, the sky above us bigger than anything.

March 4th

You raise the hood of the car and peer inside, shaking your head. After a few minutes, you stride over to your old shed and return with some tools. Lying on the dirt, you reach under

285

the car and start tugging at something on the undercarriage. I tinker in the shed too, searching for different tins—spam, sweetcorn, carrots, we've had them all. No matter what I do, our dinner always tastes like bland, over-salted mush. I pull out a dented tin of anchovies. Possible? It feels almost domestic; you and me like this. Is it the kind of thing we could keep up? Or just another kind of make-believe?

In the kitchen, as I open the tins, checking each one for mould, I look at you through the window. Now you're leaning against the car, hands propped on the bull-bar, frowning at the engine. Soon, you head into the shade under the scrubby trees and sit in the sand, wiping sweat from your forehead. I should take you out some water. But before I can, your head tilts; you're listening. Then you smile, and I follow your gaze.

There she is again, our fox.

You reach into your pocket and hold something out to her—food?

Your lips are moving.

I go out onto the veranda and hear you telling her she's a good girl, with the reddest of red coats, and the most beautiful amber eyes, things I might say to Sal.

I know you want to hate this invader, but you can't, not when she's so close, looking like that, and hungry. You want to save her; you can't help it. You want her to live, even if by living she'll kill what's around her. We love what we come to know and fear, don't we, Ty, even when we know it's bad? Sometimes we come to love it so much, we don't see anything else. Maybe there's no other way to love.

'Tell me about the woman in Banksia Drive?'

'My sister?'

'Don't be stupid, she's not your sister.'

Your laughter echoes in the quiet room we now share. 'So, who is she then?'

'Your sister had blonde hair and is fat. I saw her at our trial.'

You shrug. 'She got thin and died her hair. So? You got skinner and died your hair, too.'

'I wasn't ever fat.'

'Fitter, then.' You sigh. 'Anyway, your point?'

'She's not your sister. I've been following her online for years, and she doesn't look like that.'

'You're seriously creepy, you know? You're worse than me.'

This is the old you, trying to be funny, but it's not something I can laugh at.

'Don't lie to me,' I say. 'Did you marry someone in prison? Is that who she is? You can tell me, you know, you *should* tell me. Anyway, your sister is called Marie, not Louise.'

'How'd you know about Louise?'

I feel my lips pinching, my throat tightening. I don't want to tell you about being armpit deep in the recycling bin of 31 Banksia Drive, but I do, eventually, when you keep staring at me. After a short laugh, you shake your head at me.

'You changed names too, Kate. Remember?'

I don't like who I am right now, don't want to ask these questions; I don't want to care about their answers. But I also want to know if I meant so little to you that you fell in love with the next person who came calling. Again, though, you shake your head.

'She's my sister,' you say firmly.

March 5th

You're well enough now to go out to the car each day, bending over it for hours and poking at the engine. This morning, when I come out with water, you drink greedily.

'Fixed it yet?'

You shake your head. 'Like I said, you fucked it.'

'Maybe I did it on purpose.'

You sigh in resignation.

'Should be glad I didn't hide the key again.'

'Hmm, with your hiding skills?' You turn back to the engine.

'What'll you do if you get it going?'

'What do you think?'

'Would you take me with you?'

No reply. I guess that's a no then. I don't feel anger, as I thought I would. But I'm not sure you'll get the car fixed anyway. It still sputters each time you turn the key. And even if you did fix it, there's the petrol problem. But it might get you as far as it got me a few days ago, and then you'd get a hitch back to Perth.

'You just going to leave me here, that your plan?'

'Wasn't that your plan for me?'

'No.'

I was going to kill you. I tried to, didn't I? And when that didn't work, I tried to make you better. I'm not sure what I'm trying to do now. Something more complicated.

I shield my eyes to watch cloud shadows move across the Separates, then slip over the sand. From inside the rocks comes the shriek of an eagle. I think I'm coming around to the idea of being left here. Maybe it's never actually been about you—the wide space of this desert has always been what's most important.

288

'What about that girl in the park,' I say, lying on the bed while you trim your beard with a pair of rusty scissors. 'Tell me the truth about her.'

You turn to me and frown, scissors splayed.

'In Perth. The teenage girl who looked like me,' I prompt. 'School uniform. Short skirt. You were watching her.'

'You mean the one I was selling to? Jesus!' You go back to chopping.

I sigh, impatient. 'Oh, come on. She wasn't just some girl you were selling drugs to.'

'What was she then? Someone like you?'

'You tell me.'

You shake your head slowly, rolling your eyes to the ceiling. You put the scissors down on the bed beside you. 'So, this is what you want to hear? Really?'

'I want the truth.'

'You want something weirder than that.'

'What were you doing with her?'

'I was selling! It's what I do now, if you hadn't noticed.'

'You don't do anything now.'

'Apart from being kidnapped, okay, that's what I do. Jeez, Gem, don't look at me like that! I was trying to do other stuff in prison, I did have a plan, you know, before you got in the way.'

Those pictures you'd drawn on the back of the leaflet, all those papers in your backpack, your CV with the art prize... you'd been trying to break away, and I stopped you.

'You were at the police station that day. I saw you.'

'So? I have to check in. Parole conditions, remember? I

believe you know about those. You seem to know most things about me.'

'You had drugs with you when you went in?'

You shrug.

'Why would you be so stupid?'

'Maybe I am stupid. You ever thought of that?'

'You're a lot of shitty things, but you're not that.'

You sigh again, pick up the scissors. 'You make me up, Gem.'

'I make you better.'

A half-smile now as you look at me. 'Is that so?' you say. 'She didn't even bloody pay, you know, that girl. I was running after her to get my money when you—'

'When I stopped you.'

'Fucking teenage girls!'

The wind whips sand against the wooden walls, a million gunshots at once. A high-pitched yelp far away could be our fox. You snip, snip, snip.

'They'll come looking, you know, Gem. Someone will. They'll go searching for me when I don't show up for my next check-in.'

'Why would they care enough about you to do that?'

You laugh, a loud, splintering sound that makes me jump. 'They don't. But they care about the system. If I can't get the car going, we're both fucked. That what you want?'

You raise your eyebrows. I can no longer see obsession for me behind your eyes. You've moved on, left me behind. I feel my fingers curl into fists, frustrated at myself. At you.

March 7th

The light is soft and golden this morning. You're asleep when I step over the snake still curled at the threshold of your old room, ants feasting on the flesh. I know I should remove it, and the ants. They'll only find a way into our bedroom and attract more dangerous creatures. I should be sweeping it all outside, like I did with the debris. I should get back to fixing the house. You fix the car, and I fix the house. The perfect couple. But it's been days now since I came back, since you started to heal, and the snake remains.

I find binoculars hanging on the cupboard door in your old room. Like everything in this house, they have a new skin of dust and cobwebs, which I brush away. I should go and look from the top of the Separates, but for now, I just stand on the veranda. Even through the binoculars, I can't see any mine sites. I can only see the access track I took, cutting a straight gash through the land as it continues somewhere else. I scan the scrub on this side of the track, stretching back to our house. The other side of the track is flat, red dirt. The mine site must be beyond that.

If you do get the car going again, could we return to Perth, like you said, pretend this never happened? Has that ever been possible since the day we got here? I could drop you at a McDonald's in the outer suburbs. You could make up some excuse to your lover, or your sister, or whoever the hell she is, about being on a bender, being so out of it you don't remember a thing. The police might buy that too. And meanwhile I slip back, unnoticed, check out of my hotel, get on the plane, go home. Nothing changed.

But I no longer have a hotel booking.

And I've missed my return flight.

People will be getting suspicious. My mother, for one. The hotel staff.

It's too late to return.

'So, what else have you lied about?' I say.

'You mean this time we've been here, or last time?'

'I mean all of it.'

'Since the day I was born? You're in for a long night.'

We're on the bed again, in the vanishing light of dusk. I'm staring at you and you're staring at the ceiling. Tonight, I found tinned tomatoes and mushrooms and mixed them together.

'Getting adventurous,' I said, handing it to you on a china plate I found in a set in the shed, rather than straight out of the tin.

You didn't smile and didn't eat all your food. Neither did I. We're both sick of the tins.

You glance across at me. 'Go on then,' you say. 'Which lies you want in particular?'

'I want all the lies.'

You laugh, a deep bark. 'No one can remember all their

lies. Could you tell me everything you've not been truthful about?'

We're more relaxed with each other tonight. You sigh as you turn on your side so that we're face to face. I force myself to look at the wrinkles in your forehead and around your mouth, the puffy pockets below your eyes. I'm not attracted to you, not when I see you like this. You look so much older than Nick, than me. You look older than you are. I shift on the bed, and look at the disappearing sun instead.

'Did anyone try to hurt you in prison?'

'All the time.'

That isn't a lie; I can imagine it. Men behind bars for what you did always get it worse.

'Did you ever think you'd return here?'

You frown, clenching your jaw. Perhaps I should be warier of you now that you are stronger. Or maybe, wisely or not, I'm starting to trust you. We're starting to trust each other.

'I didn't want to return,' you say. 'Not after that court case, how they treated us.'

'But what you said, when we left—you promised you'd find me. Was that a lie?'

'I changed, Gemma. I had to.' You shut your eyes. 'Haven't you?'

I study you in the dusty light. Your hair is clean from bathing in the pool, lighter from the sun. I can believe that I've changed, but why is it so hard for me to let go of the you I want to remember? Is one's own memory a kind of coercive control too, constantly reordering into the familiar, gratifying narrative? I watch a line of sweat roll down your neck. Then I turn and watch the bright knives of sunlight on the wooden floor, the swirling dust motes.

'The Ty you were before,' I say slowly, 'with me, was that all a lie?'

You sigh. 'I don't remember him like you do.'

The words force my gaze back to you.

'I'm this person now,' you say. 'Can you live with it?'

I swallow. 'Can you live with me?'

Can we be past and present versions of ourselves at the same time? Is that how our future could work? I focus on the scar on your cheek.

'But I lied about this,' you say, touching it in response to my stare. 'I didn't get the scar because I was running from a net, or whatever shit I told you.'

I shake my head. 'You were a kid. You were running from police or social workers, or...'

You snort. 'I was probably just drunk, Gem. Can't even remember how it happened, to be honest. It's just a scar.'

'No.' I sit up, stare down at you. 'You ran, there was a net and someone beat you up. You made me feel sorry for you.'

You smile at my words. 'Sounds good that way, doesn't it?'

'Why'd you say it if it wasn't true?'

You shrug. 'Ah, fuck, I dunno. Maybe I thought you might like me more. Maybe it'd worked with all the other girls.'

You're smiling wider now, laughing at me, at the belief I once had in you.

'All the other girls?' There's that jolt of fear—could you have taken others? Did you want to?

'Jeez, Gem, it's a manner of speech!'

I turn back to the dust motes. 'You're nothing but a fake,' I say. 'You made me believe you.'

'We're all fake, Gem baby. All just made up.' And you turn and promptly fall asleep, as if none of this conversation matters.

March 8th

You're snoring softly beside me as I wake. The heat is bearable, so I slip out of bed and pull on a pair of cargo pants and a tank top, the few clean clothes left in the drawers, then head outside to the storage shed. As I walk down the aisles, I light a candle and hold it up in all the darkest corners. Today I need to search the entire shed, even the glass enclosures.

I remember doing this before, when I was sixteen and you were out hunting for food, or whatever else you did when you left me. Back then, I was looking for booze, for anything to fuck me up and get me away from this place. I hadn't got around to loving it yet, or you.

Although I'd take booze if I found it, what I'm really searching for is a gun. The lack of variety in our food is becoming a pressing concern; with a gun we could shoot a roo, get meat. Last time you were proud of your guns and showed them to me often.

I open the boxes easily; the tape you used to stick the sides down has long since dried out. I know you have guns here somewhere. Finally, I find them in a trunk that also contains a rat's nest, but thankfully no rats. Three guns. Two long ones, some sort of hunting rifles, and a smaller one. A handgun, is that what they're called? I leave the rifles and pull the smaller one out, brushing cobwebs from it. The gun fits neatly into my palm and looks like the guns you see in films. It's a nice weight. I can see why carrying a gun like this might make a person feel powerful. But could it shoot? Does it have bullets inside?

It takes me ages to work out how to open it, but when I finally manage to pull the top section back, I see the glint of a bullet in the chamber. What kind of rookie leaves a gun loaded for ten years?

I thread it through the waistband of my cargo pants and, back in the house, I hide it in the pantry. I smile to myself as I make tea and bring it to you in bed.

You're out working on the car again when I see them.

'Camels!' I shout from the veranda, peering through the binoculars.

I was looking for the mine site again, for any vehicles on the access road. But when I surveyed the land, the long, flat stretch of red leading out beyond the Separates, I saw shadows in the distance, moving closer. I thought it was just a trick of the light at first, or a dust devil. But as they approach, I see long legs, long necks, their easy loping stride. Two of them. Could one of them be ours, the one we tamed last time, come back to see us?

'Come on!' I shout. 'Camels!'

But your head is still under the hood. I go over and grab you, wrap my arms around your waist and pull you away, leading you by the hand towards the house like a small child. I let go of you once we're on the veranda, as I point to the animals.

'Let's go closer! Have you got the car going yet?'

'Oh, so you'll drive to see camels, but not to take us back to Perth?'

There's the hint of a smile on your face.

'Do you think one of them is our camel?' I ask.

'Doubt it.'

We sit on the steps and I hand you the binoculars. 'Two bulls,' you say, squinting into the lenses. 'Bachelor pack.'

And here you are again, the Ty I want, the one who can show me this land.

'Are you lying about that?'

Again, the hint of a smile. 'Could be.'

I slap your arm gently.

The camels jog across the sand, their necks impossibly floppy. I can't help laughing as their legs seem to skid out in all directions. They look make-believe, the world's strangest animal. But here they are, surviving better than us in this desert.

'They were imported, you know, to help build the railways. Then they escaped, bred like motherfuckers, and now they're like foxes and rabbits...'

'And us,' I finish.

'Probably told you all this last time. I'm getting boring.'

'I don't remember,' I say, though the tale sounds familiar. 'They're amazing, though, the way they adapt.'

'Ah, they're absurd.' You smile. 'Better hope there're no females about. Those bulls are on the rampage.'

I take the binoculars back but can't see any other animals anywhere.

'Where's our fox?' I say, scanning the mulga scrub where I know she likes to hide.

'Made a bed for her in the storage shed.'

'Seriously?' I remove the binoculars from my eyes to stare at you. Your lips are twitching. 'Thought you said she'd kill everything if we encourage her?'

'She will.'

'Then…why?'

'Ah, what's the fucking point anymore, Gem? If you don't look after the things that stick around, what else you got?'

This time you give me a broad smile, an acknowledgement that you've backed down. A change.

It's you, back.

You, almost beautiful.

You tap the hood of the car.

'It's getting there,' you say, shrugging. 'I dunno.'

I stay silent. I'm glad you're bringing something back to life, but I'm sad it's the car. If you succeed, will you still drive off without me? Or will I drive it away from you? Opening the back door of the car, you rummage through the department-store supplies, then start laughing like a jackdaw.

'What the hell?' you say, pulling out the iron. I notice a streak of your dried blood still on the base. 'Why'd you bring that out here? You nuts or something?'

I don't answer. So you don't remember I used the iron to knock you out when I took you?

You tip your head back and laugh. 'What did you think we'd be doing, going to a ball?'

You grab the cord with your right hand and, in one sharp movement, try to yank it from the iron, but it doesn't snap.

'Bloody thing. Give me your knife.'

And I do, because maybe I do trust you. Because now I'm more curious about how things will play out between us. You slit the cord and take it around to the hood of the car, where you try to tie it to something inside, swearing loudly. Suddenly,

298

the cord flies across the sand behind me.

'Fucking thing!'

I guess the iron cord is not the missing link to our departure. Your head comes up from the engine and you throw the knife at my feet. I wipe it on my shorts and smile.

'Fucking iron,' I say.

March 9th

Finally, you step into your painting shed with me. It doesn't look that different from when we were here ten years ago. Your old paintings are still on the walls, swirls of reds and yellows and browns, your impressionistic visions of this land, even though the vivid colours have faded. There are bits of vegetation and sand—your art materials—all over the floor. To add to the artistic chaos of the scene, one of the windows in the corner has been smashed, dead leaves and debris strewn underneath it.

'It looks better now,' you say, as you inspect the corner. 'Better than the shit I made here.'

I run my eyes over a part of the wall where you'd stuck millions of grains of sand. 'I told Mum about your art,' I say.

'Your mum, the big-shot art dealer?'

'I told her how you gave the desert a voice.'

You snort. 'Can't imagine my stuff would do too well in her gallery.'

'But it would,' I say. 'It's the same, really. The artists whose work she hangs are trying to get to the truth of something too.'

Scarcely glancing at what is left of your art, you're already digging about near the stash of old paint, not listening. You leap out with what looks like a piece of string, hold it up and wave it at me triumphantly.

'This should do it!' you shout as you rush out to the car.

I stay standing in the shed, remembering how strange it once felt, how the walls glowed when the sun hit them at just the right angle. The paint you made from the dirt, the heat pouring through the windows, and your hot hands on my shoulders—I felt as if I was in the centre of the earth, or at least at the centre of your painting. Your swirls seemed to stretch out from inside me. I wonder if you painted the walls of your cell like that, to feel as if you were still in the desert. I saw a documentary in which prisoners created their favourite landscapes on the walls around them—that act of creation made them happier.

I find you back rummaging in the car's engine. You look up, frowning in concentration.

'Did you paint this place in prison?' I ask, thinking how easily you must have won the art prize.

'Nah. Never painted the land there.'

'What then?'

'Portraits!' You shrug. 'I painted the crims. Ugly fuckers, most of them.' You look out towards the horizon, chewing on your lip. 'But they're good to paint. All those wrinkles, tatts, lots of stuff to draw. Sadness hangs about on a face, I reckon. Far more interesting.'

'Kind of beautiful too?'

You look at me for a moment, puzzled. 'Nuts,' you say softly. 'A murderer, beautiful?'

You return to the car.

I realise you've stopped talking about going back to Perth, and I've stopped talking about London too. We're both stalling.

Am I wrong in thinking it's you dragging your heels as much as me?

In the late afternoon, we walk to the Separates again, the sun turning everything peach, infusing us with light. A small flock of cockatiels zip past us.

'How many nights have we been here?' you say.

'I don't know. When are you meant to check in at the station?'

'I don't know.'

Like the sand, time is shifting, sliding away from us, revealing a different landscape.

I lie awake in the dark, listening to you squirming next to me as you try to get comfortable. Far away there's the rumble of what could be thunder. We go still and listen.

'What are your drugs like?' I ask, once the rumbling stops. 'The ones you had with you?'

You sigh, and I assume you're not going to answer.

'They help me let go,' you say, eventually. 'Forget what's real.'

'Freedom.'

'Sure. Drinking, fucking, drugs…the same, really. Wouldn't really call it freedom, though.'

'Nick never felt like freedom.'

'Maybe you weren't letting go.'

'I was taking you with me.'

'There's your problem.'

You turn around to me. I wonder if it would be a form of freedom to lean over and press your cracked lips to mine. We're sharing the same pillow. You breathe in the air I breathe out.

'But you made it what you wanted, didn't you?' You point to your temples. 'Imagination can sometimes make the dark bearable, no?'

You don't look away. You're challenging me. I lean forward. After a moment, you kiss back lightly.

'Better?' you ask.

March 10th

On a day that's as hot and as bright as any other, you start the car. I hear the noise when I'm looking at the busted water pipe, wondering how to fix it. I drop the pipe and run back. You are in the driver's seat, hand on the key, pumping the accelerator. And then, *vroom*. That noise again. Traitor car.

We stare at each other through the windscreen while the engine roars. You look as shocked as I am. Is this it then? Will you slam the gearstick into reverse, put your foot to the floor, and get out of here? Or will I wrestle you for the key, and escape myself? I could open the passenger door and get in with you? You even incline your head as if that's what you might like. I stand stock-still, the soles of my feet stinging from the hot sand, waiting, as you look at me. Now, the power is with you.

'So, you leaving then?' I say.

You squint at me. 'You think I should?'

I didn't expect that. 'No.'

You watch me, your hand still on the ignition. There is no longer any reason for you to be here, or for us to continue whatever this is. You could return, find a life without me. You look over at the Separates and back again. I want to see what will hold you. Without warning, you slam your hands down onto the steering wheel.

303

'It's too hot to get going now anyway!'

You step out from the driver's seat, the car still rumbling. Like me, you are waiting to play this out. You come and stand beside me, and I take a deep breath. The car sounds unwell, too loud and artificial out here.

'If you turn it off, will it die again?'

You shrug. 'Pretty sure I know how to get her going now.' You tap the hood. 'You took most of the underside off, y'know? Poor old girl didn't have a belly left.'

'Do you think the hire car company will notice?'

You grin, your eyes blue as jays' wings in the bright sun. Blue like everything innocent. Then you lean back into the car and turn the ignition off.

'Take the chance?'

Who are you now? The Ty from before, or the Ty out of prison, or a new Ty? What are you staying for? You stride past me towards the house.

'We need to cool off,' you call back. 'Don't you reckon?'

Standing with one hand clasped around a veranda post, you turn to me, the full force of the sun on your face and chest.

'If you're wanting to swim, you're going the wrong way,' I say, squinting back at you.

'Righto!' You give me the thumbs-up. 'I'll get the pool noodles!'

I walk back to wait on the veranda, listening to you thudding around inside. When you come out, your arms are full: two hats, the binoculars, a couple of towels, and a bag into which you thrust everything.

'Why so much?' I say.

'Reckon we stay out there til sunset. Really cool off. I'll

work something out with that car tomorrow.'

I pass you on the veranda and go into the house. 'Hang on, I've got another idea.'

In the kitchen, I reach my hand to the back of the pantry, behind the old jars and saucepans. The gun is not there. As I keep searching, I hear you behind me.

'Don't worry,' you say. 'I've already got it.'

I step out of the pantry, away from you. I thought I'd hidden that gun well.

'What, you think I don't know where my guns are?' you say. 'Anyway, you did good getting it out of the shed. Now we can get something decent to eat.'

I eye you warily.

'You did good,' you say again, and you open the bag of swim stuff on your shoulder so I can see the gun resting inside. 'We can shoot something for our last supper. Go out in style.'

'Last supper?'

'Sure, why not. I thought you liked the Bible references.'

You shrug, but my eyes are still on the gun. You're a good shot. I remember when you took down roos with only one pull of the trigger. You could take me down if I started to run, if I raced off in the car. Perhaps you've realised that it won't work to return to Perth with me, and that you must kill me, leave me here, then pretend you were never here in the first place. If someone found me here, with a gun beside me, it would no doubt be seen as suicide. Poor innocent Gemma couldn't cope after all.

I snatch the bag from you. 'Fine, but I'm carrying it.'

'Jeez, Gem,' you say, studying my face. 'Relax already. You've been asking for some decent food for long enough. I can shoot something.'

'Why don't you just take the car and go?' I say, sharper than I mean to.

'I will.'

But your eyes drift away from mine. This hesitation of yours is different. You don't want to go. Not yet. You want to stay.

'Well, then,' I say, 'swim with me. It's hot enough.'

As we walk to the Separates, flies swarm around us, desperate for the moisture from our sweat. It might be our hottest day here. If we don't kill each other today, this place will cook us. I look up, expecting clouds—a storm building from all this pressure—but the sky is clear.

'Death trap,' you say, glancing up too.

As we trudge through the heat, heads down, you tell me that the tracks on the sand are from thorny devils and long-tailed rats.

'Are you lying?' I say.

'Does it matter?'

We step between the boulders on our familiar pathway, you slightly ahead. In the small clearing, halfway to the pool, you pause. Tentatively, you brush aside a thatch of acacia and look down a narrow passageway between the rocks that I haven't noticed before.

'Still here,' you murmur. 'Want to see?'

Before I answer, you pull me in. It's cooler, quieter, and it's not long before the passageway opens out into another small clearing. A dead-end. You stop, drop my hand, and face me. It wouldn't take much for either of us to grab the gun right now and shoot, but you turn, your eyes fixed on the rocks all around us. I follow your gaze and see the markings on their surface, faint red and white circles, animal tracks, dogs running, human bodies and other wisp-faint images I don't know how to name, images far older than your art.

'Keep looking,' you whisper.

You crouch down, your face near two lithe figures swaying across the rock under an overhang. I can make out a man and a woman. They look almost joyful. The images are simple, elegant, and I wonder why you never showed them to me before.

'What's it all mean?'

You shrug. 'It's what happened before.'

I crouch beside you. Some of the markings are so faint you have to show them to me twice. You get down onto your belly and, when I lie down too, I find what looks like an old sailing ship, its sails out.

'From when Australia got colonised?' I say, hardly believing it. 'It can't be that old.'

You murmur a laugh. 'This art is ancient. That's one of the newer bits.'

'But how did anyone see a ship out here? How did they know?'

'Stories.'

I lean back onto my elbows and look at it all again. The art is beautiful and complicated, but so faint. So many secrets held by these rocks.

You sit cross-legged, still. After a while, you take the hats from the bag, throw me one and pull the other one over your head.

'I didn't forget you,' you say quietly. 'I just didn't want to remember. Just so you know.'

307

Now, maybe I understand why you took me here today. These rocks don't forget what's gone before, either; there's a whole history stored in their bedrock, waiting to be seen.

'Seeing you was seeing all that again.'

Then you're up and brushing dust from your knees. You grab the bag and stride away from this ancient art and back to the path.

At the pool, we both strip, unconcerned by our nakedness now. We drift into the water, sighing, and float on our backs.

'You never told me what you lied about?' you say. 'Your name, for one thing. Kate?'

You stretch out my name as if it has two syllables, as if you're trying it out.

'My name really is Kate now, no lie. I changed it officially. And I really work for a travel company. That's not a lie either. Unless they've fired me by now.'

You snort. 'This trip part of your research?'

'Maybe.'

I remember my client Rose, how I abandoned her. Apart from you, she's the only person who knows I'm in Australia. Would she tell anyone if an alarm went out again? But she doesn't know I'm Gemma, doesn't know what I look like. I don't think she could join the dots.

You dip your head underwater, come up blinking. 'And you think you don't know me?' you say. 'I have no fucking clue who you are now.' You study me, curious for once.

I tilt my head, not quite a nod, not quite a shake. 'You knew more, once.'

'Nah. Not sure I ever did.'

'Well, if you don't, no one does.'

You frown, water dripping in your eyes. 'That's fucked, Gem. *You* know you.'

Do I? Or have I only ever been made up from how others see me, how others want me? Maybe until now, I have.

You flip to standing, then wade away from me, towards the deepest part of the pool. I wait, studying your back, discovering muscles that weren't there before, or I hadn't noticed. Then I move towards you. Closer, I see the wounds from the burns, some of them already fading to scars. I reach out and touch them. The muscles stiffen, but you don't move away. I run my fingers down the red patterns on your skin, down to your waist, and you let me do this too. When I wrap my arms around you, resting my cheek against your hot, scarred back, you remain still. Are you just going along with me, thinking it's what I need to get better, or what you need to do to help you escape, or is there a part of you that is starting to enjoy it? I listen to the chime of honeyeaters above, the rattle of dry leaves.

When you finally turn towards me, you sigh and wrap your arms around me too, running your fingers down my backbone, then through my hair, no longer as short as when I arrived. This is different, this gentleness. Your fingers in the small of my back, exploring, different too. You are letting me in, surrendering. When you smile, I see a hint of the hope from before, of your misguided enthusiasm. We could turn back into the creatures we were, adapt ourselves like animals do, find scales to place on our skin, and colours to match.

'Kate,' you say, trying it out again.

It's wrong in your mouth, too ordinary.

'Gem,' I say.

'Gem.'

My fingers thread into yours. 'And your name—is it really Ty?'

You smile. 'Course.'

And I believe you. Because I want to, and because maybe things like names and classifications don't matter anymore. Only the ones we make for ourselves.

This time when I kiss you, your lips aren't dry or cracked, but wet from the pool, tasting like undergrowth. I draw you closer until we are skin to skin, my heat and your heat. I press myself into you, against the rocks that connect to the cave below. I touch your shoulders and neck, press my fingers to the scar on your cheek. This is all new, something we couldn't do before, not like this.

'Maybe we could stay,' you tell me, whispering into my neck.

And you release into me and sigh.

Afterwards, we lie on the rocks, sunning ourselves like snakes. The desert wind has dried us, so I use one of the towels as a pillow.

'Gem?'

I must have been asleep, soothed by the heat of your body next to mine. I pull myself up to where you're sitting and see how dark it is now. The air is cooler. There are goosebumps on your belly. You wrap an arm around my shoulders and draw me back to lean against your chest.

'I meant it,' you say. 'About staying. What else have we got now, anyway? Just this.'

Now when I look at you, I see something of myself in your expression, a yearning for the impossible, a spark that's going to set you on fire and destroy you. I stare at you, marvel at your sudden faith in me, and feel a wild, primal urge to smile. But I shake my head.

'One of us should take the car,' I say.

You frown. 'I fixed it for both of us.'

I nod. 'But if someone finds us together, we're both screwed. You said it yourself. If you won't take it…You could walk into the bush, couldn't you?'

'With nothing?'

'Haven't you done it before?'

I watch your Adam's apple as you swallow. I am surprising you. This isn't what you expected.

'We could make a plan,' you say. 'If anyone comes, you could take the car before they get here. Lead them away, explain. Then you come back.'

I hesitate. I always thought this was our one safe space, inside the Separates, a sanctuary. And you have just said the words I wanted to hear. I let them sink in, then take a breath.

'We are fugitives now,' I say. 'We can't go back.'

Your expression is serious as you stare at me. 'Maybe no one will come.'

But I understand, at last, that even if no one else comes here ever again, us being here isn't what I want. Not now. I want a different kind of ending. And maybe you see this thought in my eyes because your arm tightens around my shoulders, which only makes me feel more certain.

You shake your head. 'Why did you bring me here if you…?'

'You need to disappear,' I say, more firmly now. 'That's why.'

I thought this would feel good when it came. I breathe in the smell of the pool in your hair, feel your warmth against me. I'll miss this. But will I miss you? Can I be me without you? Am

I strong enough to find out?

'Where would I go, though?' you ask. 'I can't use my name, I won't have...'

'...anything,' I finish. 'I know.' I keep your gaze. Without anything, maybe you would finally understand?

You are very still as you study me.

'You'd have the land,' I say. 'You told me once about other wild places.'

'Further north.' You nod. 'Crocs and snakes and stowaways up there.' You shift behind me to sit up straighter, sliding me off your body. I press against the rock to steady myself. 'You remember that?'

'I remember more than you give me credit for.'

Your mouth curls into a small smile. As you look at me, perhaps you also remember more, too—your dreams and fantasies, all you wanted from me. Do you remember the feeling of wanting something impossible, then going to get it?

'There are islands up north like gardens of Eden,' you say. 'Beautiful wildernesses. Reckon someone who doesn't want to be found could hide there. But you could find me, I could tell you where. A new place.'

I trace my fingertips across the rock beneath me. 'There's no new place.'

You go quiet. When I turn to see you properly, your eyes are focused elsewhere, avoiding me. Are you angry, or do you know I am right? Perhaps now this feels like abandonment.

'Hungry?' you say suddenly, your eyes narrowing.

You move your chin, indicating something behind me. A lizard, come down to the pool to drink. Almost the length of my arm, fatter than a fox, he's the sandy-red colour of the rocks.

Silently, you reach behind for the gun in the bag, then you place it in my hand.

'You do it,' you say.

The lizard still hasn't sensed we're here. The sound of him lapping reminds me of Sal with milk. You put my index finger on the trigger and lean against my back, keeping me steady and warm and still. With your fingertips, you adjust the angle of my head so that I'm looking straight at the reptile. I feel your hot breath on my neck and behind my ears.

'Now, shoot,' you whisper. 'When you're ready. You're all lined up.'

I hesitate. Haven't I killed enough this trip? And this creature, with the patterns across its skin, is so beautiful.

'It'll be quick,' you add. 'And then, dinner. Meat, finally.'

When I don't move, you kiss the very top of my left ear and press your finger on top of mine, and we shoot together. After all these years, the gun still works. The lizard's tongue is darting out for water when he tips over into the dirt.

You move off me, towards the lizard, and I'm left with the gun. Are there more bullets inside? My finger still on the trigger, I aim it at you, see what it feels like. It wouldn't take much: one finger to move a couple of centimetres, to press down. It had been nothing at all to shoot that lizard. Too easy, really. One movement again, and all this would be really over.

When you turn back to me, your eyes don't even widen when you see the gun pointing at you. You stand up straighter, in fact, even more in my sights. If I shoot, you could tip straight back into the pool.

'Do it, if you want,' you say. 'I've come to reckon you deserve it.'

But do you mean I deserve this revenge for what you did to me, or do I deserve what's going to come to me after I shoot you? You don't elaborate. You just tap your chest, your heart, my target. You smile, all teeth. Maybe this is what you really want. Or what I want. True release. I put my eye up against the gun and look down the barrel.

I make a fire near where the lizard died. All the time, I wonder if it's safe, if anyone will see the smoke.

'I'll keep the flames low,' I murmur.

The lizard roasts nicely. I pick its juicy, soft flesh off the bones with my teeth, and it's good, finer than any fillet steak. I don't think about the car, or the escape plan, or what's going to happen tomorrow.

Later, I lie near you, the embers from the fire still warm. The night is not as clear as it has been, the moon waxing and cloud cover moving in. But there is little wind, no distant thunder, so it might not mean bad weather is on the way. A distant yipping is probably from a dingo, but I think of our fox. I haven't seen her for a few days, and I know she now depends on you for food. Where will she go if we both leave?

I lean up onto my elbows and stroke the hair away from where it's stuck to your face, away from your shut eyes. Perhaps you did fix the car for me, not for you. Is that your kind of sacrifice, your apology?

As I fall asleep in the middle of our rocks, to the sound of the grasses rustling and frogs croaking, I clasp your hand in mine.

I dream we dive down to find the spring beneath the rocks, the source. The pool overflows and we ride on the water across the land. I dream our journey forges a river and that we sing to make it deeper. And I swim, swim, swim for the sea.

Only you're not singing when I wake.

You're not here anymore.

March 11th

In the dawn light, I touch the ash on the cold ground beside me. The gun is still here. I lean over and pick a sliver of cold flesh off the lizard carcass, chew it slowly.

You're gone.

The binoculars are still here, the towels, everything we brought with us.

I take the gun and, picking my way through the grasses, stand at the edge of the pool. The early-morning light falling on the surface turns it pale green, and tiny fish dart like rays of underwater sun. I look down and open the barrel of the gun; there are no more bullets. Time to let it go.

I wade into the water, then dive down towards the cave, feeling the bubbles from the spring against my face. I stretch my arms out to the rock ledge, and see the cave below, then the rocks and underwater roots that could be perfectly positioned to secure something precious. I drop the gun deep into the pool's depths and imagine it sinking to a place far below, where fish will nibble at it, and where it will be safe and hidden, inside the heart of the Separates.

Gone.

I press my feet against the side of the pool for traction and angle a large root across the spring's entrance, leaving enough space for bubbles to rise, but nothing else. Then I swim back, breathe the dawn air deeply, and push myself out.

I keep watching for you as I wind through the Separates, climbing higher. I can still feel your breath on the back of my neck, your eyes on mine. I imagine you going back to the house, finally deciding to help fix it up, repair the roof, sweep that dead snake away or connect the gas cylinder to the stove.

I climb faster. I'm almost at the top of the rock, above the treeline of the Separates; soon I'll be able to look back at the house, and at everything around. I drop the binoculars around my neck so it's easier to clamber higher. A brown falcon flaps off ahead of me, soaring over the rocks towards the sand dunes. When I finally turn and look down, I see the house, the expanse of red dust threaded with the broken piping, and the car. Still there.

I can't see any movement around the house. I turn, scanning the sand and scrub, then use the binoculars to look further. The only sound is the shriek of the raptor flying off, and the rustle of leaves around me.

I lean back against the rock, shielding my eyes as the sun gets brighter. I blink when I see a dust devil, far away on the access track. Dust devils don't usually follow a man-made track; they whirl across the sand, growing as they gather more grains. I wait for this one to veer off across the red sand. When it doesn't, I hold the binoculars up to my eyes. It's definitely dust I can see, a lot of it, but whether it's caused by a dust devil or something else, I can't tell.

If it's a car, I should find you, hide you.

317

I start to scramble back down, the rock's smooth surface already heating up against my skin. I descend into the tree cover, breathing in the tobacco scent of bloodwood sap, and grasping its sticky bark, already thinking of worst scenarios of who might be coming. Police? The mining owners of this land? It was only a matter of time—we both said it.

I scoot down the boulder, grabbing onto branches, the binoculars clunking against the rock and my collarbone. It's probably just a mine truck, not coming anywhere near here. Soon, I'll see the fluorescent flag bobbing on the hood. I imagine you shaking your head at me and saying, *I told you there was a mine site nearby.* I'll watch it drive on down that straight track.

Just a mine truck. It's amazing, really, that we haven't seen one before.

But as I walk back down the path between the rocks, I remember our words from last night: *If someone finds us together, we're both screwed.*

I grab what we left beside the pool, kick dust over the fire. On the long stretch of sand before the house, I follow the old water pipe in, remembering how amazing it was when it carried the spring water to us. It was all ingenious, what you did here, how you made something out of nothing. But it was also ingenious how the land took it back, covering the plastic pipe with plants, hiding animals in its crevices. Everything always has its time.

I step up onto the veranda. No sound from inside. Through the binoculars, I check the access track and find the dust devil easily enough, although now it looks more like a dust cloud. I move the binoculars down to see what's underneath.

A car.

318

No flag bobbing.

It's hard to be certain with the dust and the distance, but I don't think it's a mine truck.

Down the corridor, past the snake and into the bedroom. You're not on the bed. You're not anywhere.

'There's a vehicle!' I shout. To nobody.

It's hopeless. You're gone. There's just me.

I run back out to the veranda, peer through the binoculars again. Definitely a vehicle. White. No mine flag. But it could have lost its flag, or never had one in the first place. It's sure to keep driving to the mine. It won't turn down here.

But what if it does? I could take the car, but where would I drive it? The only way I know out is the access track, and there's a vehicle there. I'll sit tight. That vehicle isn't coming down here; it's not coming for us. I lose sight of it for a moment—it could be in a dip, or stopped, or even driving off the track in another direction. I pull the binoculars down and squint into the distance.

You've been gone a while.

I blink, see you in the bed, then see you fixing the water pipe, then walking with your long, sure stride back to the Separates, lithe as a shadow. I blink the images away. I need water. But I can't go back to the pool now to refill. Not with this vehicle coming. Not with you missing.

Again, I look through the binoculars. The dust cloud is closer. The vehicle has turned off the access track into the scrubland. It's coming this way. Perhaps you saw it this morning and went straight into hiding. You could be deep inside the rocks, surrounded by that ancient art.

I pick up the spade that still has your blood on it and wipe it clean with the little water I have. Then I tidy the house as best I can. The iron, cordless from where you sliced it, is still lying in the sand. I pick it up, wipe it clean of your blood too, and leave it in direct sunlight, metal side up. When it's properly hot, maybe I'll use it to press your suit straight again.

I wait.

Until, through the binoculars, I see a white four-wheel drive tipping and lurching through the scrub towards me, fluorescent stripes down the side, along with the word POLICE.

Shit.

I stay on the veranda, waiting for the vehicle to come for me.

Supreme Court of Western Australia
PERTH

October 15th

Nick has finished telling the jury about me cutting him. He went over everything in intimate detail, made it sound worse than it was. He even said I chased him out of the flat with the knife at his back, that I screamed at him like a wild animal. I don't remember that bit, if it ever happened. Perhaps Nick is a bit of an embellisher. I wonder whether he's been boasting to his friends about his involvement with me. Or maybe he uses his story with me as a pick-up line, plays the wounded party with baby-blue eyes and a victim story.

I examine the jury. Do they believe him? There are six women in this jury of twelve: two older ones, four probably under forty. Maybe they approve of Nick's looks: his smart suit, clean smile, clipped city-boy accent. Your voice is so different from his, strong and slow and resonant. Your voice is the heat to Nick's cool English pitter-patter.

I watch Nick inhale deeply as he looks all around the courtroom, everywhere but at me. Is Mr Lowe about to reveal the piece of evidence Jodie warned me about? Nick shuffles from side to side while he waits. Soon enough, Mr Lowe asks for the next item of evidence to be displayed on the screen. A series of emails come up. I recognise them, of course. Mr Lowe aims at them with a red laser pointer.

'You're familiar with these emails, Mr Avery?'

'I am.'

Mr Lowe zooms in, runs his red pointer over a few lines, then clears his throat and reads out the words for the jury:

> I've recently had some bad medical news, and I'm thinking about going on a final, special trip...

An email from Rose, my sweet, sick client, the one I only ever wanted to help. I look over at the members of the jury as they struggle to see the connection between this email and the man in front of them. Mr Lowe carries on pointing at sentences.

> I want to see something beautiful—something to reset me. I would value personal recommendations.

As he shifts back to Nick, forgetting to switch off his pointer as he turns, he blinds me for a moment.

'Who is Rose? Do you know, Mr Avery?' he asks. 'What do you know about the person who wrote that email?'

'I wrote that email,' Nick says.

And here we are.

The betrayer.

The Judas.

It wasn't enough for him to invent a whole new person to rat me out; he then had to go and take her from me too. As if there wasn't enough loss in all this. And I liked Rose.

'So, you were pretending to be this Rose character, Mr Avery, this so-called client of the defendant?' asks Mr Lowe.

'Yes, I was.'

'These email exchanges occurred over several weeks, from January thirteenth until February twenty-first. Is that correct?'

'It is.'

'Why would you do that, Mr Avery?'

Nick rolls his shoulders slowly. Perhaps he can feel me glaring at him. Will he turn and look at me now? No doubt Mr Lowe has instructed him not to. *Don't be swayed by your feelings in the moment,* he'll have said, just like the lawyers told me all those years ago. *Focus on the facts.*

'I did pretend to be a client called Rose, it's true,' says Nick. 'Like I said before, I was intrigued by Kate Stone after that night, that morning. There was something...not quite right...I wanted to help her.'

He can't resist it, a glance at me, a reddening of his cheeks. He's getting flustered. Maybe there is something good hiding inside Nick, after all: a sliver of remorse.

Mr Lowe sighs, then looks at Nick with an expression that could be interpreted as concern. 'Mr Avery, was it only intrigue you felt about Kate Stone?'

Nick frowns. 'I, uh, I did feel something else. I was scared by Kate Stone, too.'

'Scared?' Mr Lowe's voice is louder now.

'And I...uh...I wanted to find out more about her, who she was. I wanted to know what she was going to do next.'

'Can you explain to the court how you did this through your email exchange masquerading as Rose?'

'I can.'

More sentences from the emails are projected onto the screen, ones in which I describe the desert, and then when I talk about getting my head together.

'I didn't know exactly,' Nick says, 'but from her descriptions I had a pretty good idea of where she might be. In the desert, that is. And I suppose I put two and two together—worked out the connection between Kate, uh, the defendant, and that prison letter I saw on her kitchen table. I looked up the name I'd seen on it—Gemma Toombs—and found a whole lot of information about an abducted school-girl from ten years ago. And then I saw the photographs of her, and even though Kate looks different now, I mean, she's still the same person…I mean, it's clear, isn't it?'

He gestures to me, and I give him a small smile. Here I am, Nick, the Gemma behind the Kate, *hello!*

Then onto the screen comes the final email I wrote to Rose: the one I typed in the petrol station on my charging phone, after I left you in the hole.

'And what was different about this email?' Mr Lowe asks.

'It was this email that made me think there could be something bad happening. See where it says that what she needed to find was dead? Gone? That got me worried.'

Mr Lowe gets his pointer out again and traces my words as he reads them out loud.

> I saw what I needed to for the last time…whatever it was I needed to find is dead, gone.

Mr Lowe repeats the words, emphasising the *dead* and *gone.*

One of the older women in the jury raises her eyebrows.

'Was that when you alerted the police?' Mr Lowe asks.

'It was.'

The start of the end. The police found Eric Symonds at the petrol station and then Tony Kowalski, the tour oper-ator. They alerted the hire-car company, who said there was a tracker on the vehicle.

Judas car. Reliable goody-two-shoes car.

Should have known.

That tracker was there when you fixed the car's under-carriage. You saw it. You had to disappear.

When Jodie gets up to cross-examine, I know what her line of argument is going to be. She questions the validity of the email exchange as evidence; she casts doubt in the jury's mind about the reliability of Nick as a witness.

'This evidence demonstrates a propensity for lying, fakery,' she says. 'Is this the kind of witness we can put our trust in? Mr Avery, I'm interested in why you decided to write that first email. How long after your altercation with the defendant was that?'

None of us is who we say, it seems.

Seven months earlier

UNMAPPED

March 11th, later

Dust hangs in the air around the police car as it stops near the den.

The man who gets out first isn't in uniform, neither is the woman who gets out after him, but that doesn't reassure me. The car doors slam, one, two.

I lean against the house, in the veranda shadows, as they peer around. They haven't seen me yet. The woman spends a moment looking up at the Separates, her hand raised to her forehead. Then they both look across at my car. The man takes out a notebook and writes. I think of the gun deep in the pool: I could've had a shootout, me and the den teaming up against the authorities. The man kicks at the camp bed, still tipped over where we left it. He makes another note. I wonder if he's seen your crumpled suit in the dirt near the bed, the iron warming to smooth it. There's never enough time to prepare, is there?

The wood creaks when I move, and they turn and stare in my direction.

'Ah, hello, miss...' the man says, taking a couple of paces towards me.

I don't know what to say, which name to use. I don't know what to do.

I want to get in my car and screech out of here, leave them in the dust. I want you to stay hidden. You used to say that if you know how to hide here, no one will find you: I want to believe that now. I must make it look like you were never here. I am a diversion, buying you time to disappear properly, helping us both. The man and the woman come closer.

'Miss...?' the man tries again.

I still don't know which of my names to give them, if I should give them a name at all. They're near the veranda now and I haven't said a word. It must look weird: me here, not speaking. I stand up straighter.

'Ms Stone,' I say eventually, moving out from the shadows and stepping off the veranda towards them. 'Can I help you?'

My tone is all lady-of-the-manor, as if this is my house and they are trespassing. They stare at me as if I've slapped them. The man takes out his notebook again and consults it.

'Miss Stone,' he says, not *Ms*. 'Miss Stone. We are searching for a missing person.'

Right. Of course. This is the scenario I thought about over and over when I was sixteen and we were here together. The police, cottoning on, finding me eventually. I imagined it all so vividly—stepping forward, presenting myself. Being returned to my parents, away from you, telling my story to the world. Back then, I wanted you to go to prison. At least, a part of me did. Now, I don't want that at all. I've come to realise that prison is not a place for either of us. You and I need space, this land and its endless horizons.

The man is still watching me. I imagine his next words: *We have reason to believe this missing person is you, Gemma Toombs, and we're here to take you back...*

But he doesn't say those words. The man introduces himself as Detective Inspector Braithewaite, and his partner as Detective Sergeant Manikham, and he says, 'We are looking for a missing man, Mr Tyler MacFarlane.'

He waits, watching me, but I don't give him anything. He glances at his partner, who nods.

'Mr MacFarlane has been missing since Friday, February fifteenth,' he continues, 'when we believe he disappeared from near his home in Perth. We have reason to believe you may know a man by that name, Miss Stone? Is that correct?'

Supreme Court of Western Australia
PERTH

October 15th

Finally, it's Louise MacFarlane. Or Marie, as she used to be known. I scrutinise her as she makes her way slowly to the stand and confirms where she lives. Turns out she is your sister, after all. I guess you really didn't lie about everything.

And I can see it now: her blonde roots coming through, the uplifted curve to her top lip, the high cheekbones. But her eyes aren't like yours. There are no other eyes like yours. As the Bible is handed to her, she turns towards me and glares. Nice, your sister, isn't she? A real treasure. No wonder she didn't come and meet you on your release date.

Quickly, Mr Lowe steps between her glare and me, and she finishes her oath. He asks her to state her name and her relationship to you.

'Sister,' she says.

Mr Lowe nods. 'Ms MacFarlane, do you recognise the defendant, Ms Kate Stone?'

'I do.'

'Could you tell the jury how you recognise her?'

'The defendant stalked my brother before he disappeared,' she says. 'I saw her, hiding across the road in the bushes like a tramp.'

She has no evidence; it's her word against mine. Jodie's calm, impassive face says she's not worried about it either.

337

'Is this the only time you have seen the defendant, Ms MacFarlane?' Mr Lowe continues.

'No. I saw her all the time when she had a different name. In my brother's trial.'

'Objection!' calls Jodie, but your sister ploughs on over her.

'I never trusted her then,' she says, her voice rising, 'even though the rest of the world liked her story, I never believed it. Bullshit that Ty kidnapped her, they ran away together, like he said.'

'Objection, Your Honour!' Jodie is on her feet. 'This information is prejudicial to a fair trial!'

But Louise MacFarlane is still going, almost shouting now. 'She knows how to get what she wants. She manipulates men. She manipulated my impressionable brother, then killed him!'

Impressionable, Ty, you? How do you feel about that one?

'Ms MacFarlane,' the judge roars. 'If you will not answer questions as you are asked, you will be removed from the court.'

Louise blinks, silenced. Mr Lowe is beckoned up to the judge. While they talk, I keep my gaze steady on Louise MacFarlane. So, it's all my fault, is it, Louise? My fault that sixteen-year-old-schoolgirl-me got kidnapped by your strong twenty-seven-year-old brother? My fault that I got taken to Australia against my will and held there, with the help of drugs and force, for months? My fault that I couldn't get your brother out of my head? Could never move on? Is it all my fault, too, if I chose to let your brother escape this time, chose to let him go?

I glare back at her; I don't care what the jury thinks

if they're watching. It's all I can do not to shake my head and raise my middle finger. Louise MacFarlane should be grateful to me. If she could only imagine the revenge I could have inflicted.

Louise MacFarlane apologises to the judge, continues to answer questions about the rehabilitation program you joined, your commitment to getting your life back on track.

'Tyler did not want to run away,' she says. 'His disappearance is out of character. My brother was significantly changed by what had happened to him, and he wanted to put things right in his life. This is the truth. He was trying to find a new path, away from his past.'

But truth is slippery, isn't it, Louise, and truth can change? And we all have a version of it.

Seven months earlier

UNMAPPED

March 11th, later

The detectives signal that we should go inside, so I show them over the threshold into the house you built for me. I don't offer them a drink, and I watch their eyes roaming across the mess I tried to tidy.

I tell them I haven't seen you. That I've come here by myself to visit the old place again. But, of course, they don't believe me. They continue asking questions, and I'm sure they know more than they're letting on. I give them what they want, some of it anyway.

'Kate Stone is not my real name,' I say. 'My name is Gemma Toombs and, yes, I used to know Tyler MacFarlane. He kidnapped me when I was sixteen and held me here for several months.'

I pause, looking out the window towards the Separates. Is it a mistake to admit all this so soon? The detectives are writing copious notes they will hold me to later.

'So why exactly did you come back?' Detective Inspector Braithwaite asks, frowning.

'Couldn't get it out of my head,' I say. 'This land. It gets into you, this place.'

Detective Sergeant Manikham nods, so I continue.

'I needed to say goodbye to this place, I never got to last time. Things wouldn't feel finished unless I did.'

I'm not sure they understand what I'm talking about, or if they believe me, or even if I care.

'Do you mind if we look around?' Detective Inspector Braithewaite asks.

What else can I say but yes? It's not my property, it's not even yours.

But your evidence is everywhere. I may have wiped the blood off the spade, the iron, but it won't take them long to know you wore the suit lying in the dirt, or fixed the car. It's impossible, Ty, to pretend you were never here. I need a new tack. I'm feeling flustered now as I trail behind them. The crickets jumping around the house have jumped inside me, swirling through my insides, stirring up my anxiety. But I can't let the detectives know. I have to keep lying, do what you and I discussed last night.

'I haven't seen him,' I repeat, 'not inside prison or since he was released.'

'How do you know he was released?' Detective Sergeant Manikham says.

'Well,' I say, 'because you just told me.'

Her eyebrows are raised. We all know I'm a liar.

And so, the story comes out. Some of it. I admit that I knew your dates because I received a letter, but that it didn't matter anyway as I was already planning to come back and see the land again. By myself. But it all seems like such a damned coincidence, doesn't it? And these detectives know it too.

As they investigate our bedroom, I see my old clothes—the ones you were wearing—laid out on the bed. I see all the things

344

I've moved, sorted. Might they think I've done all this just for me? Perhaps there's a chance they won't see signs of you here. Not immediately, anyway.

Will that give me time to sort out my story? Run?

Give you time to disappear?

Supreme Court of Western Australia
PERTH

October 15th

Mr Wynnstay is called to the stand. He has vivid red hair, pale skin and freckles. When he announces his job title, Blood-Spatter Analyst, I almost laugh: he looks like he's been living his work. Then I have to glance down as I remember your blood-spattered face, my handiwork before I tipped you into a hole. When I look back at Mr Wynnstay, I make myself see freckles, not blood, and remind myself that he was part of the forensic team who scraped and dusted all over your den and beyond, collecting specimens.

He's doing a good job for you; he sounds impressive. But, standing straight with his stiff collar and long words and reason, he's everything you're not. He nods in response to one of Mr Lowe's questions, and I realise I haven't been paying attention again.

'Yes, it is correct that Mr MacFarlane's blood was found in the hire car,' he says. 'We found blood samples in the house, and on the veranda floorboards, also.'

'Can you also confirm that blood samples were found on this spade?' Mr Lowe askes.

A picture of the spade—the one I found in your storage shed—appears on the screen.

'That's correct. Despite an apparent attempt to remove the blood samples with soap and water, the evidence there

349

was still very much detectable,' he says.

Which apparently makes the fact that I cleaned it look more suspicious. I notice a few jury members look my way as Mr Wynnstay continues to describe how much blood was found, where on the spade, and how that indicates the way a victim could be struck. It's easy to see where the argument is going.

'It's plausible, then, Mr Wynnstay, that the defendant struck Tyler MacFarlane with that very spade, and then tried to clean the spade afterwards with soap and water?'

'It is possible, yes.'

'Would you say it is likely this spade was used to dig the holes found at the side of the house, known by the defendant as the den?'

'It is.'

'And presumably this spade could dig other holes that the police never found. Could this spade dig a hole big enough to bury a body, Mr Wynnstay?'

'Objection,' says Jodie, sighing. 'Conjecture!'

The police dug hole after hole—making ours look insignificant in comparison—searching for your body. But they found no body. No murder weapon. Unless you count the spade. But I have my own defence for that. When I take the stand in two days time, and Mr Lowe asks me about it, I will say that you tried to attack me after an argument, and that I warded you off. I will say you threatened me.

When Jodie cross-examines Mr Whynnstay, she reminds the jury of the lack of evidence.

'Beyond reasonable doubt,' she says. 'Without a body, there will always be doubt. Without a clear murder weapon, without a clear motive, there will always, always be doubt.

350

Doubt runs all through this case, including through Mr Wynnstay's evidence and testimony.'

Mr Lowe stands. 'Objection! The defence is not questioning the witness.'

Jodie nods, turns back to her notes.

'Mr Wynnstay, we have seen evidence suggesting how conflicted the defendant was in her feelings for Mr Macfarlane. And yet to kill someone with a spade suggests a large degree of strength and determination would be required for death to ensue, would it not?'

'That's correct.'

'Approximately how hard and how many times might a person swing a spade to kill a fully grown man?'

'That would depend on how strong the person swinging the spade was.'

Jodie pauses to look my way. It's no accident, I'm sure, that her eyes linger on my belly, on my hands clasped across it. 'How many times do you think the defendant would need to swing that particular spade to kill Tyler MacFarlane? Is it even possible, do you think?'

I don't look at Mr Wynnstay now. Meek and mild, I look down at my hands. But I could have done it. If I'd swung one more time that day, if I'd buried your head with the rest of your body.

'I'm afraid I'm certainly not an expert in body-strength mechanics,' Mr Wynnstay says.

Jodie returns to Mr Wynnstay's evidence, and how he obtained it. She queries his methods of sample preservation in extreme heat. Charts of his results are projected onto the screen for her to scrutinise further.

'It seems there is doubt inherent in even the so-called

facts of this case,' she continues. 'Would you agree, Mr Wynnstay, that there is an element of doubt in your findings as to how long the blood found on the spade had been there?'

'Well, yes, we don't know the timing exactly, but there is no doubt that this blood is Mr MacFarlane's,' Mr Wynnstay replies. 'There is no doubt that he was there and that he sustained a serious injury from this spade.'

'But *when* is the question, Mr Wynnstay. When did this injury occur, and why? And was this injury enough to cause death?'

My eyes go heavy as the questions roll on and the objections from the prosecution continue. Everything about me is so heavy, now. I feel waterlogged, as if I've sunk to the bottom of a deep pool.

You know, Ty, I stuck to the story we agreed on for longer than was good for me. I didn't tell the police you were there with me until they got Mr Wynnstay and his team on board. Up until that point, I insisted that you never returned. But it was hard to stick with one story when your blood told a different one.

Mr Wynnstay and his team changed a lot of things. When they arrived, I was forced to admit that you came with me after all, up the Great Northern together in the hire car. And didn't the reporters go nuts about that development? Everybody loved it when they discovered that I'd lied.

After that, my story veered closer to the truth: you and I had been trying to get to know each other again, away from prying eyes and media attention; we believed we loved each other and that was why we agreed to let each other go. When I am on the witness stand, I will be asked about our final conversation—how we agreed you would disappear into the land, how it was the ultimate sacrifice for us both.

Someone coughs in the gallery, and I jolt back to the present. Mr Wynnstay is leaving the stand. I clasp my hands in my lap as I watch him go. It won't be long before it's my turn to talk.

Seven months earlier

UNMAPPED

March 11th, later

They want me to come with them. It's not an arrest, as such, but it's a strong request to take me in for questioning.

I go with them, because if I don't, they'll only keep searching. And then they might find you. You need time to disappear properly. This way, I'm protecting me and you, in a way I never did the first time around.

Detective Sergeant Manikham opens the back door of the police car and I climb in. Detective Inspector Braithwaite, in the driver's seat, blasts up the air conditioning so high that I shiver as we drive away from the den. From the front passenger seat, as the car lurches away across the dirt, Detective Sergeant Manikham watches me in the rear-view mirror. When I try to look back at the den and across to the Separates, my head slams into the window. But just for a second, I see her: our fox. Still as stone in the sand and staring back at me, watching me leave.

I turn further in the seat, so I can watch her through the rear window as she turns and heads for the horizon. Like our fox, you will also damage what you come into contact with— non-native creature that you are—but I have released you. For better or for worse, I have released us all.

357

Supreme Court of Western Australia
PERTH

October 17th

Finally, as the primary witness for the defence, it is my turn today. Jodie said from the start that I didn't have to take the stand, not if I didn't want to.

'But I'm an old hand at this sort of thing,' I said, smiling. She didn't smile back.

Maybe she's worried I'll present the wrong image to the jury. That I won't be...I don't know...weak enough, innocent enough, given the way I look now. Not as much of a victim as I looked the first time around. But perception is a strange thing. And I am older, and tougher, and I feel it. It's hard to disguise that. And why should I?

As we wait for the court to get settled, Jodie reaches across and squeezes my hand. I hope the jury sees. It's such a familiar gesture—surely someone whose hand gets squeezed couldn't be found guilty of murder. I squeeze back: *thank you.* Perhaps it's just her commitment to her job, but I think Jodie really does believe me, my story. That's one person, anyway.

When she turns to speak to Mikael, I look down at my nails. They're bitten to the quick, bleeding in places, but I don't feel nervous. Not like I did the first time around, in your trial, which is strange, because it's my freedom in the balance this time. Perhaps it is because I have nothing to feel guilty about. But you felt like that once too, didn't you? And you also pleaded not guilty. Look where it got you.

I'm not in the same remand centre as you were. They put me in the women's prison, further out from central Perth, out in the bush. You've probably heard of it. I hear wattlebirds and magpies every morning. I thought I would hate being locked away, but it's okay being alone, waiting. I spent the past decade thinking that you must have hated it, that being in a cell went against everything you stood for. But, who knows, maybe I was wrong about that too.

The clerk calls me up to the stand and I place my hand on the Bible, just like I did once before. Even though I don't believe in God or in any religion, I've always thought taking an oath, instead of just an affirmation, sounded better, stronger.

Jodie begins. She starts gently, slowly, with those dark, quiet days in London without you. She lets me tell my story in my own words, in my own way. I start to tell the jury the truth as I've been telling it to you. It's not long before she gets to our 'inciting incident'.

'Would you tell the jury, in your own words, what happened on February twelfth?' Jodie coaxes.

I explain that I followed you after your release from prison, that I was simply curious, and couldn't keep away. I don't say I stalked you, because that wasn't what it was, and you know that too. I just needed to connect and see you, that's all. And you needed that too. You would've done it yourself if you'd been allowed to, if you'd known I was there.

Then, yes, this next bit...I guess I do embellish a little. But only a little. We all do it, don't we: shape our stories in slightly different ways to make them seem more interesting, or more heroic, or truer?

I say how pleased you were to see me when we met in the park, that you came with me of your own free will, that we were running away together, just like you'd planned for us, all those years ago. I say that, this time, we were going to do it all properly. I don't mention the girl in the school uniform, and I don't mention the drugs.

I say that you were grateful I had found you again, that you wanted to come back to the desert with me, back to our sacred place. That we stayed out there watching the stars, sitting in the sun, hunting for lizards, talking, until we realised it was never going to work. That it was only a matter of time before the authorities found us.

'We knew the end was coming,' I say, 'we had to enjoy our time while we could.'

I shift in the stand, take a sip of water. I make sure all the members of the jury get a good look at my belly. I want them to see it in all its full glory; I want them to see what we made, that last night, that time in the pool. And I want them to know that you will always be with me in some way. And that this way is my way now. I wait a few moments for the jury to take in this last piece of evidence.

On the stand, your sister argued that my belly couldn't be because of you, and Mr Lowe quoted figures about the accuracy of prenatal paternity tests. But I took two tests. Both results were displayed on the screen for the jury. Positive match, twice.

How does it feel, Ty, to be a father? How does it feel to know you cannot ever meet your child?

Your sister has changed her tune, hasn't she? In your

original trial, she thought I was lying about being kidnapped, that I was the one who wanted to run away. Now I'm saying I did just what she accused me of the first time around, and she thinks I'm lying again. Guess there's no pleasing some people. One thing is certain, though: she thinks I'm lying about letting you go. To her, I'm evil. Just like you were in the eyes of Mum.

But you wanted to be let go, didn't you? It's what you once asked for. And I came to see that it had to happen, that releasing you from me like that was the only way forward. Now you're free to become something new, stay out in the land for the rest of your life.

Soon it will be Mr Lowe's cross-examination, followed by the closing statements. Jodie's statement will tell the jury that we were protecting each other. You, fixing the car for me. Me, letting you go. She will say that we were doing what we could to keep each other free.

'Ms Stone? Kate?'

I blink back to the present. My mind is wandering, dangerously so. Jodie has asked me another question; I need to concentrate.

'Ms Stone,' she says again, softly this time. 'Could you tell the jury why you lied to the police detectives? Why didn't you tell them the truth in the beginning, about Mr MacFarlane being in the house with you?'

'Lying about that was for protection,' I say. 'I was frightened, trying to buy time for Ty—Mr MacFarlane—to disappear.'

'You also lied to the detectives about an argument you had with Mr MacFarlane. You made no mention of the argument at all, not at first—is that correct?'

'Yes, that's correct.'

'But in that argument you failed to disclose at that time, an altercation took place involving a spade. You hit Mr MacFarlane with that spade, is that correct?'

'Yes. I did hit Ty, but I didn't kill him. I immediately felt bad about what I'd done and nursed him back to health. He felt guilty too for what he'd said to me. We made up. Got closer again.'

'Why did you not think to tell the detectives about this argument?'

'It seemed so long ago, after everything that had happened since. It wasn't the version of Ty I wanted to keep in my mind.'

Jodie nods. 'Ms Stone, would you tell the jury about that final night you spent with Mr MacFarlane?'

Again, Jodie lets me tell my story in the way I want to tell it, slowly and carefully. I tell the jury how you fixed the car in that blisteringly hot afternoon, and how we lay in each other's arms after swimming in the cool water in the heart of the Separates. I tell them we talked about forgiveness and love and sacrifice. I say that you finally understood what it was like for me.

'And why did you decide that you couldn't stay together, Ms Stone?'

I shrug. It seems obvious. 'Our love was impossible; we'd never be allowed to stay together. Even if the law allowed it, everyone would always question our sanity, our relationship. We'd be ostracised from society, from everything. Besides, we're not good for each other.'

The questions continue: all morning from Jodie, all afternoon from Mr Lowe. I don't tell the jury everything, but then, who does that? I don't raise the other doubts starting to creep into my head, either. There is a niggling question, isn't there, a great big fly in this ointment? The fact that you've never come forward, that you've never been found: will the jury take this to mean you didn't love me as much as Jodie is trying to prove? Or even that the prosecution is right and you couldn't return, and I really did kill you? Is our story really a whole lot more sinister? Is there another, darker version about what happened with a gun and a waterhole that day?

If you had come forward—turned up to this trial as I imagined three days ago—you could have stopped it from proceeding. The fact that there is no body—no *live* body—goes against my story, too.

But you're smart, though, aren't you, Ty? And you were feeling guilty again. Because, even with proof that you were alive, the police could still have got me for kidnap, perhaps even attempted murder, a whole host of other charges, no doubt. Your sister would have made sure of that. Unless you came forward and told the truth. My truth. Like I'm doing now. If you told this story, it would've helped me out, you know. But you won't come forward. It suits us both for the world to think that you really are gone, so that no one comes looking, and no one ever finds you. Disappeared.

I've come to see that I'm good at imagining, good at telling stories. I like knowing all the possibilities of a tale before deciding on the version of the truth I'm going to tell.

Seven months earlier

MINE SITE

March 11th, later

After almost two hours, we reach a mine site. So, we were right, there was one nearby, closer than last time. We pass squat, make-shift buildings, a security gate, sorting belts and lots of vehicles, all with mine-site flags. No shade, no trees, no green at all, just the huge mining hole and piles of dirt; it's a scene from the apoca-lypse, or as if a giant has torn the place apart and left the land gaping. It must be hot as hell here when the sun is high.

The one-room police station is next to the one-room medical centre. Detective Inspector Braithwaite and Detective Sergeant Manikham make me wait at a plastic table, on a plastic chair, while they make some calls. I can imagine the kinds of things they're saying, as they call down to the headquarters in Perth, or wherever. It must be a big deal for these coppers up here. A missing person. A single female, alone on an unregistered prop-erty. A mystery to solve. Something that's not mining-related.

They take ages, and it's sweltering; my legs are sticking to the plastic. The air-con unit is not much help, slowing down and speeding up erratically. I rest my head on the table and shut my eyes, thinking about you. I imagine where you could have gone. You told me you wanted to go further north to the islands at the top of this state: the last wilderness, you called them.

A person who doesn't want to be found could hide there.
Crocs and snakes and stowaways.

I wonder if I'll see those islands, one day. It's impossible, I think.

If I tell the police anything, I'll say you went far south. Who else have they got to believe, after all? And it might buy us more time.

Supreme Court of Western Australia
PERTH

October 18th

Mr Lowe gathers his notes and turns to the jury, about to begin his closing statement. His back is straight and stiff, his suit jacket well pressed.

He tells the jury to discard my evidence on many grounds, first and foremost regarding my pregnancy. After this pronouncement, he looks back at me, then at the jury. How typically male to start here: by undermining what I can do and he can't, sabotaging my trump card.

'Her pregnancy is just another part of the elaborate fantasy the defendant is trying to spin for you,' he says, 'the fantasy that she is perhaps even spinning for herself. Just because the defendant and Mr MacFarlane had intercourse doesn't mean it was consensual.'

The pitying expression on his face when he looks at me next makes me want to punch him.

'Let me tell you the rest of the defendant's fantasy—or, rather, let me unravel it for you.'

He turns back to the jury, his pitying expression replaced by one of utter professional seriousness.

'It was not Mr MacFarlane's choice to be in that desert house, despite what the defendant would have you believe. He was held there against his will. The ropes found at the scene would suggest he was likely tied up. The blood spatters on the spade suggest that he was violently assaulted with it, perhaps to the point of death. Mr MacFarlane's continued disappearance, despite the state's substantial efforts to find him, suggests that whether the spade was used or not, the defendant did in fact kill him. Remember, there were also guns and knives found on the property. After committing this act, it is likely she buried him out there. You've heard details about the disturbances in the ground—and seen the evidence in photographs—proof that she was trying to find the best place to do the burying.'

The jury are shuffling in their seats. Are they convinced? I want to turn around to see Mum's face, and Nick's if he's up there. Are they looking at me in a new way now?

'And why haven't the police found Mr MacFarlane's body yet?' Mr Lowe's voice booms into my thoughts. 'You've seen from the photographs just how vast that land is up there in the deserts of this state. Think of all the space that the defendant had to hide one body. With the best resources in the world, the police could never search all of it. She had a car, after all. Tyler MacFarlane's DNA was found all over that car.

'What the defendant has told you today, members of the jury, is nothing but a fantasy. Do not let her innocent look, or her pregnancy, sway you—or even the tragedy of what happened to her ten years previously. If anything, let what happened to the defendant previously make you more resolute to return a verdict of guilty. This was a revenge killing, make no mistake about that. The defendant knew exactly what she was doing. Why did she book a flight to Perth that arrived only a few days before Mr MacFarlane was released from jail? Why buy a knife from a city department store?

Why stalk Mr MacFarlane at his sister's house night and day after he was released?

'We know that Mr MacFarlane was seen in the defendant's hire car. And we know that after that last sighting of him by Mr Symonds in the desert petrol station, Mr MacFarlane was never seen again. Not by a single person, apart from the defendant. Do not let the fact that there is no body dissuade you from thinking this is a murder case. Think of the blood in the hire car. Think of the defendant's cover-up around the house, the evidence concealed. Think of the fact that the defendant lied to police.

'And the defendant says she did all this to protect Mr MacFarlane? Unlikely. This elaborate fantasy that you've heard her weave is nothing more than a selfish lie to protect herself.'

The jury are listening intently, everyone is. I can understand why: Mr Lowe's story is almost as good as mine. I look down at my clasped hands, my belly beneath them. Is that a kick I feel?

Mr Lowe continues, his smooth voice hammering home his argument until even I want to believe it.

All just a fantasy?

I'm lying when I think you're still alive?

I killed you, then said I didn't?

I imagined it all?

What do my parents think now, as they look down on me from the gallery? Has Mr Lowe finally swayed them? But you know, Ty, despite the days and money spent on this trial, it will only ever be you and me who truly understand what I can do, only you and me who know the truth of what happened in the desert. Just like you and I are the only ones who can ever say what a fitting punishment might be.

'So, is the defendant a fantasist?' Mr Lowe asks the jury. 'Can you see behind her mask? Can you see the evil behind her exterior? You heard it yourself from Ms MacFarlane, the victim's sister, that the defendant is good at manipulating, that she likes to make up stories. So, ask yourself—is this all just a story? Is she trying to convince you to believe her own private fantasy? And do you, members of the jury, want to choose her fantasy as the truth?'

Seven months earlier

MINE SITE

March 11th, later

Through the window of the hot, makeshift police station, still waiting for the detectives, I watch the men outside, driving back and forth across the mine site in their Prados and Land Cruisers, wiping their brows with the bottom of their shirts, smoking sometimes...You must have done all this once, in the time before me, when you were a young man, before I got inside you. I would have been in primary school then. And you would have had it all going for you: beautiful, tanned, strong, making mining dollars. Is that where you'd go back to if you could rewind time, when possibilities stretched like the desert around you? Back then, you could have been good or bad, could have been anything.

I feel a bit like that now: I could be anything. Is that strange? I wouldn't go back, you know, not to our time before. And, despite what I believed for so long, I'm no longer sure that I would live any of it differently.

I slide my T-shirt off my left shoulder and trace my skin underneath. That red, raw mark. Your bite. I remember your mouth last night in the pool. I remember biting back.

I touch the pattern of your teeth, enjoy how my skin feels tender there. It will bruise, but it will also fade; I don't think the detectives will notice it. I pull the material back over my shoulder and trace my fingers over the skin above my knees, and then along my collarbone. You touched all these places last night. I kept my eyes open the whole time, watching you, waiting for you to fall for me.

Afterwards, I held your body as a place I had fought for; the marks I made were shot wounds, splayed across your chest and shoulders. I hammered a stake, as hard as I could, aiming for your heart. And you went crawling from my front line, wounded. But I wanted you slain. Fully captured by me. You lay with your head in my lap, and I traced my fingers across your lips. And you spoke to me of love, of wanting to stay.

Supreme Court of Western Australia
PERTH

October 18th

As the defence, Jodie gets the final say. She asks the jury to think about one word: love. She asks what it means to them, what it can do. She describes how it can destroy, and how it can also be returned. She reminds them of the remorse I felt when you went to prison, the letters I wrote, and that the feelings I had were genuine, if misplaced.

'Kate Stone is full of love to have done what she did,' Jodie concludes. 'Love strong enough to set free her captor, love for her unborn child, even love for herself. In the end, her crime is to love her kidnapper. But can we ever really call love a crime?'

When Jodie sits down, I watch Mr Lowe exchange a look with the solicitor next to him.

'The defence are playing unnecessarily on your heart-strings,' he told the jury earlier. 'Do not be swayed by their emotional, irrational approach.'

I run my eyes over that jury: twelve strangers who will decide my fate and how we are remembered. I almost feel sorry for them: what a responsibility. One of the younger women meets my gaze, just for a moment. Although I do not smile—I cannot—I am happy she is seeing me. I look down, my fingertips outlining the patterns of rock art on the table.

We wait hours for the verdict in a small, plain room in the bowels of the courthouse. I am allowed tea and biscuits, and soon I feel sick from eating too many. When it gets dark outside, a guard says they'll take me back to the prison to wait there.

'My bet is it's going to be hours yet before they come to a decision,' Jodie says, as I am escorted back to the transport van. 'Try to get some rest while you can.'

Seven months earlier

MINE SITE

March 11th, later

Detective Inspector Braithewaite returns, hands me a bottle of water. I sip it slowly.

'We need to wait for a senior-ranking officer to arrive to interview you,' he says.

He seems more tense, doesn't meet my gaze. He's probably annoyed he hasn't been allowed to conduct the interview. Or things have got serious now that he's found out more about me.

'Anything else you need? Some food?'

'A room with working air-con would be nice.'

He nods. 'I'll get you a fan.'

After he has left, I stand in front of the window, trying to see beyond the piles of dirt and machinery outside, imagining the cooler, deeper, rusty-smelling land beneath, its ancient red rock and precious metals. It would be quiet inside that land. You would say there are worse places to end up. I touch the rough wooden windowsill and feel your scar. I return to the chair, take another sip of water, shut my eyes. Now I imagine you striding through the land, heading far away into the pounding sun of the north. Freedom. At least for me.

REMAND CENTRE

October 19th

When we still haven't heard anything by morning, Jodie tries to reassure me. 'It's such a complicated case,' she says. 'The jury have to accept that the only people who know what happened are you and Tyler MacFarlane. And Tyler's gone, so...'

She looks away, across to Mikael, and again I wonder, does she really believe me? She said early on, on the first day I met her, that it's hard for a person to just disappear, no matter how vast the land.

'There's so much surveillance these days,' she said. 'So much technology.'

But she doesn't know you. She doesn't understand how well you know that land, either. If anyone could disappear, it would be you.

Jodie, Mikael and I are sitting in one of the special rooms where people like me can talk to their legal team. If there's still no decision, Mum will come later, with Dad, during the afternoon visiting hours. Nick hasn't come, but then I suppose they wouldn't allow a prosecution witness to visit. Shame, as I'd like to ask him if he believes the things he said in court.

There are so many versions of our story now, Ty—I suppose it's my story now—it's hard to know what's true, even for me. But if I can't know, how will the jury work it out? It might simply depend on how they're feeling on the day they decide—what happened to them that morning, what they ate for breakfast, what parts of the stories they liked best. Maybe there's a different truth for each member of the jury. No wonder they can't decide.

'Do you forgive him?' Jodie asks, looking at me carefully. 'Should I?'

She smiles, turns back towards the window facing onto the courtyard. 'You know that's not for me to say.'

Do I forgive you for taking me all those years ago? And does it matter in the end if I do or I don't? I'm not sure if my forgiveness is the burning question this time around.

'Perhaps the real question is, would he forgive me?'

She turns back to me immediately, frowning. She didn't expect this; she doesn't want to hear those words. I'm sure she wants to ask what I mean, but she won't ask me anything else right now. If my version of the events is not the truth, she can't know that.

Will questions like that follow me into the future? Do I forgive you? Is that why I did what I did? Do you forgive me? Do we even care about forgiveness now?

Mikael pulls out a stack of newspapers, broadsheets and tabloids from his briefcase and dumps them onto the table in front of me. I flick through a few, reading the headlines.

Not enough evidence for murder!

No body, not guilty?

Gemma gets away with it!

'We might be okay,' Jodie says quietly. 'Most of the evidence in the prosecution's case is circumstantial anyway, unreliable. There's nothing solid to tie you to this, and you're the only witness, so...'

'Without a body, their case was always thin,' Mikael concurs.

When our time is up, I stand to go back to my cell. Jodie and Mikael stand too.

'It won't be forever,' Jodie says, 'whatever happens. You'll get out of here. Look after yourself.' I know what her glance at my belly means: I have a lot more to look after now.

I like the walk back to my cell, across the courtyard between the blocks. Usually, I hear at least three different types of birds. Today the wattlebirds are cackling. The magpies are warbling too, but I can't see them when I look up. And the raucous shriek of the mynahs is never far away. I still have an appreciation for the tiny wildernesses on the boundaries of places, even in this prison—the weeds in the cracks of the yard, the gums peering in from outside, the hot north wind bringing dust.

When I'm halfway across the courtyard, drops of rain start to fall. Cold rain, blown by an icy wind. The guard accompanying me pulls her collar up.

'Spring, eh!' she says, giving me a half-smile. 'Who'd want to be outside in this?'

But you would.

You are.

I imagine you walking across an open space, the same wind reaching you. Can you smell the sea on it? Can you smell me? Raindrops crawl down the back of my neck. I shiver and stick out my tongue to taste them. They taste like you did when we swam for the last time in the Separates.

I imagine you back there, a good place to hide. Caves above and beneath the ground in the spring, entrances leading deep inside the rocks—an easy place to disappear.

You know, I never told anyone exactly what happened on our last night, about where we were. Not even Jodie. That pool is ours. The time we spent there is for us alone. I will never tell anyone.

I never spoke about the cave at the bottom of the pool, either. If the prosecution knew about it, they would search it. And I don't want anyone to go searching there, ever. Some secrets are just for us. Just for me.

'Here we go then.' The guard holds open my cell door. 'Thank you.'

Back in my cell, the usual stash of mail is waiting for me. Letters of support mostly. Some love letters too. And some hate letters. You must have got a whole heap, I realise now; apparently men in prison get more than women. What is it with people and their obsession with prisoners? Don't people outside have lives of their own?

I flip through the envelopes and pause at a postcard—nothing written on it apart from my address here in the prison. The postmark is from Derby, up past Broome, far north. It can't be you, it's not your writing.

I study the picture of the beach on the front. Sand, creamy as churned butter, fire-red rocks and a turbulent sea. Probably from some nutter, having a laugh. You'd be surprised, the kinds of letters I get. Or maybe you wouldn't be.

I keep the card, pin it up beside my bed. It could be useful if the verdict doesn't go my way.

REMAND CENTRE

October 20th

It's early when Jodie returns—the guard raps on my door, telling me to get ready to see her. Sunshine streams through the window, the rain gone. I sit up awkwardly, dress again in my smart courtroom pant suit, and use the hairband I once took from your ponytail to tie back my hair, long now. I didn't dream last night, and my head feels clear, which is unusual, especially with my belly like this.

I'm ready.

I follow the guard across the sun-drenched courtyard. No wind this morning, and only one call from a crow. The postcard is in the pocket of my suit pants—potential evidence, if we need it. Maybe enough to reopen the case or launch an appeal.

But maybe we won't need it. And maybe I am already free. In a way, it doesn't matter what the jury says. I know what happened. Whoever is in my belly will also know it, but for now it's my story.

Jodie waits behind the glass doors to the meeting room. She's smiling.

Supreme Court of Western Australia
PERTH

October 20th

Jodie grabs my hand as the guard leads me inside.

'Feeling good?' she says.

I nod. It could be the endorphins from the new being growing inside me, but I do feel good. I feel...different. I have what I need to start again.

I hand Jodie the postcard and she smiles.

'Hopefully, we won't need it,' she says, filing it in her briefcase anyway.

I file away the image of you up north too.

As the guard hurries me along, I test out the possibility of being found guilty. I know you would not return to prove my innocence. But I smile as I imagine Louise MacFarlane's shocked reaction if you ever could return. When the guard scowls at me, I make my face neutral again; she probably thinks I'm smiling at her.

In the courtroom, I look at the faces of the jury, one by one. Each of them meets my gaze: a good sign, Jodie would say. There's no preamble today; the clerk asks for the jury's decision almost immediately.

One of the older women steps up. She confirms that she is speaking on behalf of the entire jury.

Twenty hours to deliberate. Not easy for them.

The clerk reads my crimes: kidnapping, grievous bodily

harm. And then, of course: murder.

This woman—this stranger who will never see inside my mind—responds:

'Not guilty.'

To everything.

I hear gasps from the gallery, a commotion. Mr Lowe's face remains calm, before he looks down at his briefcase and shuffles his papers. I know Jodie is looking at me, waiting for me to turn to her. The guard has moved closer; perhaps previous defendants have fainted at this point.

But I'm steady as I stand. I've won my trial. My story was believed. I won, Ty, and you lost.

'This is bullshit,' Louise MacFarlane shouts, her voice ringing across the courtroom. 'They've got it wrong!'

And maybe they have. But isn't every story wrong for someone?

The guard is stepping away from me now, and Jodie grasps my hands, pulling them away from where I've been gripping the table.

'You did it, Kate,' she says, eyes wide, grinning. 'How do you feel?'

I nod absently. 'Thank you,' I say.

It's not what I imagined. It feels more like a death. An end. Shouldn't I be punished for something? Or have I served that punishment already? Were those ten years with you inside me enough?

Jodie is still talking, moving her hands emphatically. I'm surprised by her emotion; I thought lawyers were always composed. Seems she did believe me, after all.

'She'll launch an appeal, won't she?' I say, looking up to where I see two policemen rounding on Louise MacFarlane.

'She won't. Go on, enjoy your freedom,' Jodie says. 'You can go anywhere you want, do anything. No constraints now.'

I nod and try to look reassured, but in this moment, I don't know what to celebrate: if the jury say I didn't kill you, then you are out there still and could return. Will you come back for your child one day? Maybe I should have owned your death, stamped you out entirely from everyone's minds, left no doubt.

The guard steps aside for me, and I look down the courtroom, to where reporters are milling, to where Mum is trying to push through the crowd.

'You're free to go, Ms Toombs,' the guard says. I glance at her, and she blushes and corrects herself. 'Ms Stone, I'm sorry.'

I nod. 'It's really okay,' I say.

And it is. I can decide my next name, my next me. From now on, my actions alone will determine my future. And, you know, Ty, I've now made your ending mine. I've had the last word. Your story has been told—owned—by me. I've left you unresolved.

Barrack Street
PERTH

October 20th

When I get outside, I take a deep breath, look around at the trees, flower verges and bins where foxes would be if they were here. You're not here. I no longer see your face anywhere.

On this chilly spring day in Perth, the commuters and tourists know nothing about me or you, nothing important anyway, and this ancient land beneath us doesn't care. I want to pull off my uncomfortable high heels and step onto this land that is older, more resilient, more enduring than any coloniser. But I can't go barefoot on the sodden grass, not right now. The air smells of frangipani, hot chips, lemon balm and traffic. I sigh out the courtroom.

Just like that, you're gone from me.

I feel you leave like a breeze.

The man the jury decided I did not kill is just Tyler Andrew MacFarlane of 31 Banksia Drive. A man good at fixing cars, and at art, and who had a tragic, loveless upbringing. A man who did something very stupid and terrible when he was twenty-seven years old, my age now, and who did not get away with it. Tyler Andrew MacFarlane, who I will not see again. Like a change in the season, he is out of my head, and I am left with me, all of me. And with something new too: a new love growing inside.

A release.

ACKNOWLEDGEMENTS

I am grateful for the generous support of a research grant from the Authors' Foundation, administered through the Society of Authors.

This book has been a long time in my notebooks, and an even longer time in my head. Thank you to so many of you for your faith and patience while you waited for it to come. Penny at Text, Nicola at Bent, August, Cath, Gordon, Sam, friends, family, colleagues, readers of my other books—my gratitude. Thank you, especially, to my husband, Rajiv, for all that is light and love in my world.

I acknowledge the Traditional Custodians of the land I write about, in particular the Whadjuk, Palyku, Nyangumarta and Marda people, and I pay my respects to Elders past and present, respecting their cultural heritage, beliefs and relationship with the land.